Mysterious Ways

ALSO BY WENDY WUNDER

The Probability of Miracles
The Museum of Intangible Things

Mysterious Ways

WENDY WUNDER

WEDNESDAY BOOKS
NEW YORK

For Gregg and Cadence,
my reasons for being

....

Please note that this book contains themes about
and nongraphic references to suicide.

First published in the United States by Wednesday Books,
an imprint of St. Martin's Publishing Group

MYSTERIOUS WAYS. Copyright © 2024 by Wendy Wunder. All rights reserved.
Printed in the United States of America. For information, address St. Martin's
Publishing Group, 120 Broadway, New York, NY 10271.

www.wednesdaybooks.com

Library of Congress Cataloging-in-Publication Data

Names: Wunder, Wendy, author.
Title: Mysterious ways / Wendy Wunder.
Description: First edition. | New York : Wednesday Books, 2024. | Audience:
    Ages 13–18. | Summary: Seventeen-year-old Maya struggles with her omniscient
    abilities, but when she meets a cute guy at her new school, he helps her learn how
    to cope with knowing too much.
Identifiers: LCCN 2024015446 | ISBN 9781250770202 (hardcover) |
    ISBN 9781250770219 (ebook)
Subjects: CYAC: Ability—Fiction. | Telepathy—Fiction. | Interpersonal relations—
    Fiction. | Schools—Fiction. | LCGFT: Magic realist fiction. | Novels.
Classification: LCC PZ7.W96374 My 2024 | DDC [Fic]—dc23
LC record available at https://lccn.loc.gov/2024015446

Our books may be purchased in bulk for promotional, educational, or business use.
Please contact your local bookseller or the Macmillan Corporate and Premium Sales
Department at 1-800-221-7945, extension 5442, or by email at
MacmillanSpecialMarkets@macmillan.com.

First Edition: 2024

10 9 8 7 6 5 4 3 2 1

Band Names Notebook

(or Table of Contents)

Prologue

Dear Diary (insert upside down smiley face emoji),

Amy asked me to reflect on my *origins* in order to try to understand who I am and how to move forward. I keep telling her I don't have an origin story. We don't live in the Marvel Universe, Amy. I don't have a magic hammer forged by the dwarves of Norse mythology or anything.

I mean, since I was born from my mother and born with this condition, I can only assume it comes from her, and let's face it, she is kind of a "queen" herself in common parlance. I must also assume it comes from my mother because she's the only being I cannot know *everything* about. My readings on her are fuzzy and erratic. Sometimes she comes through loud and clear, and kind of scary, actually, and other times, like when I try to know anything about her past, it's murky at best.

FACTS: None of us (including me) can fully know our mothers, and we secretly like it that way. We're not super curious about our mothers' *personhoods* as long as we are getting our needs met, right? And since I can't know Stacy, I can't confirm it comes from her, and I can't know what powers she has and what powers she hides. It's probably a recessive gene, which means Glen has it, too. Surprise, surprise.

It's getting stronger, whatever it is, gnawing at me like a constant nagging itch. It wants to grow, but I tamp it down, keep it small and local, because in the past, it's only ever gotten me in trouble. There are limits to it, too. In monotheistic religions, "god" is supposed to be omniscient, omnipotent, and omnibenevolent. But that has never truly been the case, right? God has never been "all-powerful." Because it's never been in god's wheelhouse to prevent us from destroying each other. So if god exists, god has obvious limits to their power and benevolence that no one ever talks about.

Anyway. Maybe there have always been girls like me. Girls with elusive powerful magic they can't fully understand or unleash, because the patriarchy is stronger than god and much more insidious.

Grippy Sock Vacation

Of the many ways one could choose to spend their six-week stay in the psych hospital, reading the Bible was not something Maya expected to top the list. But there were Bibles lying around. And she had always meant to look at one.

She bent the book and let the gilded pages flutter past her thumb like the wings of a moth, butterfly kisses, before stopping at a random spot. Right off the bat, she discovered something interesting. Genesis, chapter 6, verse 5. The reason God flooded the earth the first time:

> And God saw that <u>the wickedness of man was great in the earth,</u> and that every imagination of the thoughts of his heart was <u>only evil continually.</u>

A page or so later, He, or She, or They (you couldn't pretend to know God's preferred pronouns) promised never to do it again, flood the earth ... but Maya was suspicious. Even gods could break promises, right? Because according to the most recent drastic flooding reports from climatologists everywhere, it seemed that God must once again have become discontented. (Insert lightning bolt emoji.) And the thoughts in people's hearts must, once again, have become: Only. Evil. Continually.

There was evidence of this, Maya knew. Just look at the headlines:

Report: Hate Crimes in the US Rise to Highest Level in More than a Decade / Flooding Death Toll Soars to 11,300 in Libya's Coastal City of Derna

US Man Charged for Shooting Black Teen Who Approached Wrong House / Floods in Turkey Kill 13 People in Earthquake-Affected Provinces

Texas Man Pleads Guilty to Setting Fire to Synagogue / Huge Southeast Texas Sinkhole Suddenly Starts Expanding

Montana Man Convicted of Shooting to Rid Community of the Lesbian and Gay Members / Thousands Forced from Their Homes amid Southern Malaysia Floods

Hate Crimes Rose 44% Last Year in Study of Major Cities / Flooding and Heavy Rains Rise 50% Worldwide in a Decade, Figures Show

Sus.

But was the evil causing the flood?

Even though the flood was inevitable (we'd waited too long to stop it!), and even though the evil was continuous (and the wickedness of man, great!), there was no evidence, yet, that one thing caused the other. Correlation, you eventually learn in your first statistics class, does not imply Causation.

In other words, it might be just a *coincidence* that people had become awful, hateful trolls at the exact same time in history that the ice caps were melting, unleashing not only their regular watery potential for destruction but also the thawed-out deadly pathogens of yesteryear—bubonic plague, Spanish flu, polio, smallpox—that would kill the rest of those who'd fled for higher ground. It might be just a coincidence.

The wickedness of man was great in the earth, though. Maya knew this for sure. Which begged the question, would you save it? The world? If you could? Was it even worth it? Or would you leave it to its watery, fiery fate? She spun a pencil over the Bible in her lap and thought about illuminating the book in the margins.

This was the ultimatum of their generation, she thought. The ultimate ultimatum. If they didn't do *something,* they would die young, likely clutching their small children to their breasts in some kind of cataclysmic war or weather or, like, cannibal event. 2050. Everyone had envisioned it, in part because it was already happening, except maybe for the cannibals. Cannibalism was still a little ways down the road, after people realized they couldn't get enough nutrition from bugs and lichens. And this dim version of the future was the core anxiety of her z-generation, aside from trying to become relevant on social media. It pulsed beneath everything, ruining their youths, when on the surface, all they really wanted to do was have a good time.

But even if Gen Z wanted to do something to save the world, they had no power, because: old men. Maya began to lose her cool and put her pencil to the Bible. She drew an angry bearded old man in the margin, waving his fist. The old men stood in the way, she thought. It was the boomer's last stand. The boomers wanted to go out with a bang and leave nothing behind for future generations. The boomers wanted to doom the zoomers. They were bent on it. And with advances in healthcare, they just kept hobbling to the polls.

And you couldn't depend on Gen X. Maya shook her head and drew a big blocky *X* in the bottom margin of the Bible page. The boomers "raised" them, sort of. They berated their Gen X children and left them alone to latch-key-raise themselves while the boomers hightailed it out of their marriages and into sports cars and trophy wives. Gen X was completely traumatized and inept. Maya shook her head. It was up to Gen Z, and maybe the millennials if they learned to curb their whiny overconfidence with the right rhetoric.

So. In conclusion, Maya thought to herself, if Gen Z did nothing, the earth would once again become a deserted hellscape, relying on tiny future microorganisms to evolve and repopulate it with some unknowable future species. Dragons maybe? She drew a dragon whose tail wound down the side of Genesis. Definitely something reptilian for sure. Or a phoenix. Rising out of the ashes.

But what could Gen Z do? If the *evil* was causing the *flood*, how could you make people love one another? How could you make people like *people* more than they liked *money*?

She thought about all this ontological bullshit, because, hello? She had landed herself in an *institution*. She was on a grippy sock vacation, as they say on TikTok (Grippy Sock Vacation being an excellent band name that she added to the notebook of collected band-name ideas she shared with her mother. It was their only mother-daughter pastime.)

Anyway, she was on a grippy sock vacation where she was forced to think about how to proceed as a human girl in the Anthropocene. She was forced to think about it, too, because she had inherited, or acquired, or been *afflicted* with certain attributes that perhaps made her privy to what god (and everyone) was thinking.

She had certain *abilities* that sometimes led her to believe that she might actually, kind of, *be* god?

No one knew about this, obvs. She had never written it down. It didn't show up on her Myers-Briggs test on career day.

If things like statistics could actually measure people, which they could not, her Myers-Briggs career test results would *not* have been ENTJ: Possible Careers: Attorney, Psychologist, Entrepreneur; but rather ENTJ: Possible Careers: Bartender, Acrobat, God (?).

- *Bartender* because she had always had a way with those who were down-and-out. And because there were always bartender jobs to be *had*, which was something the career test did not take into account.

It did not consider the economic prospects of the subject taking the test. (Who did they think would foot the bill for law school?)

+ *Acrobat* because she was uberflexible and sometimes fantasized about joining a circus. She could stay on the move, the exertion of her muscles working the world's grief out of her body. She could make temporary friends with the nihilistic Eastern European acrobats, who wore thick, garish makeup and only smiled after two shots of vodka. This was her fantasy, because wouldn't it be ironic, in these times, to *actually* run away with the circus?

+ And *god*. Well, god, because of the things she could do.

Pretend Teardrops or Reaganomics

She currently sat in the "all-purpose" room of Whispering Pines (a stupid name for a psych hospital, because if people were apt to hear *voices*, why surround them with the prospect of *talking trees?*). Anyway. She sat in the all-purpose room of Whispering Pines where she was forced to stay after the incident (!).

The room buzzed with the thoughts of the humans milling about. *I will never have main character energy. Everyone needs to take several !@%& seats. She hates me. I'm so bored. I hate everyone. I only have two vibes: salty and ashamed. I can't stop letting him live rent-free in my head. I swear this is the last time I (use, cut, binge, etc.)... . I can't believe I (used, cut, binged, etc.) again. I'm useless. I can't stop choosing drama. Can sixteen-year-olds have heart attacks?*

The humans—once trusting toddlers sitting crisscross applesauce at circle time—were now the overgrown, lumbering victims of decades of Reaganomics gone wrong. Meaning that in the seventies, Maya knew (because she just knew all "the things" and didn't know why she knew them), America was on the right track. The vibes were about "brotherhood" and "equal rights" and "save the earth." *Roe v. Wade* passed. Carter put solar panels on the White House. There was beginning to be representation in literature and television. Things were on the love-is-love up-and-up! But then Reagan was elected by a Christian Moral Majority (thanks to Phyllis Schlafly), and unless you were a white male, things got worse for you. But even white males won't survive the climate apocalypse. And here we are.

As she sat in the all-purpose room of Whispering Pines, Maya was thrust into the depths of Gen Z sadness.

Bobby could not stop crying. His face was splotchy, like pink parchment paper, and every time he tried to stop, exerting the muscles behind his nasal cavity and biting his tongue, a new hot well of tears would bubble up and then spill down his face in two straight streaks, like errant drips of paint.

"Bobby," Maya whispered. "You have to stop."

He sniffled next to her and a new tear dropped from his chin to his chest. She had to get his mood stabilized because they—the absolute powers that be—were going to do anything they could (more Zoloft, Zyprexa, Haldol, ECT) to neutralize his emotions, and sometimes they went overboard. It was all a big experiment and Maya wanted to help it along. Because if Bobby refused treatment and fled or checked himself out, his insurance company would not pay for the ten days he'd already been here. His parents would be stuck with the $100,000 bill, forced to drain his entire already insufficient college fund.

I'm such a simp loser, Bobby thought, and because Maya sat next to him, and because she was whatever the heck she was, she had to hear it all. *What were my parents thinking, giving birth to me?* he lamented. *Is wishing you were never born the same as wanting to kill yourself?* he wondered. But he didn't think so, ultimately. Ultimately, he didn't think he belonged here, quasi-incarcerated, and that added *injustice* to the many layered reasons why he couldn't stop crying. He was also crying *because he was crying,* if that made any sense.

Maya handed him a tissue from the box that was strategically placed on the coffee table shaped like an enormous clothespin turned on its side. A touch of whimsy to delight the delinquents. Strategically, there were no mirrors anywhere.

"Stop," she urged Bobby again as she took a quick glance at Nurse Abby behind the raised whorl of the nurse's station. Luckily, she was too preoccupied—rattling out pills into tiny paper cups, preparing to make her rounds with the meds cart—to take notice of Bobby's "state." "They'll take the constant crying as a sign of worsening depression, Bobby, and they'll increase your meds, again."

"Which is why I'm crying," he said.

"I know. It's a vicious loop."

"How can I convince them to stop the meds? They make me feel so weird." *I just want to feel like myself again.* The last part he did not speak out loud. She heard him think it.

"'Yourself' was really struggling, though, right?" she asked.

"Just for a second! The thought was *fleeting.* It wasn't even a full thought, it was a thought-ling. A thought-ino. A tiny baby thought. It was not, like, *ideation,*" he snuffled. "I don't need medication. I didn't, like, have a plan to hurt myself or anything." He raised his voice and the tears welled up again and the pink splotches on his face glowed like jigsaw puzzle pieces. Maya zoomed into his brain and body and realized this was true; he wouldn't hurt himself, but she also saw the powerful strangling black vines of self-loathing that were winding their way around his organs.

Come on, she thought at Bobby, and he heard her without realizing she hadn't spoken.

She hoisted herself out of the foam block chair and led him to the heavy industrial door to the outside grounds. It was risky, but she had to get him to a place where he wasn't being watched. She heard the humming buzz of the nosy security camera craning its neck toward them and she punched in the codes to deactivate the alarms. She knew the codes because, well. Bartender, Acrobat . . . She just knew.

Bobby blew his nose and whimpered a little, like a toy poodle, though if you had to compare him to a dog based on his physique, you would choose Bernese Mountain Dog. He had thick, feathery black hair, a block head, and a brisket built for knocking people over on the football field. A large boy-man who'd been wrecked and ravaged by love. As love is wont to do to a person. Especially with one's first experience of it. And especially when love's spurned participant is a white boy used to getting what he wants.

She led Bobby across the well-maintained Garden State Jersey grass to the parking lot where they hid behind a tall, boxy black Mercedes SUV.

"Look at me," she told him. But he was too messy to make eye contact. "Bobby! You need to look at me."

The twins, Aidan and Jacob, were dressed in their volunteer scrubs and had just disembarked from the douchebag BMW their surgeon father had gotten them for their sixteenth birthday. They were already straight A high school students headed for Harvard Medical School, and for some reason (nepotism), the Whispering Pines administration felt it was copacetic for them to intern at the psych ward where they could lord over their suffering peers. It was difficult to deny them the opportunity. They were already publishing papers about adolescent development in the age of plastic, in which they presented their findings about how all those estrogens in the BPA GladWare containers were destroying the brains of our young people.

So far, Maya and Bobby had avoided them in the cafeteria, but had not avoided them entirely, she knew. Maya glanced at them now for a second. They both had close-cut, looping black curls that clung tightly to their heads and sparsely freckled profiles. She tried to get a reading on them, but their brains were so intertwined, she had trouble sussing it all out. They had trouble forming independent thoughts of their own. They spoke in the language of twins. Cryptophasia. More than one, less than two, Maya thought. Creepy. Aidan started thinking at Jacob, *What's our plan of attack?* And Jacob thought back at him, *Hot candy striper? Last time I*—and Aidan finished, *Unbuttoned her cutoffs.*

Maya grabbed Bobby's enormous wrist, where she surreptitiously felt for a scratch, and scurried with him to the other side of the car. "Get down," she told him and they slid to the hot macadam, one in front of each tire so no one would see them beneath the car's underbelly. "The twins are here," Maya whispered to him.

"I'll never live it down if they see me."

But Maya suspected they already *had* seen him and had begun calling him "Cry Bobby." Bobby had concocted an elaborate cover story, telling everyone he was spending some time at his aunt's in California, but the twins, or someone?, had blown his cover. They told the whole school his whereabouts and christened him, now and forever, Cry Bobby. He would never live it down. There was even a CryBobby Finsta account dedicated solely to pictures of his pretend teardrops. (*Only. Evil. Continually.*)

You would think teenagers would tread lightly with this kind of thing, too. You would think they would know the "There, but for the grace of God, go I" concept.

At any moment, at the whim of their fluctuating hormones, exhausted by their grueling college-prep schedules, any one of them could snap. Each and every one of them was just one pregnancy, giant zit, tab of acid, breakup, failed test, strong marijuana gummy, college rejection, date rape, public humiliation, bad selfie, STD, borg, or instance of parental neglect away from the big house. You would think they could *see* that and be *empathetic*, but, sadly, empathy was not the strong suit of the seventeen-year-old brain. Anyway, whether they knew it or not, they all probably belonged in the psych ward at some point. She and old Cry Bobby, here, were just stupid (or lucky?) enough to get caught.

AIDAN AND JACOB

They sat on the grassy knoll killing some time, having a snack, and think-talking to each other before their shift began at Whispering Pines, when they caught sight of Maya and Bobby sneaking around the parking lot and then crouching behind a Mercedes. It was impossible to know which of the twins was thinking which thoughts in their combined consciousness. They couldn't really explain it, and it's what got them interested in neuroscience in the first place.

Ooo Bobby's getting some
I don't think so; he had snot hanging from his nose
Should we report them?
Oh Bobby
It wasn't our fault. Stop thinking it was our fault
We could have done more to help him. Been better
    friends
He was like doomed from the get-go
He wasn't good at baseball . . .
Or soccer
Ball sports in general
Dooms a dude for life if he throws like a girl

There's no recovering from it
Even in the new millennium
Girls don't even throw like girls anymore
But he should have pivoted . . . to like swimming
A lot of boys are bad at swimming
Not enough fat
Yeah, remember when you saved me from drowning
I do. Effing wave pools
Death traps
Maybe he should have done martial arts
He eventually got to the football team
Second-string lineman
He tried to be an inventor slash entrepreneur once
Ohhh. Yeahh. Remember seventh grade? Fanny Ham?
The clear hamster fanny pack for bringing your hamster
    to school
He did not hear the end of it
It's curious, though, because someone else could have
    pulled it off
True. Like here we are, eating yogurt from toddler tubes
And no one would make fun of us
That should be our next paper
How some folks garner social capital in middle school
And others are destined to be targets
And how that shapes the rest of your life
He needs to laugh at himself
He needs to embody his weird
He needs to embobby himself

Ack. True. Hey, you should take it down
CryBobby Finsta? I didn't make it
Get it taken down
Maybe we can replace it with something more Bobby
    positive
We can be better friends to him
Agreed
From now on
Bobby positivity

Then they fist-bumped.

The Incident

The incident that finally landed Maya here was, unfortunately, a very public affair. She had been isolating because she couldn't take the constant chatter of people's thoughts. She didn't want to keep hearing the self-deprecating, self-defeating stories people told themselves all the time. She didn't want to hear all the *wishing of other people dead*, which happened a lot more than you would imagine.

The thoughts that really weighed on her, though, were the ones that other girls had about her. Girls, it must be said, could make the world a very dangerous place for other girls. Girls had to navigate a psychic minefield every day, and it was curious how everyone just shrugged it off. Even worse than "boys will be boys" was how people (adults) just accepted the fact that, in middle school, "girls will be mean."

Maya didn't have to wonder what other girls thought of her. But maybe that was better. Maybe it was easier to know for sure, as she walked by them, that the other girls thought she was a *Freak, Dork, Slut, Bitch, Whore, Sleaze, Nerd, Suck-up, Asswipe, Hermione, Brownnose, Knob gobbler.* Maya at least always knew where she stood. But it didn't make her less lonely.

She, being who or what she was, understood it. The patriarchy wasn't going to give a girl-child (or any child who was not a boy) any power, so if girls wanted any power at all, they had to try to wrestle it from each other. Boys weren't just going to surrender any power to them; boys were content to bask in the golden glow of their princely superiority, which was so subtly but ubiquitously bestowed upon them by everyone in every sphere of life. And who could blame them? It was just a mood. They were born into it. They didn't ask for the power. So girls often took each other down, and they did it by being mean because they didn't realize (and no one told them) there was already enough power to go around in the universe and they didn't have to make other girls feel bad in order to feel good about themselves.

Long story short, girls sometimes hated Maya, because Maya actually did have power. They couldn't put a finger on exactly what it was, but they knew she had some kind of leg up that made people like her. And as soon as that started happening, as soon as the boys started chasing her on the playground as she ran free and coltish through the long grass, or as soon as the teachers started giving her gold stars or special responsibilities like escorting the pukey kid to the nurse's office, there arrived a target on Maya's back and girls began to shoot at it.

It was called "relational aggression" according to the experts. But no one ever did anything to address it. If there were any relational-aggression experts in the state of Pennsylvania they did not venture out to her county of residence.

Before iPhones, it was bad enough, but when they turned twelve, they took to sharing pictures of her accidental temporary camel toe, say. Or a close-up of an errant nose hair sticking out of her nostril. They called her Maya the Pariah. It was a witch hunt, and they were creative in the rumors they started about her: herpes, prostitution with the Amish, masturbating with vegetables. They would say anything, and she was outcast. And the message she took away from it all . . . The world was a dangerous place.

So, eventually, in high school, she holed up for a couple of months in her basement bedroom, alone, with her headphones and her computer. People did ask what was wrong with her of course. But relational aggression is so subtle as to be indescribable. And who wants to be a snitch. And Maya began to believe what other girls thought about her. She was, and this is the worst thing a girl can be in the new millennium, awkward.

Eventually her parents staged an intervention with the help of the school guidance counselor. They forced her out of the basement. Challenged her to attend a school event. "Just once," they pleaded. "See what it's like to be caught up in a crowd filled with school spirit. It will make you feel like you're a part of something." She needed to try, they said. "You love swimming. It will be revelatory."

It wasn't.

Well, it was a little. If you wanted the incessant sexual fantasies of fifteen-year-old boys sitting in the bleachers of a swim meet to be *revealed* to you, which, trust her, you didn't. She doesn't know why she agreed to a swim meet. Without her headphones. No one at school had ever seen her without her headphones. It was like leaving the house without her shirt. But she did it. She let her parents take her to the pool. The natatorium. The echoey vault where reflections of the ripples moving on the water projected themselves onto the walls and made it feel like the entire room was swaying.

Someone turned on some loud music that bounced around the torture chamber, and it thankfully drowned out the mental chatter Maya could hear around her in the bleachers. The boy swimmers stormed out of the locker room and burst through a paper banner held by the girls' swim team. (The girls didn't get to burst through anything, which goes without saying.)

The boys started jumping and boinging elastically to the music, loosening up their muscles, their onesie swimsuits pulled only halfway up, with the shirt part hanging down so they looked like half-peeled bananas. Some of them had peeled the banana so dangerously low that you could almost see their pubes. The girls looked for pubes. There was a pube hunt going on in the minds of the girls in the bleachers. *Did they shave them?* Then everyone cheered. And then, it quieted down, and the swimmers of the first events stretched and snapped on their ridiculous caps and fastened their goggles into their eye sockets. The girls' swim team came and surrounded Maya in the bleachers. She was inundated with their self-hatred.

They just started thinking, right next to her. Their thoughts drowned out the announcement of the first event, and the starter pistol, and the splashing of the boys' oversized feet in the water.

Maya heard that Jamie was sleeping with a scary, aggressive

college dude whom she didn't really know how to handle, and that Emma had failed another history exam. She heard Katherine hate her butt, Ella hate her thighs, Maddie hate her outfit, and Lillie hate her eyes. She heard Abby hate her stomach, Margot hate her zits, Lara hate her freckles, and Izzy hate her tits. She heard the twins hate on each other. She heard Ava May break down. She knew that Maritza Gore would throw up and that Charlotte Jones sucked down two Adderall to get her through her Chem test. She knew Olivia had ripped her shirt off and sexted her boobs to David Smalls. And knew that Alex had called Olivia the sluttiest of them all on Snapchat.

Before she knew what she was doing, Maya stood up, screaming, "Stop! Stop! Stop it! Just stop!" She screamed and held her hands over her ears.

The girls looked up at her, kind of blue-faced and horrified in the aquatic light of the pool. Reflections of ripples undulated across their shocked expressions. But the thoughts kept coming at her: *Freak. WTF. Now what? Aw jeez. Oy, her poor parents. Oh Pariah.* They pitied her. These people who couldn't even be chill and comfortable in their own youthful, hot bodies pitied *her*. Thought after thought after pitying thought came at her, and the only way she could think to escape them was, regrettably, to push people out of her way, hop awkwardly down the metal clanging bleachers and jump, fully clothed, into the pool right in the middle of a race.

Her nickname, forevermore: Cannonball.

Patient Belongings

"Bobby," she said now, the hot black of the Mercedes tire wall burning through her shirt. "Just look at me for one second." When he could finally comply, she locked into his dark, brown-eyed stare and let herself get sucked through his optic nerve and into his memory banks where she found images of his girlfriend Eliza everywhere. She was tiny. Only five foot two, but she had enormous, innocent, doe-like eyes that radiated her love for him when she caught him in her gaze. Her love was real and deep and true, and it was no wonder Bobby felt so much pain in losing her.

Maya vacuumed out his pain. Repaired the resentment and anger that fueled some of his violent feelings toward himself and Eliza. Then she sealed the fragmented tendons of his memories, connecting the bad (Eliza screaming through her tears at him when she discovered the truth about his drunken hookup with Tess) to the good (the first time they held hands, the first time they kissed, the first time they walked the beach, the first time they secretly shared the same bed and felt magically transformed into adults upon rising for the first time together).

She sealed them together so they made sense as a whole. She zapped away his humiliation and shame and tried to leave him with some shred of mental strength and dignity. She linked all the images into a neurological slideshow and set it to "Into the Mystic" by Van Morrison, so he would have something to digest and reconcile and appreciate as timeless and forever. She made the entire relationship feel bittersweet, like nostalgia, instead of desperate, like *the end of the world*.

All of this, his brain would have done on its own, eventually. But they didn't have time. She had no idea how she did it. It was just a thing she could do sometimes. Bartender, Acrobat, etc. . . .

"Whoa," he said, his tears suddenly drying in two muddy rivulets on his face. "I feel cleansed."

"A good cry can do that for people," Maya said. "Boys don't cry enough to know that."

"I stopped crying."

"I see that."

Maya looked at him. New chinks opened up in the wall of sadness behind his eyes and rays of light shot through them. He had a thought that was hopeful, instead of humiliating and hateful. *I hope I get into Bucknell*, he thought.

"You know what you need?" Maya said.

"What?" he asked, jumping up from his squat behind the car tire and holding a hand out for Maya.

"An anthem. Everyone needs an old rock anthem to play loudly in their head. To drown out all the noise."

"'Basket Case.' Green Day."

"Too literal and, like, negative. Try again."

"No, I think it's good. I'm owning my shit and moving on. That's my anthem."

"Fine. Let's go."

They crouched down and Bobby hummed "Basket Case" as they ran tree to tree through the woods so the surveillance cameras wouldn't find them, then snuck back in with the eating disorders unit waiting to be let in their door after their daily slow walk around the grounds. Finally, Maya and Bobby made it back to the lounge.

"Where were you?" asked Nurse Abby, holding out tiny paper cups for each of them.

"Smoke break," Maya answered. And she heard, or perceived, or whatever she could do, Nurse Abby's thoughts. *Oh god please don't let them be having sex on my watch. I should have kept a closer eye on them. Dammit.*

"It was just a smoke break," Maya assured her. And then Nurse Abby thought, *They don't smell like smoke. But they also don't smell like sex, so* . . . "Right," Maya said. "We're clean. I promise." And then she wondered what the heck sex smelled like, having never had the privilege of finding out. Could you smell it on people? And then she knew, because her brain never let her guess at anything for too long. She was never given the luxury of just wondering something. She knew. She could smell it: a salty, sweaty sock floating in the ocean and then trapped for a week in the hamper. Or in a Ziploc. And then spritzed with a little hot lilac. The smell of sex had some undertones of hot, wilted lilac.

Nurse Abby, whose long, tired face would now be forever associated in Maya's brain with the smell of sex, turned back to her and said, "Don't forget, Maya. I have your discharge papers ready. Your parents are coming at three. Make sure you're packed."

"You're leaving?" Bobby asked, his puppy eyes sinking in desperation at the prospect of being abandoned.

"You got this, Basket Case. I'll see you in a few days."

"A few days? You think?"

"You're healed. Just tell them what they want to hear."

"How do I know what that is?"

"Easy," she said, although she knew it wasn't as easy for other people as it was for her. "Just tell them you were wrong about not needing help. They were right all along, and you're grateful. Thank them for their wisdom. Keep sucking up to them, until you're the flipping teacher's pet and they'll let you out."

"I wasn't wrong. I don't deserve to be here."

"Well, you kind of cried constantly for ten days straight. But I think you're better now. Speak truth to power and they'll see your truth and let you out."

She was a little nervous, though, because people in power never wanted to hear the truth. Especially coming from the mouth of a young person. She had tried to shed light before. There was the time when she was six and she told Kristen Jensen's mom that Kristen was dyslexic, and the grown woman slapped Maya across the face. There was the time when she was nine and she told Brian Lester's dad that he dreamed about torturing kittens. Brian's dad told the teacher, and she had to sit with her head down during recess for a whole week. (In the meantime, Brian actually did kill two kittens and scalded his baby sister in the bathtub.)

The thing about telling people the truth was that they always, always shot the messenger to keep the truth at bay. The truth made people very uncomfortable, and therefore, so did Maya.

"You got this," she reminded Bobby, and then gave him a little encouraging nudge on the shoulder on her way out.

....

In the hospital room that she shared with Jenna—the self-harming girl who was making strides—Maya gathered her belongings.

"You going?" Jenna asked. She was reading *The Bell Jar* on top of her brick-red and apricot-scratchy institutional bedspread.

"Yes. And don't."

"Don't what?"

"Don't use the pages of your book to give yourself paper cuts. And why are you reading *that* of all things?"

"I . . . wasn't . . . going to . . . ," Jenna lied. "How did . . . ? Man, you're freakier than all of us combined. How does it feel to be the queen of the freaks?"

Maya ignored that question and walked over to Jenna's bed. "Hey, Jenna, do I have something in my eye?" she asked.

"Why don't you ask Nurse Abby? I'm not a nurse."

"Just look for a second," Maya said, bending over and pulling down the red rim of her lower eyelid so Jenna would look at her.

When she finally did, Maya zoomed in and saw the mostly angry, sad, critical, blaming barbs targeted at Jenna throughout her childhood. *Only you would think that, I wish you were never born, Leave me alone, Pain in the ass, You can't, etc.* The kind of things that resonated the loudest and landed with a heavy thud and dug into the moonscape of your brain and basically stayed there forever because no one else went up to your moon-brain to sweep it all up.

When you're shamed, your brain just gets littered with this moon-junk of heavy garbage-thoughts that make you feel bad about yourself forever. The praise and happy thoughts never land in quite the same way. Any compliments you receive float and drift over the shame junk and never quite do the heavy lifting of sweeping away the criticisms.

Maya tried to blast the moon-junk away as if she were playing a video game. She tried to untie the knotted-up strands of pain and energize Jenna's brain to think one good positive deserving thought about herself. *Love yourself,* she said to Jenna's brain. *No one else can do it for you.* She injected a soundtrack of "Electric Lady" by Janelle Monáe. Then she closed her eyes, and when she opened them, Jenna seemed a little better.

"Why do I have a Janelle Monáe song in my head?" she said. Sadly looking up at Maya and realizing that yet another human was abandoning her, she commented, "That is one piece-of-shit piece of luggage. Vera Bradley? What are you, a Real Housewife from New Jersey?"

"I don't know. My mother packed it. It is hideous, though, isn't it?"

"You look like you're taking the ferry to *Mahtha's* Vineyard or something with your lover who wears salmon-colored shorts and whales on his belt."

Jenna hopped off the bed and headed toward their bathroom, where Maya could hear her rattling around under the sink. "Use these instead," she said, holding up two white plastic bags with hard plastic handles that said PATIENT BELONGINGS in bright blue across the front. "They're more badass."

"True," Maya said, mentally adding Patient Belongings to her list of potential band names. She stuffed her clothes in them, and then she donned the thin, floppy hospital-issued Styrofoam flip-flops over her big fluffy grippy socks she'd worn since they'd taken away her shoelaces. If they wanted her to be a mental patient, she may as well play the part until the bitter end. "What do we do with this?" Maya asked, holding up the hideous calico sack.

"With that, we make hats," Jenna said, tearing it in half with the superhuman strength of her pent-up frustrations, and for the first time in six weeks, Maya actually laughed.

Luckily, they have art therapy in the "Pines," Jenna thought. She was messed up for sure, but the art showed her that deep down inside herself, at her very core, there was courage. She was powerful as heck, maybe too powerful for this world, in fact, and that's why she had to hurt herself. She did it in order to bring her whole vibe back in line with the meekness and weakness people expected from a girl.

She hobbled herself to fit in. It was an old story, like that sixties TV show *Bewitched,* where Samantha, even though she could have dominated the mortal world with her magic, suppressed her power to become Darrin's bitch. The whole show was a warning to any woman who dared to embody her power. Men needed to keep women in line. So they invested big Hollywood dollars in big propaganda to make women think that power was shameful. It worked.

We all know now that powerful women are unlovable, and Jenna wanted to be loved more than she wanted to be herself.

It helped when she painted. She painted her urges, and they looked like raw meat, or fire, or acid rain, or white rage. She got them out of her system and then made them more palatable by decorating them with bucolic vines of flowers around the edges, or rabbits, or teapots, or some other icon of domesticity, because what are we all if not walking palimpsests covered in layers and layers of deceptive paint illusions. Art therapy helped.

While Jenna painted what it *felt* like to have demons, Bobby, sitting across from her now, painted his actual demons. He painted violent, bloody war-torn depictions of his monsters and what they would do to innocent beings if left to their own devices.

Jenna feared he was perhaps misdiagnosed. He hid these from the art therapist, of course, and showed her instead his drawings of roses and rainbows. Jenna feared he was not being helped at all and should probably not be let loose on the world any time soon, but she knew, because he was a bro with parents who were "involved," he'd be sprung well before she would.

No matter. She painted him a note with a thick stiff brush you would use in preschool.

ARE YOU OKAY? it said.

Bobby flipped it over and, using his finger dipped in black paint, wrote, *IDK*.

Frankendaughter

"Hi, honey," her mother said, enveloping her in their familiar interlocking embrace. Maya looked like her mom—voluminous strawberry-blond waves that grew in every direction, milk white skin, a smattering of caramel-colored freckles—but she had always been a few inches shorter, so she could fit right into her mother's body like yin to yang.

It's worse than I thought, she heard her father think, as he took in Maya's yellow calico Vera Bradley hat and matching bra-top she and Jenna had had the extra material to make. He looked at Maya's pale, doughy complexion, her grease-stained floor-length hippie skirt, her hospital slippers, and the overflowing patient-belongings bags they give to homeless people. Maya wore big, round dark sunglasses so she wouldn't see directly into anyone's eyes.

"You look great," he finally managed to say, but was thinking, *Jesus, she looks worse. We should never have let this happen. She wasn't like this when we dropped her off.*

Like what? Maya wondered, adjusting the cone-shaped hat so it tipped a little more jauntily to the side. *Maybe I should have washed my hair,* she thought, trying to calculate when she had washed it last and coming up blank.

"What do you want to eat?" her mom asked.

"It's three o'clock," Maya answered. "That's not really a mealtime. I'm programmed to eat at six. Lights out at ten. I'm regulated now. You've had me regulated. Automated. Frankendaughtered."

"That's good, though, right, honey? I think what you *needed* was some *limits*, right? I've been thinking a lot about this, you know, because it's always the mother's fucking fault, right? Fuck." Apparently, estrogen was the sole chemical responsible for keeping people from cursing. As her mother's slowly drained from her body during menopause, her language became a litany of curses that would shame most truck drivers. She had no filter left. Words rushed to her brain all at once and she had no time to choose the correct ones. She just blurted what she could manage.

"Stace," her dad said. "Language."

"We're picking up our daughter from a f . . . mental hospital, Glen," her mother said. "I don't think we need to worry about propriety anymore. It's time for real communication."

"You were the one *just* talking about limits . . . ," he mumbled as he opened the creaky door of the truck for them.

Poor Glen, Maya thought. He had a lot on his plate managing her mother and the household she neglected for her perpetually unfinished creative "pursuits," not to mention helping to manage her "business" that threatened to thrust them into bankruptcy. He was tired and resigned and hopelessly enmeshed in his fading love for her mother. Even his name was sort of pathetic. Glen. It was the topographic equivalent to a ditch. Well, not exactly, but it was a peaceful, gradual thing. Nothing like the drama of a valley or gorge. Poor Glen. He got into the driver's seat, which was a place he rarely inhabited metaphorically.

The family car had always been a pickup truck because the family business was a record store, and they needed the truck bed for carting around the inventory. Maya climbed into the half bench behind her parents and sat between them like she always did. A three-headed monster.

"Yes. Limits," her mother went on, and Maya knew that while picking up her daughter from Whispering Pines was almost her worst nightmare, analyzing how she'd ended up there would keep her mother's mind busy for a very long time. She tended to overanalyze. "Hon. I've been thinking about this, and we should have set limits. You've never even made your bed."

"Well, you don't make your bed . . ."

"That's what I'm talking about. I don't have limits. You don't have limits. No one ever drew any lines. People need lines and boundaries and rituals. Kids need them and I didn't give them to you. It *is* my fault. As much as I don't want to admit it."

"So I'll make my bed."

Some old Beatles song about thumb-sucking and a bathroom window came on the radio, and her mother, who had just calmed down, piped up again.

"And another thing," she said. "You young people don't have *albums*. It's affecting your psyche."

Uh oh, here we go, thought Maya. This was, being a vintage vinyl salesperson and a devotee to the magic of music, one of her mother's standard Rants.

"How can your young brains make connections when there is no *conversation* happening in your music? You download some tinkly bullshit song set to a drum machine and it's not related in any way to any other song on your playlist. Your music is just another distraction. Fragmented pieces that never create a whole. Albums, my dear Maya, *heal* people. With their cohesive stories and characters and imagery and transitions. You listen to an *album* and you become whole. You don't listen to 'She Came in Through the Bathroom Window' without also listening to 'Golden Slumbers' into 'Carry That Weight' into 'The End.' You don't listen to individual songs on *Abbey Road*. You just don't. They work together as a medicine for your mind. Which is why all you young people are going cr . . . um, struggling. No albums."

"Stace!" Glen said again.

"It's okay, Dad," Maya said. "I know I'm crazy. In the sense that everyone's fucking crazy."

"Don't *you* start with the language. See," he said to Stacy. "Now she's starting with the language. Can you tone it down?"

"I really can't. It's a fucking problem," her mother mumbled, turning her attention to her phone, aimlessly scrolling through her Facebook page and her Instagram and then her email account filled with sales announcements from the retailers she'd recently blown a month's salary on.

Her online shopping mania was an effing problem, too, Maya thought. There really was no money for college. She'd have to get into an Ivy, where they gave out pity tuition to those whose parents made less than a hundred grand. If she went to college at all. She could just get a coding job and work forever out of their basement.

"I mean, Joni Mitchell's *Blue?*" her mother piped up again. "That record *healed* me when I moved away from my lover in California. *The Very Best of Sinatra?* Even that compilation tells a story."

"Yeah. That the lady was a tramp," her dad deadpanned, and Maya could see that he was still thinking about the words California and "lover" and how that word strategically did not specify gender. He had always wondered about her time in California before they'd met.

At the same time, Maya could see her mother remembering the lovers. There had been seven. *It was San Francisco, after all. Before the flipping dot-com yuppies ruined everything,* her mother thought.

It wasn't easy having even very occasional access to your mother's brain. Thankfully Maya had been born to a woman who blurted out most of her thoughts as soon as they entered her mind, anyway. So it wasn't enormously surprising to sometimes know what was going on intimately behind the scenes. And most people, as a survival instinct, could tell what their mothers were thinking just by looking at their faces. Disappointment. Disapproval. Dismay. And the occasional Pride and then maybe Envy in an infinite loop. Disappointment. Disapproval. Dismay. Pride. Envy. Repeat. Most people already knew.

That's the way it was with mothers and daughters, anyway.

The loop was different with the mothers of boys. The mother-son loop was a little more like: Delusional Pride. Overestimation of Son's Abilities. Slight Disappointment. Forgiveness of All Transgressions. Boys Will Be Boys. Repeat. This, she knew, was somewhat at the root of all the evils of the patriarchy. The way mothers fell in love with their sons.

"Home sweet home," her father said as they pulled into the driveway of their tiny cottage on Derby Street in New Hope, Pennsylvania. It was set back into the woods and built of stone with decorative wooden eaves cut out like doilies and ancient wooden shutters with tiny hearts cut out of the bottom. Straight out of "Goldilocks and the Three Bears." Behind it ran a babbling brook that was filled with stepping stones and stretched, if you followed it, to the Delaware River, which sometimes thundered behind the quaint village and used to power its mill. The mill was now a playhouse, which, because of the town's location smack-dab in between New York and Philadelphia, drew some significant talent during summer stock. Zendaya had come one summer, and of course Timothée Chalamet, who was always everywhere all the time doing all the things.

Aaron Burr lived here once, in this exact house, and it had drawn some attention a few years ago as the wacko play-pro apostles of the show *Hamilton* sometimes drove through town singing "I'm not throwing away my shot!" and occasionally throwing eggs at the onetime house of the man who shot Alexander. That was truly the only excitement they really ever experienced here in the woods. And Maya liked it that way.

She was happy to be home. Especially happy to see Maurice, their black mini poodle mix who was named after a character in a Steve Miller song. He almost wiggled himself to death in greeting Maya. She picked him up and let him lick her face and then asked him if he wanted to go out back to the brook so they could turn over some rocks in search of crayfish. That was their favorite thing to do together. The rush of the brook and whistle of the breeze through the trees drowned out any noisy thinking in a three-mile radius, and Maya could find peace and quiet back there.

Maurice could read *her* mind in a way. He always knew when she was awake in the middle of the night even when she lay there pretending to be asleep. She would slowly drift out of an intense dream, and before she even opened her eyes, as if he, too, had been watching her dream come to an end, he would jump on her bed and lick her face and beg her to let him out at three in the morning. She didn't, though, for fear of the enormous coyotes who had drifted down from their yuppie-pillaged habitats of upstate New York to terrorize Pennsylvania's catkind and the safety of local tiny dogdom.

Maurice could read her mind. But she couldn't hear his. Which made him her favorite being on the planet. She also used this as a gauge. She knew if one day she could hear Maurice's thoughts, she'd have finally, truly gone off the deep end.

"Going out back," Maya said and Maurice followed her, leaping two feet at a time like a bunny down toward the brook where he would show Maya which rocks to flip in order to find a tiny skittering gray crayfish. She'd grab its torso and place it on a dry rock, letting him batter it around for a bit before plopping it back into the brook.

When this got boring she walked upstream by moving

rock to rock, the rushing water drowning out the sounds of everything, while Maurice followed behind, walking in the water and biting at its surface for an occasional drink or to eat a water bug that balanced on top of it like an arachnoid figure skater. She went to her favorite rock, a gray boulder slightly bigger than a basketball, worn down to almost a perfect sphere. She'd marked the water level last spring with a silver sharpie and now it was fully submerged by at least two inches. The water was rising. . . . If you believed that the flood was happening as a result of our bad behavior as humans, which Maya hadn't really established, but thought was an interesting hypothesis . . . then the wickedness, as evidenced by this drowning boulder, was great in the earth.

She was so tired of thinking about it, though, so she took a deep breath. The best part of home was that it was damp and dark and cool. She could shy away from the light, the light of knowing everything, and simply be herself. She let the hem of her black skirt drag through the water and could feel the water climbing up the fabric.

"Maya," she heard her dad call. And she knew she should answer him. She could sense his anxiety and felt him wondering if she'd thought about drowning herself in these six (now eight) inches of water.

She hadn't. In spite of everything, she still had a will to live.

MAURICE THE DOG

Some people call me Maurice / 'Cause I speak of the pompatus of love. This is from the Steve Miller song after which I am named.

Do I speak *of* the pompatus of love or speak *from* the pompatus of love? It doesn't matter, because no one knows what pompatus means. Steve Miller made it up because it had the right number of syllables and sounded like a magnificent place to speak from . . . or of. I choose from. I imagine the "pompatus of love" as a godly *place* like a pulpit, or a mount, like the Sermon on the Mount, or like Delphi, the place where the oracle sat and told the future. The pompatus is a place, from which Maurice speaks. The pompatus lends Maurice-from-the-song the authority he needs to convince his lover that he is not, in fact, a dog. Which, ironically, I am. But dogs are loyal. We're always "right here at home" like the song says.

We're right here at home, tamed and detached from the original intent of our instincts. I can still feel the instincts, though. They feel like certainty. They feel like god sending electric currents through my body that say "Chase squirrel!" But the humans don't like instincts, and so they don't feel the electric currents from god telling them how to behave. This is what I've noticed. Or maybe they listen to the wrong instincts from their fear place instead of the right instincts that come from the pompatus of love.

Take Maya for example. God is speaking to her, I can see it. And instead of feeling the certainty of that, instead of knowing what she knows, she lets bad people tell her she's sick. They want her to be part of the pack, which you can't be when you're the alpha. Every dog knows this. Alphas exist. But the humans don't like to fall in line behind alphas, especially a female alpha, so they make the female alphas feel bad or something.

If I were able to speak to Maya in human barks, I would tell her the things of the songs I have to listen to all day in the record store. There's one about not giving a damn about your bad reputation or "girls who run this mutha" or the one that says "you don't own me."

She also needs to speak from the pompatus of love. That's how to be a good alpha leader. But it's so hard to do that when everyone else is so afraid and they want you to be afraid along with them.

Squirrel!

Womb Music

Maurice shot off in pursuit of a squirrel and, chasing him, Maya ran into Scott the town hermit, who had lived off the grid since before there was a grid.

Most women walking alone in the woods would be terrified of Scott. He seemed dirty. He let his gray ponytail just grow matted with the earth and twigs he slept on. He had a knife scar down his left cheek from having been, well, knifed, in the service. As he aged, the scar became less noticeable because it had folded itself between the layers of his face creases, which were bronzed over from his rugged outdoor life. He'd been living in the woods ever since his tours in the army, the best way for him to grapple with the evil he'd witnessed in another senseless war that didn't need to happen. He couldn't take it anymore. The evil being continuous. The wickedness being great.

Maya thought of him as a mentor really. If he could live out here without all the chatter of humanity getting him down, then so could she one day, right? Maybe she could get him to show her the ropes.

He squatted on the bank to wash his tin camping dishes in the brook, and it just went to show what living off the land could do for a body. His easy sinewy limbs folded up next to him like a frog, and he could do things most American bodies couldn't because of the centuries-long tradition of sitting on chairs. What was the most detrimental invention to humankind? It was the lowly chair. Sitting in one for hours a day atrophied your hip flexors. Most men his age could never squat this way or spring into action to catch a squirrel or swing up onto a tree branch with the gymnastic ease of an orangutan. We are supposed to be able to do these things but sadly cannot because of hours spent sitting in chairs.

"Hi, Scott," Maya said.

"Oh, hey, Maya. Did you hear about the ordinance?" he asked. Scott was a man of few words, obvs.

"No. What ordinance?"

"Bobcats," he said, and rather than explain, he held out a ripped piece of newsprint from the part of the paper no one reads. Maya skimmed the small print. Yadda yadda yadda bobcats. Yadda yadda open season. Town council vote.

"Huh," Maya said.

"Sad," Scott said. "They want to hunt them. But bobcats don't really hurt anyone, and you can't eat them. I've tried."

It wasn't looking good for bobcats. People here liked to hunt. In fact, the only hunting ordinance that had ever been denied in town history was the one that tried to create an open season for Bigfoot in 2005. It got shot down (pun intended) because Bigfoot was too humanoid and because they were afraid hunters would unintentionally shoot Scott.

"You shouldn't aspire to be me," he said, completely out of the blue, as he filled his cup in the brook and then took a sip.

"What?" Maya asked. Could he hear *her* thoughts? "What do you mean? Wait, is that, like, potable water?"

"Well, I hear the gossip," Scott said, holding another full cup of brook out to her as if to say "cheers." "And I know how you sometimes like to isolate. How you went to the hospital. I don't think you should do that. I think you should make connections," he said.

"Connections?"

"Yeah. With other people."

"But people are terrible. And the good ones don't seem to like me. I make people uncomfortable, I think."

"Waaah," Scott cried sarcastically. "Try harder."

"For people to like me? Why?"

"Not *all* people. Some people, though. Because when we truly see each other, like you and I are seeing each other right now?"

Scott paused here for dramatic effect and peeled a piece of jerky from his jerky stick with a giant pocketknife, then stuck it in his mouth.

"Yeah?"

"That is god," he said.

"Whoa," Maya said. "Thanks."

"Don't mention it." Scott nodded, and then Maya heard the obnoxious clang of the cowbell her mother used to call her in from the woods when she was ten. Tensions seemed to be mounting in her parents' house, and she would have to talk her parents out of their respective trees.

"Duty calls," Maya said. "See you later, Scott."

"Peace be with you," Scott said, but he held up a hand in what looked like a gesture from Star Trek.

Her mother, the firstborn overachiever, obviously took this mental hospital stint as a referendum on her entire performance as a parent. For her sake, Maya would have to begin to act like a normal teenager. God, what did that even mean? She would need to make, as much as it made her cringe, *friends*. *Connections*, like Scott said. Well, maybe one singular friend. If she could make a friend and get her diploma, her parents might feel somewhat redeemed. That was her job now. She was the Redeemer. That was her superpower.

Back inside, the air in the house hung close. That was what they always said in old-timey books. The air was close. It clung to Maya in a panoply of steamy smells. Her life was passing before her nose. The musty scent of the record collection boxes in the corner, the dewy rot of the roses outside, the meaty crackle of chicken skin, the sharp bite of her dad's hair gel, her mother's sweet hippie funk—it all combined and enveloped her.

The giant record console in the living room—the one Maya used to lie next to when she was sad, leaning her head against the speakers, so close that she could taste their bitter vibrating metallic screens—currently blared *Songs in the Key of Life*. Her mother's choice for life's new beginnings. (For endings, she also chose Stevie Wonder. His *Fulfillingness' First*

·*Finale* was for her grief.) "Isn't She Lovely" came on, the baby cooing and gurgling for almost a full minute before cuing the famous bass line, and Maya scooted up their tiny staircase before her mother could tell her *again* the specific choreography she envisioned for the three of them dancing to this at Maya's wedding. She even planned to hire a special harmonica-ist. Maybe, after all this, her mother's wedding fantasies were finally fading. Maya could only hope. The only song they could dance to now was "Isn't she awkward / Why will she not glow up...."

Upstairs in his room, her father plucked his guitar from its special wall hanger, which chased away the cat. The cat hated the guitar.

"Everyone's a critic," he said as Maya sat down on their unmade bed.

He picked around on the strings and eventually landed on the lick for the Beatles' "Blackbird," which he mastered when her mom was pregnant so he could play it for Maya every day in the womb. It was her womb music; but sadly, it didn't trigger any prenatal memories for her. She humored him, though, swayed a little, and pretended to be consoled. He sang the line about waiting for moments to arrive and looked her right in the eye.

"This moment?" Maya asked, sweeping her pointer finger around her handmade bra-shirt and her foam hospital slippers.

"Any moment," Glen replied. "That's the magic of the song. Every moment is a chance to start over, so the song always works."

"Does it work now?" Maya asked.

"Yes."

"How 'bout now?"

"Yup," he said, avoiding the instinct to turn even *this* into a real argument. "How 'bout a hug?"

"Sounds good," Maya said.

"Try to take it easy on your mom," he said. "At least for tonight."

"Since this is all about her."

"Everything is always about her." He smiled on one side of his lips.

"Right."

"I think that's what we like about her, though."

"All of her her-ness."

"Yeah."

Maya's mom tried to be chill at dinner. But that was never her natural state, so it was awkward. She set the table with an actual tablecloth and flowers and pewter napkin rings in the shape of standing-up poodles that had cannonballs shot through their bellies.

"What are these?" Maya asked.

"They reminded me of Maurice. I thought you'd like them."

"I do. They're great. Perfect touch of whimsy."

Maya had to pretend to like them. Her mother couldn't always say what she wanted to say (Gen X, raised by boomers, etc., there was no emotional intelligence proffered or gleaned), Maya knew. So all the love went into stupid shit like napkin rings.

"What's for dinner?" Maya asked, changing the subject, and then she thought into her mother's brain because she knew that Stacy needed to hear it: *I love you, Mama.*

An unexpected sob caught in Stacy's throat. The certain inflection of the word "Mama" disarmed her. *Mama* was everything she was and everything she seemed to be failing at and the only thing that mattered. Words still eluded her and she pulled Maya in for a hug and kissed her on the top of her head. "Lasagna," she said.

They sat around the table and passed things around, everyone avoiding conversation. Her dad said something about the weather. And that was about as much small talk her mother could take. She canceled her chill and pulled out a list. "So they say these are the things we have to do. Next steps," she said, waving a brochure in the air. "Thing one, therapy. Twice a week. Thing two, school."

"Wait, no," Maya said. "Please no school. I don't need school. Everyone at Harvard these days is homeschooled."

"The only people who are homeschooled are those quiver people," Stacy said.

"You mean Quakers?" Glen asked.

"No, quivers. The ones who turn their wives' uteruses into clown cars. Filling up their quivers with the arrow-children for Christ or something. The ones with nineteen children."

"Are they clowns or arrows?" Maya asked. "You're mixing your metaphors."

"I don't know, but all of those kids . . . It's like a litter. How can they think that's what God wants?"

"No one knows what God wants," said Glen.

"Exactly," Maya's mom agreed.

Maya wanted this conversation to be over. She had a feeling, in perhaps being god, that "what God wanted" was never really going to matter.

"I'm not going to school," she said.

"Maya, what did we just talk about upstairs?" Glen asked.

Glen didn't know it, but she was already three steps ahead of him. Acting recalcitrant and obstreperous. (They made her study vocab at the "Pines.") Performing for them a typical teen. She could just go along with the plan, but that would seem compliant and obsequious. That would send up a red flag. Her resistance was more believable teen behavior. She had to show a little spunk.

Maya's mother held the brochure up in the air again. "I defer to the experts. School will be good for you. Come on, Maya. You have to start having some goals. It will feel good to have goals. You're so brilliant," she said and reached out to squeeze Maya's cheeks together. Maya could see her mother trying to convince herself that this was true. Whatever brilliance Maya could muster would always be tarnished by the doubt she could sometimes read in her mother's mind.

"I have a goal," Maya said to her mother instead.

"Good. That's great, Maya. Let's hear it."

"You know that YouTube video with the couple who adopts a baby lion, and then the lion gets too big for the apartment, so they set him free in Tanzania or something, and then they go to Tanzania ten years later, and the lion, now a full-grown wild beast, just recognizes them on the savanna and runs over and gives them a giant lion hug?"

"Yeah?"

"We should do that. Adopt a lion cub. Set it free. Wait ten years and then see if it recognizes us in the wild. That's my goal."

"That would be cool," Glen said without irony, which is why Glen always won for favorite parent and her mother always won for best actual *parent*.

"Ugh," Stacy said and took a giant forkful of lasagna without taking her eyes off Maya. Maya kept her in her gaze and tried to invisibly convince her *I am going to be okay*, and then she winked, which drove her mother crazy because it indicated she wasn't taking this seriously enough.

"Fine," Maya said before her mother could go off again.

"Fine, what?" her mother asked.

"I'll go to school."

"You will?"

"Yes. But please can it be the public school?" She knew that Bobby went there, and she wanted to keep an eye on him. And there must be some kids there she knew from her toddler days. "I don't want to go back to Concordia Academy," Maya said, recalling her parents' dwindling bank account and the disappointed glances from the admissions team who secretly knew they shouldn't have taken a chance on her in the first place—an artsy financial-aid kid from the wrong side of the tracks. She was now a mark on the Academy's precious reputation. She couldn't face them and their cold, Ivy-educated attempts at empathy.

"I've already spoken to someone at New Town High," her mother said. "You can start as early as tomorrow."

Maya had already known this, of course, and had been mentally preparing herself for the larger, institutional experience. She hoped she'd have some anonymity at New Town High. She'd just become another number, floating around in a faceless pool of infinite adolescence. She could easily get lost. "Tomorrow, then," Maya replied. "Let's do it."

"Are you sure?" said Glen. "You don't have to rush into things." To which both of them exasperatedly replied, "Glen!"

Hidey-Hole

The facade of New Town High School did what facades are designed to do: deceive. The sturdy, well-built brick exterior of yesteryear, flanked by wise old oak trees, evoked a simpler time when all folks had to do was learn how to use a slide rule to get into the college of their choice. (Though even that idea was deceiving, because it was only true for white male folks.) Upon stepping through the large arched doorway and into the echoing portico, there was no time to catch one's breath before being ricocheted into a series of additional labs and wings and hallways from different decades, latched on to the front like an awkward freight train. Maya and her mom followed the inlaid tile paw prints on the floor (Go Bobcats!), which led them to The Office.

After the principal welcomed them, he gave them a schedule, a locker combination, and a "Just Maddie" to show them around.

"Is it short for Madison or Madeleine?" her mother asked.

"Just Maddie," Maddie chirped.

Maya gave her mother a warning gaze, a shot across the

bow, to make sure she didn't editorialize or criticize. The child was not responsible for her own naming.

"Just Maddie" may not have been named by human parents, though. She may have been hatched from a 3D printer or put together in a lab like a cyborg or an android—what's the difference again?—not only because of the way she mechanically recited her lines on her millionth tour of the school, but also because her stature was something only a horny mad scientist could have dreamed up. She seemed chiseled from the composite dreams of everyone who had ever attended a comic-con. Long, smooth, powerful legs encased in shiny futuristic Lycra pants dead-ended into platform sneakers that padded the institutional tile as she walked powerfully toward the cafeteria. Thankfully, on top, just to leave a little to the imagination, she wore a baggy sweater that hung loosely off her left shoulder.

"So, this is the cafeteria," Maddie said while checking her phone and waving her manicured hand around the mostly empty space that hosted clusters of male children in sports garb who couldn't keep their hands off one another, constantly touching with fake punches and faux headlocks, incessantly and inadvertently grazing each other's balls and nipples—the homoerotic stuff of their still-repressed culture of gender binaries.

Scattered among them were teams of girls looking at computers and doing all the actual work of high school. Busy beavers, they. Maya saw her mother take them in, hunting like a she-bear for a person she thought Maya could relate to. Her mother homed in on Helen, a lonely, bespectacled girl, reading an analog book in the corner, pretending to stay focused while footballs and paper airplanes and conversations zoomed past her head.

"Who's that?" her mom asked her, and Maya's heart sunk. This was the companion her mother would choose for her. The saddest, loneliest girl in the room. Maya just stared at her mother and thought, *Give me a little credit*. Her mother could not read her mind, per se, but she could read her eyes. "What? She likes books," she said.

"A lot of people like books, Mom. You like books, don't you, Maddie? What's your favorite book?"

Her mother stared at Maya with a snide sideways smile and her thought came through: *Of Mice and Men, Mockingbird, or Gatsby. She's only read the books that are required.*

"Oh, definitely *To Kill a Mockingbird*. Such a good book."

"Totally," said Maya, and she wished her mother would wipe that smug look off her face.

Maybe I should show them the library, thought Maddie, and though Maddie tried not to judge, Maya watched Maddie look her up and down and gather data about Maya's hair, face, nails, and outfit. *Forgettable . . . Drab*, Maddie thought, which was almost good. Maya would not be seen as a threat by the popular girls if she could just lie low.

"I think I'm set here," Maya said. After all, she did know everything already. "I'll figure out the rest on my own. But thanks so much for your help."

"Okay," Maddie said. "Well, if you got this, I'll go study for a history quiz. Here's your schedule. Oh, and I'm supposed to show you my senior capstone project. It's room one forty-three. We turned it into a wellness center for, you know, when you're feeling anxious and stuff? Too many people were feeling anxious because of all the homework and the pressure to get, like, recruited or, like, you know, the end of the world. It's a lot. So it's, like, filled with pillows and stress balls and slime and incense and yoga mats and friends to talk to, you know? So you don't feel alone with all this," Maddie said with another sweep of the manicured hand. "It can be a lot. I know."

Maya looked into Maddie's greenish eyes to see if she really *knew, knew* or if she signed up for peer counseling and dreamed up Room 143 to amp up her college résumé, to create her *brand*: the hot girl with a heart. It was all about the branding. On the Common App, she would be Mental Health Maddie™. Maya scanned Maddie's memory banks, searching for a chink in the hot-girl armor: a learning disability, perhaps? A controlling mother, a deceased father, a disabled sibling, a battle with cancer, a dead pet, divorce? Did she know any of these things? Did she know true pain? And then she found it, because True Pain™ walked by in his chinos and oversized flannel right then, and Maddie flinched. Voldemort in a pair of Vans. *It wasn't worth it to report him,* she heard Maddie remind herself. *Of course he thought I wanted to. But I didn't want to. I just have to get through this year.* They all did.

Room 143 was the last place Maya wanted to be; she'd just been released from hearing the sad thoughts of a whole hospital full of depressed children, but she needed to show her mom she was trying. And after what she'd just learned about True Pain, she wanted to show Maddie some support, so she said, "Thanks, Maddie, I'd love to see that."

They, the powers that be, didn't have a ton of real estate to share with Maddie and her wellness-room initiative. It wasn't a thing (like football!) that attracted the big donors. So they gave her an old closet beneath the stairs, like the muggle Dursleys gave to Harry Potter. Still, as young people are wont to do, they made the best of it.

Strands of beaded macramé hung in the doorway, and Maya rattled them as she ducked in. Painted on the cinder block back wall were the numbers 1-4-3 and, above them in a rainbow shape, I LOVE YOU. It was Mr. Rogers who was obsessed with the number 143 because of the "mystical" (coincidental) connection to the number of letters in I Love You, and apparently Ms. Hirsch, Maddie's faculty advisor who was raised on reruns of *Mister Rogers* and whose moral code was entirely Mr. Rogerian, came up with the idea to name the room "143." She took it as a sign that there hadn't already been a room 143 in the school's initial floor plan. There was also a small poster of Mr. Rogers, inexpertly laminated and peeling up a bit in the corners, that depicted him smiling in his red sweater. WON'T YOU BE MY NEIGHBOR? in big seventies bubble letter font spread out in an arch over his head. It was soothing, Maya had to admit. The world could use more neighbors. Someone, lovingly Maya hoped, had given him a Sharpie mustache and soul patch.

A circular mandala rug sat in the center of the floor of 143 and was held in place by dark green cushions arranged as if this were a beach campfire. Instead of a fire, in the center stood a potted plant, offering oxygen to the humans slouched on the paisley couch strumming an old acoustic guitar. A mini fridge in the corner held the promise of healthy snacks.

Requisite rolled-up yoga mats hung against another wall in a smart-looking rack made of recycled wood. What caught her mother's attention was the record player in the corner and the Post-its stuck at random onto a mirror that read, *You're amazing. So Smart. I see you. Be Bold. Today will be the best. Breathe.* Etc.

"This is great, isn't it, Maya? I wish they had this at your old school." This is what she said. But what Maya assumed she thought (she couldn't actually read it like she read everyone else) was *Oh great. She's going to sit in here all day wearing her headphones. Just what she needs, another basement hidey-hole.* Maya particularly hated that phrase for some reason, and she visibly cringed. "We can donate some records. Only happy ones, of course. We own the record store over in New Hope."

"Cool. But sad ones are okay, too. We strive to acknowledge all of our feelings," said the boy strumming the guitar.

"Yeah. Sometimes we come in here and listen to breakup songs for an hour and just cry our eyes out," the girl next to him agreed. She had big round brown eyes and a sheet of ombré hair that was dip-dyed light blue, like the bottom of a beachy skirt.

"Great," said Stacy. "Do you have Leonard Cohen's 'Chelsea Hotel #2'? I think I have a forty-five. Can you play forty-fives? He wrote it for Janis Joplin, you know. And you *need* 'Hallelujah.' Also Leonard Cohen, but I will allow the Brandi Carlile cover, in spite of her unfortunate name. The *i* at the end just kills me. But her voice. Warbly. Appalachian. Gorgeous."

Maya watched the couch-people take her mother in. The flared jeans, the earthy brown T-shirt (was she wearing a bra?), the dozens of mostly organic beaded bracelets, the thumb rings, the too-long-for-her-age wavy strawberry-blond hair. They tried to process it. *Who is this person?* they thought. *Do we like her? She seems desperate. Do we trust her?* Maya saw the thoughts as they pinged around the kids' brains like pinballs. *No,* they decided. *Tilt. Game Over.* They got back to whatever they were doing before Maya walked in.

Great, thought Maya. She was already persona non grata in "the neighborhood." *And these could have been "my people."* They were at least striving for emotional intelligence. She was searching for signs of any kind of intelligence, particularly in people who didn't "borg." These could have been her "friends." That was her goal here. Maya only needed one or two people and a diploma. Why couldn't her mother keep her mouth shut?

Stacy looked at Maya then, and Maya could see the pain that wove itself in and around all of her mother's organs like a net. Her entire insides were enmeshed in a thick white net of pain and fear, like a salted imported ham hanging in a deli. Maya saw the same thing in all the mothers who came to visit their kids at Whispering Pines. The mothers felt their kids' pain more acutely than the kids themselves did. They walked into group therapy with heavy steps, barely able to move their limbs and remove their trendy handbags from their shoulders. Kids weren't supposed to notice it, but Maya noticed everything. She'd have to double down on the plan to become a Normal Teenager™, if only for her mother's sake.

"I'm okay, Mom," Maya told her as they stepped back into the bustling hallway.

Maya felt Stacy's breath catch for a second, snagged on a rare psychic outcrop of her own empathy. "You have to do this, but high school really is often a piece of shit, Maya. Things will get better. Later. When you're released from the group-think. When so many people aren't judging you all the time. When there's less pressure to be the same as all these idiots."

"I know. I can do this. And they're not idiots. And people will always be judging us all of the time." This was something she knew for sure. The trick was not to care, which she knew wasn't as easy as it sounded. "You should go."

And off her mother trudged, her bracelets jangling a little, looking down so Maya wouldn't see her tears. It was like being dropped off for the first day of kindergarten.

....

School. Maya walked away from room 143 and into the stream of it. Other people's thoughts rushed into her head. Most of them were *I'm going to fail. I need to copy Abby's notes. I have six minutes to finish my essay. I forgot my baseball glove. I don't know my lines. I have no idea what's going on in Calc.* Then she had a thought of her own. What if people stopped pushing kids to complete the learning of college in high school? What if everyone just did high school in high school and college in college and slowed everything the eff down? *What if we all just did that? Then we wouldn't need room 143. Everyone just slow down.* She almost screamed it out loud when two lacrosse players rushed by her, and the backdraft alone pushed her into the lockers.

She fought the urge to cry. The weight of everything gathered in the back of her throat, pushed upward, threatening to
erupt through her tear ducts. *Do not cry at your new school!*
she told herself. But that made it worse. She shook her hair
in front of her face and moved onward, sloshing through the
student soup. *Why hasn't he opened my Snap? I hate my hair
today. She's such a bitch. I hate her. I wish she would die. Why
can't I be like Isabel. Look at that fine ass. I need her to sit on my
face. I'm starving. I'm fat. A C—???? Fuuuckk.*

She reached in her bag for the Bible she'd stolen from
Whispering Pines, wondering briefly about the moral implications of stealing a Bible. Spreading "the Word" would probably
trump "Thou shalt not steal"? Or at least cancel it out. She had
developed a habit of soothing herself by flipping the soft pages
past her thumb. Basically, the Bible had become her "wubby,"
which was probably not an authorized use of a Bible. But there
it was. Everyone needed to self-soothe somehow.

She flipped the soft pages against her thumb and randomly
stopped at 1 Samuel, chapter 16, verse 23.

> *And it came to pass, when the evil spirit from God was
> upon Saul, that David took an harp, and played with his
> hand: so Saul was refreshed, and was well, and the evil
> spirit departed from him.*

It looked like there was some other stuff going on between David and Saul, too. David and Saul were definitely
doing it. She vowed to investigate further to squelch all the
homophobia that was rising up again in these parts. But the

main gist of this particular passage was: Music soothes the savage beast.

It was the perfect reminder for Maya to put on her headphones. She had promised herself not to use them as a crutch, but just this once, just to get her down the hall to math class, she plugged in to her Spotify playlist for The Invoking of Immediate Chill that was mostly populated with Khalid, and trudged onward down the hall.

The shoebox took a full hour to decorate. She cut a slot in the lid wide enough to accommodate a thick envelope, hypothetically filled with a three-page letter, say, and perhaps an encouraging insert, like a sticker that said *You got this!*, or a patch with a smiley face on it, or a fidget spinner, or a photograph from happier times. These were the instructions she delineated in her Sunshine Club newsletter:

> *. . . PLEASE FOLD YOUR LETTER AND PUT IT IN AN* **UNSEALED** *BUSINESS-SIZED ENVELOPE. FEEL FREE TO DECORATE IT. IN THE LETTER, INCLUDE PLAYLISTS, BOOK AND PODCAST RECOMMENDATIONS, COLLAGES, ENCOURAG-ING MEMES, STICKERS, AND OTHER CHEERFUL MISCELLANY.*

The letters needed to be unsealed so "the staff" could check for drugs, pornography, or other contraband that could be used for self-harm or the injury of others.

She wrapped the shoebox in red wrapping paper that she'd found in her mother's closet. It was covered with brightly colored hedgehogs and hailed from a different era when hedgehogs were trendier than mushrooms. Everything now was covered in mushrooms.

She installed the box on a shelf in the cafeteria next to the cereal bins where everyone would see it, and she labeled it in loopy script from bright gel pens, *Cheer for Bobby!*

She sent out five reminders on the LISTSERV.

Two days after the fifth reminder, she collected the box in a rush after spring rowing practice and threw it in the trunk with her gym bag. It did feel a little light, but there were things sliding around inside it, so she was emboldened!

At home, she prayed for at least seven letters. Bobby could really use the support. He was suffering a bout of such severe depression that he had been hospitalized for a few weeks, which could happen to anyone, Maddie knew. There was no shame in it.

She took a breath and lifted the lid.

Inside was

1. a condom,
2. a slice of ham from the sandwich bar, curling slightly around the edges, and
3. a tightly rolled joint.

Mortification set in quick. The very outside layer of her epidermis (the *stratum corneum,* she remembered, because what was all this for if not to eventually get into med school?) burned with humiliation, while the rest of her body felt blank. Other feelings crept back, and she felt sad for Bobby, and she felt sad for herself, because neither of them, even when teamed together, were popular enough to elicit a modicum of sympathy. Meanwhile, every time quarterback Aidan Fiorello got concussed, people waited in line to bake him cookies and do his homework for him.

A fat tear wormed its way to the corner of her eye and pressed against her duct, but she blinked it away. "Fuck, fuck, fuck, fuck," she said, then she lit the fucking joint, and got to work.

She scrolled and scrolled and scrolled through the Instagram feeds of all Bobby's followers, printing any screenshots she could find of Bobby in a big group. She cut them out and glued them with her little sister's glue stick to different pieces of stationery and construction paper. She cut out encouraging words and snippets of positivity from the headlines of her *Cosmo*. She created caring, thoughtful collages, wrote letters in the small chicken scratch of boy-writing and the fat, luscious loops of girlhand, and she wished Bobby well in twenty distinct voices, then collapsed at 4:00 A.M. without even touching her homework.

She thought a few times of what people might say if Bobby thanked them, but figured she'd cross that bridge when she came to it. She'd deliver the box. And hope that Bobby felt seen.

Group Project or Maximum Glow

Math class.

Guess what was new in the world of pedagogy for teenagers? *Design Thinking! Project-Based Learning!* Which meant there was no instruction, per se. Which meant teens were left to figure things out by themselves. Which meant *Group Projects*. Which meant what it has always meant: One person did the work, and no one else in the group really learned a thing. But this was how they did it at MIT. If you chose to work on a project by yourself at MIT, you could only achieve 80 percent of the possible points.

So, this was what they'd started to model in high school. And people here wanted all the points. Everyone wanted 100 percent of the points all the time. Their points were even publicized on the school website so that everyone knew each teen's rank, value, and inherent worth to the rest of society. And this wasn't even a dystopian novel. This was real life. In real life, all the teenagers were publicly ranked and set against one another to fight to the death in math class. At least this was what it felt like in A/B Pre-Calculus. A fight to the death. Because even when they were *mathematicians* and should realize things about probability and number theory and how there could only be one person at the top and it was usually random chance that got that person there, they were still intent on being number one.

Maya was placed here because, well. She knew all the things. She could do all the maths. It just made sense to her. But her GPA had transferred over from her old school, which meant that she had very few of the points. If you wanted to find her and her sorry GPA on the school website you'd have to scroll for a long time until you got to the bottom. She and a person named John Ackroyd were neck and neck, duking it out for last in class. She hadn't seen John Ackroyd yet and wondered if they just put him there as a phantom placeholder so that no one felt terrible about finishing last. That was okay, though, because she was not here for a blue ribbon. She was striving to stay here and finish with one of those pathetic white ribbons they hand out at kiddie swim meets that say: PARTICIPANT.

The room was organized into four different tables, one for each group, and Maya didn't know where to sit, so she just kind of awkwardly stood in the back and waited, her crazy hair accidentally erasing tiny threads into the Expo marker formulas written on the whiteboard. The thoughts of the pre-calc class drifted through the static air of the classroom and wedged themselves up beneath the padding of her headphones: *Loser, What is she wearing?, I'd tap it, Eyeroll.*

Instead of visibly rolling their eyes, some girls simply

thought *Eyeroll* while others thought *Bring it*, as if by simply showing up, Maya had thrown down some kind of psycho-social gauntlet. The straight boys separately, dully, almost obligatorily thought about which appendage they wanted to stick into which of her orifices. Maya instinctively crossed her legs and hugged her arms around her chest. The teacher, a thin white man in his twenties who had the kind of pristine micro-biome that supercharged his metabolism so that he could eat foot-long steak bombs for lunch but still keep his 29W belt buckled on the tightest setting, rushed in and set his laptop on his desk. He scrolled through it before looking up and seeing Maya standing there in the shadows. He shuddered for a second, he was so disturbed by her appearance. *Ugh*, he thought. *I'm a math teacher, not a sociologist. Where am I going to put her where she'll best fit in?* Then he actually ran some numbers from his grade book in his head, wrote down some formulas on a Post-it, and mathed the heck out of the situation, gather-ing data, before announcing, "Maya, you're in 'District Twelve.' Lucy will get you up to speed." To their credit, "District Twelve" did not audibly groan. To her credit, Lucy stood up for herself.

"Mr. Randall, I do not have an inherent ability for math just because my ancestors were Korean. I've never even seen an abacus."

"Ha! Abacus," shouted Eddie Jacobs, blond white wres-tling phenom with cauliflower ears, who somehow heard the conversation through the AirPods wedged into them. He slid into his seat and kicked off his plastic sandal slides (thankfully he was also wearing black crew socks) to watch the drama.

"First of all, this has nothing to do with your ancestral

background," said Mr. Randall. "I'm asking you for a favor. Just bring her up to speed. It says in your file that you tutor."

"In history," Lucy replied. "I suck at math."

"Okay, Kevin . . ."

"Also Asian!" Lucy said. "God."

"Fine," said Mr. Randall. "Victoria . . ."

Maya looked over at Victoria "Tori" Williams and instantly knew her story. She was the star of every production here at NTHS and was often auditioning for *American Idol* or *The Voice* or whatever when she wasn't constantly hawking her new studio-produced single, "You," on her social media channels. She got up at five every morning because her expert makeup routine (she could contour like the best of them) was extra grueling. It made her tired and cranky and impatient.

Maya stared at Tori and her makeup. She looked as if she lived inside the Juno filter, everything smooth and soft and perfectly lit. She used the highlighter so expertly that it caught the light in the right places on her face, but didn't make her look shiny and metallic like the Tin Man in *The Wizard of Oz*. A lot of unfortunate highlighter incidents walked these halls, everyone trying to achieve maximum Glow. Maya wished she could swipe left and see Tori's actual #nofilter human face. Sadly, she could hear her no-filter thoughts.

Tori looked Maya up and down and took in her unwashed hair, her pale, sallow, six-weeks-in-a-psych-hospital complexion, and thought, *I don't have time for this piece of garbage.* She actually thought that, which, Maya knew because she knew all things, meant that she had heard it from someone else. People weren't born like this. Wickedness was taught. The Wickedness is great in the earth. Luckily, Lucy sized up the situation and grew a conscience on the spot.

"Hey, you know what, Mr. Randall? I got this. I wouldn't mind adding this to my tutoring résumé or whatever."

"Great."

"Thanks," Maya whispered to Lucy as she sat next to her.

"Don't mention it," Lucy said and then turned to Maya. "I couldn't do it to you. Tori is like, um . . . How do I describe it? Like the Demogorgon in *Stranger Things*, maybe, mixed with the flying monkeys in *The Wizard of Oz* with shades of . . . like, Gunther and Tinka from *Shake It Up* and also Sharpay."

"Wow, you watch a lot of . . ."

"Shhh," hissed someone from across the room. Lucy gave them an open-mouthed stare that dared them to continue shushing.

"So let me get you up to speed. Basically, it doesn't matter what you do here, because Tori is going to go home and redo it. You can do the problem set, or ignore the problem set and just let Tori do it because that's what she's going to do anyway. You are now up to speed."

Tori heard her, obviously, because it was meant to be heard, but she chose to ignore it and passed back everyone's work from last night covered in red ink.

"See."

"But how do you know she's right?" Maya whispered.

"It doesn't matter. You just have to let her do it. She cannot *not* be in control. She needs to just get laid already. I think. I wouldn't know, having not had the pleasure of getting laid myself. But I imagine it would just chill her out. Or maybe

I've just been conditioned to think that from the patriarchal media. I don't know what she needs. But for the time being she needs to control this math group. So we let her do it."

"That's kind of you."

"I like to think so."

Maya zoomed in on Tori for a second to see what she really needed. Attention, obviously, since she was seeking fame at such a young age without yet realizing if she had any true talent. But why? Why the perfect face, perfect grades, perfect voice? What was she hiding? Why the dark need to be so "relevant" on social media? For what was she overcompensating?

Maya looked in Tori's eyes and captured a quick snapshot of her life—poverty (she lived in a double-wide) and alcoholism and a rageful paternal presence barking at Tori. A meek mother pretending everything was okay and that rage was just the way men operated in the world. Tori knew she was less. Her parents had less money, less education, less experience. They couldn't help her with her homework. They knew nothing about college or how to get there. She swallowed up all these facts and let them become her. She was less. She wanted more. She had to prove that she deserved it. But she was never certain that she did. In fact, she knew for certain that she didn't, because running over and over in her head were her father's words, "Who the hell do you think you are?" And though it was a rhetorical question, the implied answer, and the one Tori always mumbled to herself was, of course, *nobody*.

Thankfully the people around Maya started thinking about math, and she was carried away on a sine wave of formulas and frustrations, always seeing for herself the ultimate answer to the problems but pretending not to know them right away. People, she knew, hated her for knowing all the answers. She let them discuss the new problems for a bit, Tori seemingly tolerating some input from Kevin and Lucy and the rest of the group, but ultimately criticizing their attempts, so they gave up.

"I think it's negative three," Maya finally interjected meekly. "Your math is all correct, but you added wrong right here."

Tori looked at the Google Doc they all shared and, realizing Maya was correct, turned a bright red, but because it was covered by so much foundation, her face turned a puce color. The color of her unwarranted shame. She and Maya had the problem up on their screens and fixed it because everyone else had already moved on to something else.

Lucy toggled between eBay, a sneaker website, and an app where she sold used clothing to people on the internet. She had created a tiny fashion empire called Gilding the Monster, and she was trying to save enough to bypass college altogether. *You can't tell me Stella McCartney would deign to attend an American Zoomiversity*, she thought. Lucy might consider a design school in Europe or merchandising at FIT. Her mother was bent on Harvard for economics or maybe Wharton. No way Lucy was doing that. She'd have to send herself to fashion merchandising school. She was on her own, because she knew if her mom didn't disown her for her career choice, she'd definitely do it for her sexual preference.

Anyway, recognizing that her mom was sadly a temporary being in her life ignited Lucy's hustle. Her Instagram tagline was: *I'm in imports and exports.* She ran a tight business and currently waited patiently for her bid to be accepted for a pair of vintage '84 unworn white Reebok high-tops.

"How we doing?" she asked as she opened the Google Doc and looked Maya in the eye. *Damn, she's cute but super straight,* Lucy thought. "You getting the hang of this? You sort of engage for a bit, get the gist of the problem, and then just let Tori do it."

"Seems pretty straightforward," said Maya and the bell rang.

·················

Lunch.

Maya was already exhausted and couldn't imagine the terror of lunch in the cafeteria followed by three more classes. Impossible. She caught her reflection in the math class window, and it seemed ghostly white and drawn; she felt a little woozy, when Lucy swooped in from behind her and linked arms with her.

"I got you," she said, and she swept Maya away to room 143. *Maybe I can flip her,* Lucy thought. Then she thought, *No, I have sworn off straight girls. I have sworn off straight girls.* She repeated it six times in her head, and earlier this morning had written it fourteen times in her journal, which, according to some self-help book, was a magic number for making things manifest.

The last straight girl Lucy had loved, Emma, had crushed her so entirely, her GPA had crossed over the point of no return. That tenth percentile line, which would define you forevermore if you weren't an athlete. *Go beneath the top ten percent,* Lucy thought, *and you are doomed to a state school and rejected even from their pathetic honors programs.*

Lucy had thought Emma loved her. There was the soft stroking of her knees and shoulders at random moments. And there was winking. And pink Post-it notes of positivity stuck to her locker. Wasn't that what love looked like? But it was all a cruel tease, which she found out when she excitedly leapt into the cafeteria one day to find Emma on Aidan's lap, her arms looped loosely around his neck before she leaned in for a soft, very practiced peck on the lips. *That* was what love looked like. And that was when Lucy's heartache set in. The heartache and the mortification. *How could I have been so stupid?* That heaviness that sinks to the bottom of your chest and makes it hard to move. Maya felt it. Luckily Lucy still propped her up.

In room 143, someone had turned on the bubble machine, which the PTA had stocked along with the coloring books and jigsaw puzzles, so the room was filled with a joyful floaty lightness like the scene toward the end of *Willy Wonka & the Chocolate Factory* when Charlie and Grandpa Joe had to burp their way to the ground.

"I feel like I'm in a bottle of kombucha," Lucy said. "Speaking of kombucha—" She reached into the mini fridge and pulled one out for Maya, who hated the stuff and made a face. "I think it's gross but it's like six dollars a bottle, so it must be good for you."

"You seem too cool for this place," Maya whispered to Lucy.

"I am. I'm in it for the free stuff," she said, rustling around in the mini fridge for a yogurt parfait and a banana, which she tossed to Maya, and then they flopped together on the couch. "You just have to listen to that crap for a bit, but I've come to find it soothing."

Lucy pointed to the right of the couch, and wedged into the corner there was a thin boy with a broad muscular chest who sat on a pillow in lotus position with his eyes closed. Every five or so seconds he let out a deep, vibrating "Aum . . ."

The boy's pristine white vintage eighties Hard Rock London T-shirt billowed a little with each of his belly breaths. His spine sat perfectly erect like a tower of LEGOs. His vertebrae had not yet morphed into the S-curve spines of Gen Z adolescents, whose necks were permanently stooped from looking constantly at their iPhones. His biceps were not insignificant, Maya noticed. They pushed at the limits of his short sleeves and were covered tightly with smooth, thin olive skin that was latticed only here and there with slightly bulging greenish veins. He was the picture of "wellness," almost plant-like in the way he was both rooted to the earth and reaching for the light.

Maya tuned in to get a reading on him, but he was actually meditating properly. She could see him pushing his thoughts aside with each audible exhale. His mind was quiet.

"Who is that?" Maya asked.

"Tyler." Lucy sighed and thought, *God, I'm so stupid. I'm just delivering my catch to my superior, like a pet cat leaving a dead mouse in her owner's slipper as a gift. Here you go, Tyler, take my flipping dead mouse.*

"Expound," Maya said and caught herself before adding, *And I'm not your dead mouse.*

"No."

"Why no?"

"I'm protecting you. Tyler is a self-proclaimed quasi-Buddhist, so he lives without attachments. You can extrapolate. Attachments to friends. Attachments to girls. Attachments to goals. His religion basically excuses him from any type of follow-through."

"Can't he hear us?" Maya whispered.

"I don't know. Can you hear us, Tyler?"

"Yessss," Tyler chanted with his next exhale.

"Oh good. So, Maya, what that means is that his desires—which he's not supposed to have in the first place, right, Tyler?—are, shall we say, mercurial. He'll love you and ditch you and use his faux 'spirituality'—finger quotes around spirituality in case you can't see them, Tyler—as an excuse to use you and move on." She paused to take a sip of her kombucha and cringed with the taste of it, then continued. "He's destined to become one of those fake American yoga gurus who builds a Lycra pants empire and sexually harasses all the women who run it for him. Can you major in that, Tyler? Fake, predatory American yoga guru economics?"

Tyler's bright eyes blinked open then. He looked first at Lucy, and said, "Why so negative, Lucy? It isn't healthy." Then he locked eyes with Maya for what seemed like an infinite second, and they both had the same thought at the same time.

Uh-oh.

The 36

The last thing Maya needed was a *Tyler*. The only time Maya had had any experience at all with a boy happened in her living room with the supposed best friend from her toddlerhood, who'd moved away before kindergarten in the perennial search for better schools. She couldn't remember toddlerhood, obvs. Her only memory of this boy, Justin, was the amalgam she'd made from old photographs. Her and Justin on the swings. Her and Justin on the beach in their swimmy diapers eating sand. Etc.

They had both swollen into preteens, knobby in some places, chubby in others, growing different protuberances from all parts of their anatomies and struggling with the routines of regular hygiene, and this was the moment their parents decided to reintroduce them. After dinner, the adults polished off the third bottle of wine around the dining room table while Maya and Justin retreated to the den to play video games. They heard the soothing chatter of their parents in the background, punctuated every now and then by a fortissimo blast of laughter.

Anyway, because of her thing, because of who she was, Maya could hear what Justin wanted. It was so *insistent*. He sat next to her on the floor wiggling the controller with his thumbs but imagining Maya placing her hand on his inner thigh and inching it toward the crotch of his sweatpants, which had instantly, with the thought of it, become stretched tight and rock-hard. He imagined them kissing and lying on top of each other and kind of rolling around on the floor and that's where the fantasy stopped because he couldn't even fathom any specifics of what would come next. They were still only twelve years old.

He seemed desperate, though. Aching. And so Maya, happy to relieve some of his torment, used one hand to continue building their Minecraft fortress as she slid her left hand up toward Justin's crotch. Justin's mind turned to blank white heat. Compelled by something inside herself now, Maya dropped the controller and started kissing him. Lightly at first, and then attempting to kiss more languorously, like she'd seen on *High School Musical*. It was wet and sloppy and delicious—until Justin brusquely pushed her aside with a stiff arm to her sternum.

"What are you doing?!" he asked. He was white and appalled and embarrassed and afraid all at once.

Maya was mortified.

"I thought that's what you wanted," Maya admitted, tears pooling in her eyes.

The parents, as if on cue, came in to collect Justin, and the two had never seen each other again, except, of course, on Instagram. Justin was grown now, easily and comfortably posing shirtless in his board shorts with his hand around the waist of a girl in a bikini. Clearly, he wasn't scarred by the incident. But for Maya it stood out as a shameful reminder to keep her hands to herself.

Tyler, because of the way he'd looked at her, was the first person to challenge—even if just for a millisecond—the idea of her self-imposed celibacy.

After meeting Tyler, which seemed to really irritate Lucy, Maya had asked for Lucy's cell phone number. "Digits," she called them, which according to Lucy's eye-rolling scowl, was apparently no longer a thing. "Just add me on Snap," she said, but when this was met with a blank stare she capitulated. "God. Okay, but also, I am warning you about Tyler," she said.

"Thanks," said Maya. "I could use a friend."

"Don't mention it," said Lucy and then tried to engage Maya in a fist-bumping handshake, which Maya could only maneuver because she could read the choreography of the thing in Lucy's mind. Bump. Clasp. Grip. Fly Away. "Not bad for a white girl," Lucy said.

"Thanks, I think." And having achieved the monumental goal of meeting one possible friend, Maya left school for the day, skipping a couple of classes, only a couple, and arrived at Whispering Pines Conditions for Release #1. Therapy. With Amy, the in-house therapist whom she'd been seeing for the past six weeks. She was almost excited about it, because it was familiar. And quiet.

Amy's little office, so clinical and institutional on the outside with its shiny blue tile hallway and plain white door, was warm and inviting on the inside. Like a Tootsie Pop with its warm and gooey center. They must have a class in how to decorate your shrink office, Maya thought, so that there was enough interest to entertain the patients without distracting them with too much clutter.

Maya had spent hours staring at the family of three elephant tchotchkes on the coffee table, imagining they came from a service trip to Africa. Everyone, these days, was doing "service trips."

Just to pass the time, she'd envision "Africa Amy" in a sarong, milking goats, feeding peanut butter to infants, and starting micro businesses, when in fact she knew, because she knew all things, that Amy just picked up the elephants on sale at Home-Goods, which is where she also acquired the hippie tapestry she slung over the couch and the coasters that looked like Moroccan tile.

It took Maya two weeks in captivity at Whispering Pines before she said anything at all to Amy, and Amy, a fortyish white woman with a tangle of wavy hair of indeterminate color, patiently sat with her for fifty minutes every day for two straight weeks. Then finally Maya got so bored she started to use the time to wax poetic on the inevitable collapse of humankind.

"The last white rhino died today," she said now. "And no one gives any shits. I'm literally the only person in high school, perhaps the universe, recognizing the writing on wall."

"Really. There are no, like, PhDs in eco-diversity who might also be concerned. You're the only one."

Maya liked Amy.

"Can you get a PhD in eco-diversity? Is that even a thing?" Maya countered.

"I don't know. I made it up. But you know what I mean. It's grandiose to think you're the only one."

Amy talked a lot about grandiosity, which was why Maya could never tell her the truth about the fact that she might be you-know-what. It was Amy's job to diagnose Maya's gift and turn it into an illness. So Maya made the job as difficult as possible for her.

"If I'm not the only one, then why isn't anyone else freaking out? Because if the rhinos can go, then so can the rabbits and chickens and cows and avocados and almonds. There's already no water in California. When the rest of it goes, we'll end up eating each other until no one is left. Dark times, those."

Amy just looked at her. She'd heard it all before.

"Sometimes I pray for an asteroid. Just to get it over with. Humanity . . . the Anthropocene," Maya continued. "But maybe we won't need an asteroid. Do you think climate change is really God calling us out again for our wickedness, like they did in the time of Noah?"

"Maybe. Is there any way you can turn these dark thoughts into something more positive?" Amy asked. "Nothing good can come from all this constant dark thinking."

"Really?" Maya said.

"Really," she said.

Maya didn't believe her. Dark thoughts were necessary for survival. She could hear Amy's own dark thoughts all the time during sessions.

For example, Amy (while pretend-listening) now poked at the testicular flesh around her eyes and tried to imagine at what impossible angles the surgeon could cut it in order to pull it taut. The serums were not working anymore. She was getting old, she thought. Yesterday she even pulled a muscle in her forearm trying to squeeze out the last of the wrinkle cream. *The aging makes it hard to stay positive*, Amy thought.

See, Maya thought as she looked right into Amy's eyes.

And I'm so tired of listening to people make the same mistakes over and over again. Because everyone fails, right? We're all just assholes. That's what it has finally come down to. Everyone's an asshole, Amy thought.

"That's a pretty dark thought right there," Maya mumbled at her while tracing the geometric design of the couch upholstery with her unpolished fingernail.

"What?" Amy asked. "Wait. What?" Amy asked again.

"Nothing," Maya said. "Hey, do you know that whole vavnik theory in fringe Judaism?"

"Remind me," Amy said, still bothered by Maya's seeming response to her ruminations.

"Well, the theory goes ... everyone," Maya paused for effect, with a grand, sweeping gesture of her hand, "is an asshole," she deadpanned.

"Wow, Judaism really resonates with me," Amy said. "Go on."

"That's it ..." Maya laughed and Amy gave her the sardonic smirk she so enjoyed, so Maya continued. "No. Just kidding. Everyone is an asshole, right, but *God* continues to save the world because there are, in each generation, thirty-six pure and beneficent and selfless people who are worth saving the world *for*. They're called the lamed vavniks."

"Thirty-six seems about right."

"Yeah. I don't know, like RBG or Nelson Mandela, Mr.

Rogers, etcetera, and the rest of us are just kind of pieces of shit, so it's hard to find the motivation," Maya mumbled, dropping her head in defeat.

"Um, motivation for what, Maya?" Amy's fun smirk crinkled into a concerned knit of her eyebrows.

"Saving the world, I guess," Maya answered honestly.

"And that is your job, because . . ."

"Come on, Amy. We're Generation Z. The last generation. It ends with us, obvs, unless we do something. And if it fell to any other generation, they would just, like, party until it was over. They would do coke until their noses fell off and then jackknife into the rising sea levels, chanting 'U-S-A,' while still holding tight to their Bud cans. Gen Z is anxious about it precisely because you aren't. But I fear we're so anxious that we're paralyzed by the whole thing."

"I don't drink Bud cans or do coke," Amy said. *I thought they were anxious because of the phones*, she thought to herself.

"Good for you, and yeah, it's the phones, too."

Wait, did I say "phones" out loud? Amy wondered. The middle-aged-ness was even decaying her mind. She was in a constant state of decay. She needed to do more crossword puzzles. Eat more fish. Get more exercise. Maybe she could go for a run after this.

"I think it's going to rain, though," Maya said in response, completely by accident and without skipping a beat because she had become so comfortable on this damn couch with the coffee table and the little wooden family of elephants. Stupid elephants. She had become too acclimated. A crucial misstep.

"Which is apropos of what, Maya?" Amy asked, becoming more suspicious. Not just suspicious; kind of alarmed.

"Just making small talk. You told me to practice that, the small talk. Talk about the weather. Stop the dark conversations. Although the weather is one of the darkest conversations we can have these days, living as we are, in the midst of the climate apocalypse," she said, trying to get back to her normal Maya mode.

"Maya," Amy said, staring her right in the eyes.

"Amy," Maya said, staring right back.

"Well, it's time," Amy said, sighing, conceding defeat, and glancing at the clock, before capturing Maya again in her suspicious stare, this time with an upturned eyebrow.

Maya hoisted herself off the couch and pet the mother elephant on the head, as she always did, for good luck.

Amy walked her to the door and thought, *That was weird.* And, *Shit, we didn't even talk about school.*

And because something inside her, deep inside her, could suddenly be alone with it no longer. And because something inside her, deep inside her, kind of *loved* Amy in a way that could be analyzed for months and months on this couch. And because something inside her suddenly felt the wisdom of that old adage, *You're only as sick as your secrets,* Maya said, out loud, "School was fine, Amy," before closing the door and walking away.

EDDIE

Eddie was a builder. He built his body first. It was a thing he could control. He could use discipline; he could *be* disciplined; it was a thing he admired in people, discipline, and he was turned off a little when it seemed they didn't have it. His better self knew it was misogynist and body-shaming, but he couldn't stomach girls with soft bodies. He tried, but no matter what he read about their generation's mutated microbiomes, and the hormones in the milk, and how birth control pills could bloat a young woman's body, he saw any pudge as a weakness, so he was often alone. He tried not to judge, he sweared, and tried, instead, to focus on himself.

He might join the marines, in fact, because of the rush he got in pushing himself, in denying himself certain pleasures. It was just a shame that the ultimate goal of being a marine was killing people, no matter how you sliced it, no matter how the recruiters tried to sell it to you. You had to pledge your life to the country, but they never talked about what that meant on the ground. On the ground, it meant you had to kill—exterminate bright young lives on the cusp of their own excellence, who had just been brainwashed, like you, by adults with a different message. No matter how you sliced it.

For now, he channeled his discipline into wrestling. It was

the perfect sport for exercising self-denial. He could starve, spit, sweat, and purge, and when he made weight, there was no more gratifying victory. The victory of self-control.

He knew it all derived from survivor's guilt. His brother could not control his own limbs. His brother was born ultraprematurely with cerebral palsy, and walked and talked in halting, jolting spurts that exhausted him when he simply tried to get his point across. Eddie had first built up his body to protect Max. You would think no one would kick a kid like Max when he was down, but the teasing was relentless, the mimicry absurd, and only bolstered by the ex-president who mocked anyone without an able body in public . . . in front of the whole world. As people kept saying, there was no decency left, and people like Max, as much as they hated it, were sometimes dependent upon people's decency.

In grade school Eddie had tried to pound it into them, the decency. He'd get into trouble at school, scraping bullies' faces against the playground asphalt if they dared say anything about Max's disability. But Max said it only made things worse, urged Eddie to let him fight his own battles with his wit, which was something he had in droves to compensate for his broken body.

They sat now in the dark of the high school's makerspace, meticulously building a drone-like hovercraft with Arduino and Raspberry Pi. It was meant to one day lift Max and his entire wheelchair off the ground. It was meant to make him fly.

"Hand me the soldering iron," he told Max. "I think this is the last connection."

"I'm flipping the switch," Max said when he got the thumbs-up from Eddie.

They had attached the hoverboard to each of the wheels of

an empty test-wheelchair, and when Max flipped the switch, the whole contraption vibrated a little and then shorted out with a zap.

"Ugh! I can't get it up," Eddie said, to which Max replied, of course, "That's what she said."

Someday they would do it, though. Eddie was a builder, and one day, he'd help his brother soar.

Thomas Edison's Mother

Local hero Thomas Edison had ruined everything with his damn invention of the electric light bulb. (Actually, you could blame Thomas Edison's mother, who lovingly homeschooled him after being told by his teacher that he was "addled" and no longer welcome at real school. It was a charming anecdote darting around the internet.) Anyway, because of Thomas Edison or Thomas Edison's mother, who believed in his genius despite all evidence to the contrary, a day in the life of the American teenager had become inhumanly long. Exhaustively long. Unhealthily and dangerously long. A consequence Edison probably didn't anticipate.

Teen children could no longer hit the actual *hay* after eating a huge supper of chops and mashed potatoes and milking the cow in the pink twilight that glowed through the cracks in the barn. Nope. They could no longer calmly and casually read the transcendentalists by candlelight before snubbing out the flame between their farm-chore-callused fingertips. No. Today's teens were expected to jam an absurd amount of homework, activities, lessons, jobs, practices, media consumption, and social posturing into their waking hours, which could be defined as all twenty-four of the hours in a day thanks to Thomas Edison and his light bulb. Luckily this was remedied by coffee and, if you were a risk-taker and desperate grade-grubber, Adderall.

After therapy, Maya was expected to work at her parents' store on Main Street, which, right now, seemed impossible. She'd gotten used to the measured pace of the mental hospital. The sanatorium. Three squares, therapy, some daily constitutionals around the grounds, a little reading, and in bed by ten. She hadn't really had any squares today and bedtime seemed days away because she hadn't even looked at what homework she was expected to complete after work.

She took the bus home from Whispering Pines and then dragged herself to Antonio's Café, whose owners had known her all her life because she'd grown up there, on retail row.

Inside Sheila's coffee shop, she approached the highly polished, intricate vintage steampunk monster of an espresso machine imported from Milan two generations ago. Sheila stood behind the counter in her ruffled purple apron.

"¡Amore mio!" Sheila cried, taking Maya in for a second before busting through the little swinging gate in the counter to envelop Maya in a big, cushiony hug. Maya did a quick scan of Sheila's heartbeat and circulation, general cardiac health, and it all seemed good.

Main Street was the only place where Maya felt a modicum of control. It was her little storybook universe.

"How are you?" Sheila asked. "Life is good, right?" She held Maya at arm's length and shook her a little for emphasis. "No more of these sad thoughts," she said in reference to Maya's recent hospitalization. "We need to find you a boyfriend, that's all, right?" Then Maya saw Sheila's mind open the mental file of her nephews, sifting through them one by one to assess them as potential dates for Maya as if swiping on Tinder. None of them measured up. Too old. Too lazy. Too lecherous. Too gay. Too too. "Ah," she said out loud, waving her hand in front of her face. "You will find someone. In the meantime, welcome back! The neighborhood has not been the same. You want a coffee, yes? And a cake? You can't have a coffee without a cake. Or a biscotti. I made them fresh."

They weren't building shrines to Maya or anything, but everyone on the street—the butcher, the baker, the candlestick maker, the potter, the dressmaker, the chef, the palm reader, the historian, the dramatist, the bookseller, the waitress, and Scott, the hermit who lived off the grid before there even was a grid—all of them knew she was special. She had helped each of them in ways they couldn't define. She just seemed like a special child to them. The only thing she could not control here on Main Street were matters of life and death. She couldn't even save Antonio. He had died a year or two ago, leaving Sheila to manage alone.

There was a freedom in it, widowhood, she heard Sheila think as she looked at Antonio's photo peering down at them. Sheila missed him, of course. The way she could make him laugh. Sometimes "the missing" swirled around itself in a vortex of sadness and pulled everything into it. But other times, she felt free.

Antonio, as much as he revered her, was of the make-me-a-sandwich generation. The generation of men, spoiled by their mothers and the patriarchy, who ruled their worlds like tiny toddlers did, by throwing tantrums and expecting immediate satisfaction from the minions around them. Sometimes she felt liberated from all that. *It's okay,* she said to herself. *Everything's okay,* she thought, but betrayed herself by choking back a surprise tear. The tears still caught her unawares sometimes, the gasping, gripping suddenness of them that hit her from out of the blue.

"Everything's okay," Maya said out loud. She quickly glanced into Sheila's eyes, gathered up the splintered cords of her grief, and plugged them into the tune "Que Sera, Sera" by Doris Day.

"Yeah," Sheila said, looking her in the eye and thinking about how she dreaded going to Bingo tonight but that she really should because she'd feel better about seeing everyone once she dragged herself there.

"You going to Bingo, Sheil?" Maya asked, just to cement the deal Sheila had with herself.

Maya got a text. It buzzed in her pocket and took her as much by surprise as Sheila's tiny sob did. Maya never got texts. She was not a typical teen accustomed to typical teen communications.

"Go to Bingo, Sheil," she said. "I'll see you tomorrow?"

"Yes, Maya. I'll go to Bingo. Que será, será." She whipped a rag out from her apron and wiped some things down. "So good to see you. Say hi to your mama."

Outside, Maya pulled her phone out of her cargo pants pocket. She slid it slowly against her thigh and then flipped it.

LUCY
Tchyou doin?

It was Lucy!

                                                    MAYA
                                                Nothing.

So I need to confess.

                                            About what?

This was such an exhilarating, spontaneous, and refreshing way to communicate. She actually didn't know what Lucy was going to text next, because she was physically too far away for mind reading or whatever.

He got it out of me.

                                            Who? What?

Tyler. He was so convincing, that wolf.
That fucking yoga pants player.

Wolves were actually monogamous, Maya knew. Not players at all. They mated for life like bald eagles and swans and vultures and seahorses, probably because their lives were so short, so wolf was a bad metaphor, but friendship necessitated letting the facts slide. Nobody liked a know-it-all.

                                                What?

I showed him your Snapchat, and you, because
of your seeming technological naivete, have
left yourself on the map.

What map?

Snapchat. You're on the map.

Then she sent a photo of Maya's wild-haired Bitmoji standing right there on Main between Antonio's and The Flip Side, her place of employment.

Whoa. I didn't know it could do that.

She hadn't looked at Snapchat since eighth grade.

Well. He will find you if he wants to. He's a fan of face-to-face communication. It's part of his religion.

Thanks for the heads up.

Sure.

Maya ignored the little sneeze of hope that bubbled up inside her. She wished she'd worn some mascara. Her lashes were a big part of her overall aesthetic. Without them she was far less appealing, she knew because she knew all things.

She stepped down two steps to the purple basement door of The Flip Side and tapped, for good luck, the handmade wooden sign that creaked on its rusted hinges above her head. She took a thick sip of her latte before turning the knob and letting the door slam behind her. Despite the David Bowie loudly piping through the entire store, her mother heard her come in. She was hawkish and alert, awaiting her daughter's return so she could swoop in and ask, "How did it go?" She was unduly curious about Maya's day because (1) it was more interesting than her own; (2) she had to know that Maya was okay, because she cared for Maya; and (3) she wanted to stop failing as a parent.

Her desperation left Maya no choice but to lie. "It was great," Maya said.

"Details," Stacy demanded, flipping a long piece of hair out of her eyes and leaning against the wooden carrels built just at waist height, perfect for flipping through the albums arranged in alphabetical order. Stacy leaned on Broadway Musicals H–L. Carol Channing's *Hello, Dolly!* faced out, but they also had the Streisand and Midler versions leaned up right behind hers. Their inventory was exhaustively complete, but they still couldn't keep the *Hamilton* record in stock.

"I went to math," Maya said.

"And?"

"Just math. I'm easing in."

"Maya. One class?" She gave Maya the look: Disappointment. Disapproval. Dismay. Pride. Envy. Disappointment.

"It was a good class. I got a lot out of it. And I may have made a friend."

"Please tell me you didn't blow off therapy."

"You know I didn't." Stacy had one of those apps on her phone that could track Maya's every move as long as she kept her phone on, and she was sure Stacy was checking every ten minutes.

"Who's the friend?"

"A girl named Lucy. She's in the fashion industry."

"Like a model or something?"

"No. She sells vintage clothes online. She's taking on the evils of fast fashion. It's a social enterprise."

"Cool."

"Yeah," Maya said. "Tomorrow I'll go to all the classes."

"Great. One day at a time, right? You can do it." She was in therapy herself at Whispering Pines and it had given her some parenting scripts.

"Was that a script from the parent group?"

"You bet your sweet bippy," Stacy said. "We got a few boxes if you want to check them in." And she gave Maya a wink. "Love you," she said, but Maya could tell she was disappointed and was probably thinking, *Shit. One class? Seriously?*

"Love you, too, Mom," Maya said and she retreated to a corner of the store where she unpacked boxes and checked things in. Maurice slept there on a circular bed in the shape of an LP with his name embroidered on it. He wagged his butt off when he saw her and jumped into her lap as she started opening the boxes. She had to be careful not to get near him with the box cutter, but they had a system for it, a kind of symbiotic dance.

She enjoyed getting boxes of used albums the best, because sometimes little secrets slipped out. Photographs, letters, receipts, tickets, recipes, sprafka—the Yiddish-y word her father made up for paper miscellany. She created a little sprafka museum back in her hole, taping each found item to the cinder block wall. She could sometimes hold the items that slipped out of the album covers and feel the entire stories behind them. Today she opened a box, pulled out *Moondance* by Van Morrison, and saw a note slip out. It was handwritten, and all it said was: *I love you, but nothing changes and it hurts too much. Please let me go.*

Maya held it and tried to channel the person who wrote the note to see if they made a permanent decision about a temporary problem. Maya could understand the inclination, which scared the fuck out of her honestly, and which made her glad she was still in therapy.

Maya taped the note up next to the rest of her sprafka collage: A picture of a one-year-old smashing his fist into his first birthday cake. A ticket to Jerry's last show with the Dead, July 9, 1995, Soldier Field, Chicago. A restaurant receipt with a tip for $5,000, enough to pay off the waitress's student loans. A note to self, written shakily on a cocktail napkin: *The only one who can beat you is . . . you.* A photo of a group of young hikers at Yosemite, with one girl's face cut out of it—a jagged empty oval.

Hot Wiggle
(Fruit Salad or B Minus)

Tyler walked into the record store five minutes and ten seconds into "Suite: Judy Blue Eyes," by Crosby, Stills & Nash—a song whose harmonies basically encapsulated all of life lived at once. Stacy played it at least once a month, but no more, so as not to diminish its power. Like a handful of other songs, it was prayer for them. Church. Maya didn't want to admit that she loved the song as much as her mother did, but it had a mathematical beauty to it. In ancient India the gurus studied the mathematical variations of music in an attempt to decode the pathways to god. "Suite: Judy Blue Eyes" got right to the essence of god. Maya could tell by the way it vibrated inside her. So whenever her mother played it, she gave it its due reverence. She stopped assessing the dusty used albums' warptitude, their playability, stopped entering their titles into their ancient creaky database, and just sat through the entire seven minutes and twenty-five seconds of the harmonies.

Today, though, at precisely five minutes and ten seconds into "Suite," exactly when the characters in the lyrics stopped trying to figure out their relationship and just let nature take its course, right then, at "Chestnut brown canary . . . ," Tyler from school burst through the door, letting the sleigh bells tied to the knob slam against it, alerting them to the intrusion. It was rare that "Suite: Judy Blue Eyes" was ever interrupted. They usually played it during off-hours.

Stacy, annoyed, looked at Tyler with her famous side-eye, and she kept it on him as he stepped down into the store.

Tyler ignored her, though, and pretended to flip through the Ps by the door: Panic! At The Disco, Pearl Jam, Phoebe Bridgers, the Police, Post Malone, Prince, Purple Haze. He heard the sitar-like music transition "Suite" into its magical, nonsensical universe, and he looked a little sheepishly across the room at Maya and, precisely at the right moment, began to lip-synch. He did the whole verse, then spun like Michael Jackson and pointed at Maya to take the next verse, and, surprising even herself, she went with it. *Wow. He knows "Suite,"* she thought.

"Um, you got this, Maya?" Stacy asked suspiciously from behind the register, pretending to busy herself by stamping their paper bags with the Flip Side logo. She was suspicious yet probably secretly elated that Maya might actually know this boy. Any boy.

"Yes, Mom," Maya said. The song ended with its Spanish verse, an elegiac if nonsequitous ode to Cuba, and Tyler collapsed into the inflatable sparkle chair propped up next to the life-sized cardboard cutout of the Bee Gees wearing white tuxedos.

Maya approached Tyler. His polyester pants were so tight,

she could see how the developed muscles of his quadriceps tucked themselves behind his kneecaps. She wanted to grab his knees. Squeeze them. Was that normal? His thick dark hair swept in waves in front of his left eye, but his right eye fully focused on Maya as she stepped toward him, and when she stopped right in front of him and sat down on an overturned milk crate, his very expressive and very black bushy right eyebrow arched in curiosity.

Tyler stared at Maya, and then pointed at the Bee Gees with the back of his long thumb as if he were hitchhiking. "You know that doctors use 'Stayin' Alive' as the exact beat for administering CPR?" he asked.

"That works on a couple levels," she said. "Because you want the person to like . . ." and then she stopped, realizing a pun wasn't a pun if you had to explain it. God.

"Exactly," he said. "I love the music of the seventies. So eclectic."

Really, she thought, *say more, cute boy,* and she kind of tilted her head like a puppy, suddenly intrigued by this wily creature. Did they truly have this in common? Maybe it's because she was raised an only child in a used record store in a town full of hippies, but seventies music was the only decade of music Maya truly vibed with. America was just reborn. Finding its voice. Discovering its soul. Launched by the summer of '69, she thought. In what other decade could you put Jimi Hendrix up against Earth, Wind & Fire up against Led Zeppelin up against the Clash and Springsteen and Dylan and Stevie Wonder and Michael Jackson and Kool & the Gang against Funkadelic against Pink Floyd against Marvin

Gaye against the Ramones against Fleetwood Mac, and have them all come out winning? There was no other decade of music that was so, like, generative, if that was a word.

Maya could tell by the way he sat there and by the way his mind worked that, like a lot of boys her age, his confidence far exceeded his competence. This was a great way to move through the world if you could pull it off, because most people would never know *you had no effing idea what you were talking about.* Maya wished it wasn't the opposite for most of the girls she knew.

"Your confidence far exceeds your competence," Maya said to him.

"Is that so?" he asked. *Damn,* she heard him think. *She's not much for small talk. Those freckles, though. They're killing me.*

"So can I help you find something?" Maya asked, standing upright and letting his thoughts roll off her in a shiver of not disgust exactly but maybe disappointment. She wanted to hope he was different.

"Find something?"

"Yes. You're in a record store. Can I get you a record? Are you looking for anything in particular? We're closing in a couple minutes," Maya said, and she nervously looked at her wrist, to indicate the time, even though she wasn't wearing a watch.

"Freckle past a hair?" Tyler asked, hoisting himself out of the ridiculous chair. He stared down at her from his newly constructed, recently completed, now open for business, six-foot-two physique. Maya hadn't noticed how tall he was when he was sitting on the meditation pillow at school.

"Who says that? Freckle past a hair," she said out loud. "Do people even know what that means anymore?"

At that moment, Stacy, bursting with curiosity, could restrain herself no longer. She blinked the store lights. Then she resurrected the old PA system microphone, which they hadn't used in decades, blew some dust off it, and (even though they were the only people in the store) pressed the button. The sound system let out a scratchy, avian screech and then boomed with her mother's voice. "Attention, customers," Stacy said, while staring facetiously at Maya. "The Flip Side will be closing in five minutes. Please plan accordingly and bring all purchases to the front desk. Thank you." Then she silently whispered at Maya across the room, *Who is he???*

Maya tensed her entire body, and she knew her mother could read her body language, which said, "I am going to kill you."

"Whoa," Tyler said cluelessly. "It's go time." He grabbed a random record out of the bin to his left and held it in front of his face. "Is this any good?"

"Um, the Wiggles?" Maya asked.

"What's the Wiggles?"

"Kids' music. 'Fruit salad . . . yummy yummy.' Ring a bell?"

"Why do you have that on vinyl?"

"You'd be surprised. There's a cult following. Especially of Anthony the hot blue Wiggle."

"There's a hot Wiggle?"

"Apparently. Here," Maya said, and without looking away from him she reached far behind her and yanked Carole King's *Tapestry* out of a bin. "You said you liked the seventies."

He held it in front of him. "Hmm. It seems a little female empowerment-y."

"It's actually surprisingly doormatty and masochistic. But she was behind it all. She wrote *all* the songs of the seventies. Well. Her and Dolly Parton."

"I'll take it," he said, since he knew that Dolly Parton was having a moment, so maybe this chick would slap, too.

Ugh. *Chick*, Maya thought, and *slap*. Beige flags. She'd have to forgive so much in people if she was ever to actually hang with them. *I mean, he just thought "chick," right? He didn't say it.* She'd have to give people the benefit of the doubt, maybe.

He brought the album up to Stacy at the register, and while he was digging his wallet out of his tight pants, Maya shot another warning stare at her mother. This one said, "Do not embarrass me further."

Her mother registered the glare, stood at attention, and gave Maya a little ten-four salute before ringing up Tyler and saying, officiously, facetiously, with a little nod, "It was a pleasure doing business with you, kind sir."

"The pleasure was all mine," Tyler said politely.

Maurice, drinking water from his bowl at Stacy's feet, looked up at Tyler and uncharacteristically started to growl, even showing his teeth a little. *Traitor*, Maya thought at him. They were all, in different ways, conspiring to humiliate her. "Don't mind him," Maya said. "He's just cranky because we had to put him on a diet, right, Porker?" Maya asked him, and he growled again and then issued a sharp little bark. A warning? Or was he jealous? Thankfully, she had no way of knowing. He really was her favorite being on the planet.

Maya escorted Tyler to the door, needing to get him out of her mother's purview. Maya was mortified, but as she kind of overzealously pushed Tyler out the door, she realized he'd registered none of it: her mother's quirky, overeager display, her own mortification, Maurice's disapproval. He was just pleasantly being Tyler in a moment, and he thought, *I wonder if she'd want to get ice cream.*

"Want to get some ice cream?" Maya asked. "I know just the place."

As the door slammed behind them, she heard her mother say, "Wait, Maya . . ." and then babble to herself something about Whispering Pines conditions of release, even though Maya could tell her mother was secretly elated. *A boy on her first day!*

She and Tyler brought their cones to the bridge and sat on the pedestrian path with their feet dangling high over the Delaware River. Her feet felt rubbery, as if they didn't trust Maya not to jump. Her palms sweat a bit and she grabbed a little tighter to the railing under her armpits. The slow rush of the water and the intermittent zooms of the cars passing over the metal grate surface of the Erector set bridge acted like a white noise machine and helped to drown out some of Tyler's thinking. She focused on what he said, which was, "That song is deep, you know?"

"Which one?"

"'Suite: Judy Blue Eyes,'" he said. "It's about, like, how love and freedom are incompatible. It's what drove Sartre and Simone de Beauvoir crazy. They discovered it, the existentialists."

"Discovered what?" Maya asked, shivering a bit. It was

technically spring, but the icy breeze swept in from the west, carrying the bite of the dwindling Poconos snowcaps. (Man-made snowcaps because of the climate apocalypse, Maya thought, but snowcaps nonetheless.)

"Discovered the fact that once you fall in love, you can never again be truly free. So, you have to decide. Love or Freedom. You can't have both," he said, and he handed Maya his black hoodie.

She wrapped it around her shoulders (penetrating the sleeves felt too intimate) and thought for a second about his theory. "Vague," she said. "I feel like you're not defining your terms. B minus. That is a B minus theory. I can't tell if it's genius or totally obvious. And how is that in 'Suite'?"

"The singer keeps wanting both his freedom and his lady at the same time, and she makes it hard."

"That's what he said . . ." Maya whisper-laughed.

"Maya. Storm," Tyler chided. "No! No dick jokes while we are philosophizing. Bad!" he said, laughing, and he tapped her on the bridge of her nose with his emptied sugar cone. But secretly she knew he was elated that she could turn from high to low on a dime. She could meet him where he was, which was the dark, murky swamp of adolescence, and he liked it. She was doing it. Flirting with a boy!

"So which one do you choose?" she asked now. "Love or Freedom?"

"Freedom," he said with conviction, but there was a sadness in it. She looked into his one unobstructed eye, and she saw, surprisingly, that in his brain was a Venn diagram called "Divorce."

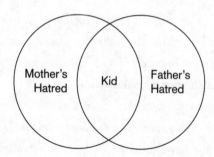

He was still philosophizing, thinking how when a kid's parents divorce, the kid gets caught in the intersection of their parents' hatred and therefore cannot love themselves. *When you're with your dad, he hates you for your Mom parts, and when you're with your mom, she hates you for your Dad parts,* he thought.

Aw, Maya thought. *Ouch.*

"I definitely choose Freedom," he said. "Love is too painful and complicated," which seemed like a good cue for Maya to hand him back his sweatshirt.

Self-Help for Superheroes

School again? Wasn't she just there yesterday? It didn't stop; the rush of it was like that mighty Delaware. There was no stopping the rush of school, its constant powerful hum. You couldn't even stand up and look around for a second, especially in the turbulent parts, or you'd be smashed upon the rocks. You just needed to sit in the current with your feet up and let it bump your ass peacefully downstream until you could climb out in the sandbar of June. You were powerless against it. The constant flow of school.

Stacy almost lost her mind that morning because Maya had gotten all the way to the car with her shoes untied, her backpack leaking all kinds of shit, as if she were Hansel and Gretel leaving a path of school supplies to help find the way home, when she realized she had forgotten her laptop and had to run back inside.

"Ugh! You're going to be late," Stacy screamed. She even scared away the first robin of spring.

"You just scared away the first robin of spring," Maya pointed out.

"Get your laptop!"

Maya stood on the passenger side of the car and reminded Stacy once again of John Ackroyd and Maya's rank at the very bottom of the class. "You know John Ackroyd is probably just a placeholder, right? So, I can't be doing any worse. It doesn't matter if I'm late. There's a freedom in that."

Her mother tried some yoga breathing and then opened the driver's side door. "I can't be the only one who cares, Maya. Get your father to bring you. I give up."

"Seriously. Already, on day two, you give up? You're not modeling the resilience."

"Get your laptop and get your father," she said as she jumped out of the pickup and slammed the old rusted door with an ugly, vibrating clang. "I'm not going to try until you do."

"Oooh tough love."

"Maya." Her mother stared at her, exhausted by all her decades of womanhood and all the desperate attempts at proving her worth. This was about her. How she was a failure if she couldn't even get her kid to school on time. It was too much for Maya to untangle before first period.

"Fine. I'll get Dad," she said, capitulating.

Glen drove her peacefully to school, emboldened as he was by his lifelong princely reign on the top of the patriarchy food chain. He was unruffled by tardiness and felt no need to prove anything at all to the world. Late as they were, he obeyed all the traffic rules and never inched above the speed limit. He even stopped for a family of geese to cross the road. He was a different animal from Stacy, kind of sloth-like and oblivious to convention.

"I think it's time for the annual Stormies," he said as he waited for the geese. Their last name was Storm, which was super apropos, turbulent as things usually were. The Stormies was an annual family awards show in which they made up whacky award categories for the family stuff that happened that year—Worst Tantrum, Best Vacation Moment, Most Disastrous Recipe, Home Improvement Fails, Messiest Cabinet.

"Maybe we should cancel it this year? It's hard to have a sense of humor about it all right now."

"Maybe that's when we need it most."

"Maybe," Maya said, but she had her doubts. She knew it was probably a bad idea. And she had to trust what she knew.

....

She was standing in the middle of the hallway in a trance when Lucy swept up behind her and tucked her arm beneath Maya's armpit. "Come on, space cadet. Time for math. Did you do the homework?"

"You told me not to, remember? Let Tori do it?"

"Tori's absent today."

"Great."

"District Twelve is going down," Lucy lamented. "We have, like, an oral exam."

"May the odds be ever in our favor," Maya mumbled as Lucy dragged her down the hall.

In math, they got through the oral exam. Maya communicated the answers to Lucy and Kevin with a kind of Morse code tip-tapping on the desk with her pen. They picked it up immediately, so it didn't look like Maya was the only one who knew what was going on. In that way, District Twelve, despite all odds against it, was able to communicate and collaborate and fake their way through another lesson on trigonometry, but right in the middle of it, Maya was called to the office.

"Ooooo," said Eddie, the wrestler, as if he were in middle school and Maya were in some kind of trouble. If she was, she had no idea what she'd done wrong this time.

Maya took the long way to the office, trying to avoid any chance encounters with people's thoughts. She ducked downstairs, swung past the orchestra room, wound through the basement, past room 143, and back upstairs to the office, where the receptionist was not thinking a thing except for what to have for lunch. She was calculating her Weight Watchers meals on her app and reveling in the fact that eggs were zero points.

Behind her stood Amy! Therapist Amy. It was weird to see her out of context, without the elephants, the tapestry. It was like being six and seeing your first-grade teacher in the grocery store and realizing for the first time that she was human and not some chalk-wielding goddess who lived at school and existed on a diet of graham crackers and tiny cartons of orange juice. It was even weird to see Amy standing up. She was shorter than Maya remembered, almost pixieish, whereas in her office, sitting down, she loomed so large. She wore a dress and a long sweater with funky sneakers and a colorful rag tied about her tangle of hair. Her glasses frames were big, black, and bold.

"Maya," Amy said.

"Amy," Maya said back. "What are you doing here?"

"We have to talk."

Maya tried to get a reading on Amy. *How unusual was this?* she wondered. Did therapists normally drop by in the middle of the school day just to chat? Was this an ambush? She was nervous, palms sweating, remembering the way she left their last session. It was basically a passive-aggressive cry for help. She revealed her deepest, innermost secret and read Amy's mind out loud. But she was hoping Amy had just shrugged it off as a coincidence.

"Um, okay?" Amy wasn't carrying anything larger than a macramé purse, and she wasn't followed by two goons dressed in white who could throw Maya in restraints, so, filled with a sense of doom, Maya started walking toward room 143.

She led Amy down beneath the stairs, where she pushed the beads aside. The scent of Tyler's incense lingered a bit and reminded Maya to breathe.

They sat down awkwardly on the thrifted couch, whose decades-old cushions allowed them to sink so deeply into it that Amy's feet barely touched the floor.

"So," Amy said. She hadn't forgotten how they'd left things, Maya could see now. She'd been perseverating over it for days. Tossing and turning at night, wondering how Maya seemed to know what she was thinking in that exact moment.

"So," Maya said back. "What do you think of the wellness

center?" Someone had left the white noise machine on, so it sounded like they were in a rainforest standing next to a trickling waterfall. The sound-activated LED light strips blinked purple and green with every fake rainforest birdcall.

"They should just give kids less homework. Everyone would be well."

"Exactly. Kombucha?" Maya asked as she opened the refrigerator door adorned with a new magnet that said, *Not All Who Wander Are Lost.*

"Is that what you're struggling with? The homework?"

"Um. Sort of. It's complicated."

"Most people are. Complicated. It helps to talk about it. You seem to maybe want to talk about it. The way you left our last session . . . I feel like you were trying to tell me something. I felt like I needed to follow up." *It was a little eerie. Finishing my sentences . . . or was I imagining it?*

"I don't know where to start. I just . . ." *Don't you dare cry,* Maya reminded herself. She took a deep breath. "It's just that I can get overwhelmed."

"We all get overwhelmed by too much thinking. I can help you with that. There are strategies." Amy, so tentative when she walked in, tried to regain confidence in her shrinkmanship.

"It's . . ." Maya said and then stopped. She couldn't tell the truth. They'd lock her up for good at Whispering Pines, wouldn't they? She took a glance over at Mr. Rogers and remembered his favorite thing to tell children when there was a crisis. "Look for the helpers," he would say. Someone is always there to help. It was supposed to make kids feel safe and restore their faith in humanity. "Look for the helpers," Maya whispered.

"Yes, Maya. Look for the helpers. I am a licensed helper."

Maya took a deep breath. "It's not my thinking I'm worried about. . . . It's everyone else's."

"What do you mean?" Amy said.

"Sometimes . . . ," (*all the time*, she thought), "I know what people are thinking."

Amy just stared at her, inhaled, and thought, *What she thinks are her instincts about what people think could really be her imagination. She's just imagining what other people think, to try to stay one step ahead of them. She's doing it to protect herself.*

"Protect myself from what?" Maya asked.

Amy shuddered. She took a deep breath, and her eyes went wide, steady on Maya's as she thought, *Okay. This is something else. There was a unit in grad school about perception. Extrasensory perception and how it could be a biological function of the brain. Something about serotonin, the blood-brain barrier, what was it, dammit? Why didn't I pay attention in grad school? Maybe because I was trying to get James to marry me. That's a valid reason people go to grad school, too, isn't it? To get married. Dammit.* "Um," she said. "Can we turn that thing off?" she asked about the white noise and the rainforest and the birds and the blinking lights. *These kids are only at peace if they are constantly stimulated*, she thought. Maya flipped a switch, and it was quiet. "So, how long has this been going on?"

"Since I was bitten by the radioactive spider."

"Very funny."

"Since my birth parents sent me here from Krypton in a space capsule that landed on the Kents' farm? Since I arrived here from Themyscira in an invisible plane?"

"You think you're a superhero?"

"No. That would be absurd," Maya said.

"Then how do you explain it?" Amy asked.

Bartender, Acrobat, God, Maya thought. "If I told you, you'd think I was crazy," she said.

Amy smiled. "Try me." *It never fails to astonish me how these young people think I haven't already heard it all. . . . The girl who skipped her period and thought it was immaculate conception, the boy who thought he could get his parents back together if he kept breaking bones, the girl who thought she could speak dog. I've heard everything, but these kids think I'm newly hatched on this planet like Mork from Ork.*

"Wow," Maya said under her breath, "That is just . . . such a strange, outdated reference." Maya shook her head, feeling less confident in this one human being she was about to divulge everything to. "Let's see," Maya started. "Um. I am the alpha and the omega? The almighty, like, creator of the universe? Maybe?"

"Maya," Amy exhaled.

"See. Oh god. Why did I say anything?"

"You're smart enough to know that this particular kind of grandiosity is part of a very serious diagnosis." She was re-thinking her decision to sign Maya's release. She never fathomed Maya was psychotic. To think you were . . . her religion prevented her from even saying the name out loud—was not on the scale of Maya's mild dysthymia diagnosis. How could she have been so far-off?

"So, maybe . . . ," Amy said, pacing and then picking up a fidget spinner from the coffee table and letting it spin between her thumb and forefinger. Taking a moment to figure out her next move. She didn't want to spook her.

"Fine," Maya said.

"Fine, what, fine?" Amy replied.

"Fine, you're going to make me do this."

"Do what?"

"Can you just look at me for one sec?"

Amy was a good sport. All that therapy. She lifted the heavy frames of her glasses to the top of her head and looked straight into Maya's eyes. Maya had never noticed how blue they were. Turquoise, really. Like the chunks of rock in the faux Native silver jewelry her mother appropriated in her attempts to look like Jim Morrison or something, or Wilma Mankiller or Sacajawea. Stacyjawea.

"Willy Wonka," Maya said after a second.

"What?" Amy said.

"Something about the film version moves you to your very core. The Gene Wilder version, obviously. Not the Johnny Depp. Anyway. The glass elevator, Charlie winning the golden ticket, the sheer justice of that, and how Gene Wilder validated the fact that there were so many bad kids who usually won everything. Like your brother. But this time they didn't. He didn't let them. Wonka rewarded Charlie. The good boy who was good in spite of his lost innocence, in spite of the travails that had stolen his childhood. There were people—Grandpa

Joe, Willy Wonka—who were trying to make up for it. Trying to give Charlie back his childhood . . . restore his pure imagination. If only someone had done that for you. Did people know what it was like trying to be a kid in the seventies? Have they seen *The Bad News Bears?* Walter Matthau makes you cry, too, by the way. How his sad dog face reminds you of the good half of your father."

"How do you know who Walter Matthau is?"

"How did I know who Mork from Ork is?" she said under her breath, seriously wondering herself. "Your father was a Gemini and he had a very bad half," Maya continued. "But you also appreciated Gene Wilder's knowing irony. Something about the *way* he sang that song . . . 'Pure Imagination' . . . revealed that he knew you were never really going to view paradise. You could try, but paradise, happiness, was an asymptote that you never really arrived at. A mythical location.

"He did all that in one song, and when your seven-year-old daughter had to dance to the Broadway version in her dance recital, you had to lock yourself in the school auditorium bathroom stall and try to stop yourself from hyperventilating, while tracing the crudely drawn letters f-u-c-k that were scratched into the steel wall with the end of a geometry-class compass."

Amy blinked. She sat down and took a deep breath. "Okay. Um. Holy shit! Sorry. This is just . . ."

"It's more than intuition. I know you; I know everyone; I know everything, especially if I'm in close proximity. And I don't want to know it," Maya whispered. Choking back a tear, she grabbed a tissue from the box on top of the plush pink cube end table that someone's mom had recently donated to the room.

"Um, wait." Amy paused. She was struggling to regain her composure, snapping and unsnapping the magnetic clasp on her macramé purse. "You seem to be shouldering a lot of responsibility here," she finally said, staring Maya in the eye.

"I've got the whole world in my hands, Amy."

Amy stared at her for a second, and her eyes were wet. "Let me try to help you."

Argh. Dogs! thought Lucy. She did not do dogs. She wondered if 23andMe could check for a gene that predicted affinity for dogs. This would be more useful than logging on there only to find that your dad's not your dad. Or that you have seventeen half sisters from the time when your dad donated sperm to a sperm bank— Seventeen Half Sisters being an excellent band name, which she would add to her list that she kept on her Notability app. She'd put it right after Soggy Schnitzel, which she came up with at Oktoberfest one year. She was going to do a line of concert tees of fake band names and had already sketched a few out.

And she digressed. Again! She was always digressing, in part, she had to admit, because her mind was so much more interesting than anything else happening in these parts, which made her afraid that she might have a superiority complex, and that didn't fit with her brand, so she needed to cut it out.

A fat brindle pit bull mix barked sharply and stood and slammed his front paws against a chain-link fence that shivered with the weight of him.

Lucy felt unwelcome, as one is wont to feel, being greeted as she was, by a pit bull and a chain-link fence!

She started to turn around, but then redoubled her resolve.

The dog slobbered and wagged his tail, which Lucy thought might be signs of affection. She had no instincts for this. But before she could google "body language of guard dogs" (this, too, an amazing band name!), Tori came to the screen door and whistled the dog away.

She and Tori were friends once. It was a sad, boring friends-to-enemies-to-frenemies trope, but in Lucy's mind—which she tended to believe was superior to others but was working on it—childhood friends were friends for life. Because Lucy was the only person alive who knew what it was like to try to sleep through the thunderous shouts as Tori's drunken father harangued her mother, stopping just short of physical abuse but threatening to grab her by the neck and throw her against the wall.

Lucy had slept over on nights like this when her mom, Jeanne, was first divorced and working nights at the Red Fox Inn. Abandoned and alone and broke in a town full of white people, Jeanne needed help, and Laurie, Tori's mom (rhyming intentional), was the only one to reach out, understanding herself what it was like being alone and scared and saddled with debt and childcare needs.

On nights like these, six-year-old Tori and Lucy, obsessed as they were by *The Paper Bag Princess,* would scribble on grocery bags with pastels, creating the pinkest and purplest of paper-bag armor, and cut out holes for their head and arms. They would then make swords from the cardboard centers of paper towel rolls, lances from rolls of wrapping paper, and a chariot for the gerbil, whose cage they duct-taped to a skateboard. Then they would sneak out, ducking beneath the insults Tori's parents hurled at each other, and crawling to the front door. They'd traipse through the woods, swishing and swashing at the underbrush with their swords and pulling the gerbil behind them, before they arrived at Lucy's house, and she'd open the door with the key in the same gray ceramic frog in which everyone on the block left their spare keys. Why would you make a frog for the purpose of hiding keys and sell a lot of them, so that everyone knew where everyone else was hiding their spare keys? *Argh. I digress,* Lucy thought.

She hadn't been to Tori's in ages; had it been six months? More? But after she missed class the other day, Lucy was worried about her.

Tori stood now at the door, pale, pasty, and sad without her makeup on, and Lucy knew it had been a rough patch of road.

"Here," she said to Tori, and she handed her a long tube of cardboard, before Tori ducked inside to get her things.

Promposal

Someone had announced the date and venue for prom over the loudspeaker that morning during announcements. As Maya slogged down the hall, *thoughts* about prom were pinging and zooming everywhere, but *feelings* about the prom only fell into three categories. There was ebullience, dread, and feigned indifference (which was what some people used to cover up their dread); so, two categories. There were only two ways people felt about it. It was pretty black-and-white.

Maya actually felt actual indifference until she thought of her mom catching wind of the event and trying to nudge her into going, and then she felt actual dread.

Her dread combined with the compounded dread of the entire dreading half of the school was too much to dread before first block, so she used it as an excuse to duck into room 143 to catch some much-needed wellness, in finger quotes, which in this case was the ability to write herself a late pass. Maddie had written that into the bylaws. You could go to the wellness center and write yourself a pass, as long as you were a junior or above. More people should take advantage of this perk, Maya thought, but they were too interested in being on time and getting all the points.

Plus mental health still = stigma, so people were reluctant to publicly avail themselves of the wellness center.

She pushed aside the beads in the doorway, and surprise! Tyler was there. Was she really surprised that Tyler was there? Was Maya actually, in fact, hoping he was there? Was she really, in fact, not seeking wellness at all, but desperately seeking Tyler?

Signs pointed to yes, if she had to be honest and if she happened to speak to herself like a Magic 8 Ball.

She reached again into her backpack for her Bible and stroked the soft golden pages to calm herself down.

"What's that?" Tyler asked. Because he was present with her and noticed her every move.

"Oh, it's just a . . . I don't know, it's nothing," she said, taking the book out of her backpack and flopping it back and forth a little. "Just a thing I carry around."

"I didn't take you for religious," he said. "In the Judeo-Christian sense. Seems incongruent." Maya just realized his T-shirt said FEMINIST in red seventies bubble letter font and it was so cute, she resisted an inner squeal.

"Yeah. I've actually never been to church." Can you imagine the thoughts she'd read in a church? she thought. Talk about incongruent. "It's kind of like a souvenir, really. I guess. I was curious about it."

"It's all good, Maya. I think we should all be curious about it. We should have one in here. I think there's already a Book of Mormon in a drawer somewhere."

"Really?"

"Yeah."

"You have a 'Read Banned Books' T-shirt, too, don't you?" she said, pointing at his FEMINIST shirt and trying not to be distracted by his pecs.

"Maybe," he said sheepishly.

"Maybe I'll leave this here," she said, plopping the Bible onto the coffee table. Did she really need a reminder of the mental hospital? And she got the gist of the Bible: Love your neighbor.

"Needs a warning label, though." Tyler ripped a neon pink Post-it from the Positivity Wall and wrote: *Please do not try to read this literally or use weird, obscure, ancient passages to justify your vile hatreds.*

"Fair," Maya said.

"A lot of people think Jesus spent some of that time in between Christmas and Easter in India, but all we get is Christmas and Easter," he said, holding up his hands in an adorable shrug that accentuated his shoulder muscles. "Where's the middle?" he asked. "The middle is where he learned to meditate. It's actually kind of what he describes as thinking of God first. You just focus all your thoughts on god for a bit and let the mundane, toxic, real-world thoughts drift away. You can focus on god or a candle or your breath. I actually see a tiny purple light when I close my eyes and I focus on that. It can be anything, just not your thoughts. And when you notice yourself thinking thoughts that lead to other thoughts, just snap yourself out of it and begin again."

He sat on his regular pillow wedged between the side

of the couch and the wall, using his fingers to close off one nostril at a time, while he inhaled or exhaled through the alternating open one. And that gave Maya an idea. Maybe she could achieve wellness through Tyler. If he could teach her to meditate, she could truly block out other people's thoughts. Amy had also suggested this, but she didn't think normal teens had meditation practices, so she hadn't taken it seriously.

"It kind of looks like you're snorting cocaine," Maya said.

Tyler just smiled serenely and kept breathing loudly through alternate nostrils with his eyes closed.

"Not that I've ever seen anyone snort cocaine," Maya continued. "That's just what it looks like when they do it on TV."

Tyler's mind flashed to the times he *did* see people snorting cocaine as a child and how it terrified him as he lay on his stomach on the rug in his footie pajamas and peeked through a crack in his bedroom door.

But then, instead of wallowing in the sadness and self-pity of that moment (like Maya was currently doing for him), he put the thought away!

It was a miracle. It was as if his inhale sucked the memory into a compartment of his brain and closed it off, so he didn't have to feel the sad repercussions of it. Then he exhaled and thought only, *Exhale.*

"Can you teach me to do that?" she asked.

She saw Tyler register her voice but then he envisioned the voice drifting away with the force of his next exhale. He literally just blew her off.

"Are you meditating or dismissing me?" Maya asked him.

"Both, I guess," Tyler said in a deep resonant baritone that rang through Maya like a tuning fork. When he opened his eyes and stared at her bravely, taking in her entire face without looking away, she saw a kind of cute version of herself reflected in his mind. It was different from the way she saw herself. Kind of herself but in HD.

Then, in spite of herself, Maya's zooming, pinging thoughts imagined: her and Tyler holding hands; her and Tyler making out on his meditation pillow in some weird upside-down yoga posture; her and Tyler at goat yoga; her and Tyler eating a heart-shaped vegan promposal pizza; her and Tyler having a prom photo shoot at their house in front of the hydrangeas, where Stacy would say only the most embarrassing things and where Maurice would pee on his tux. . . . Her thoughts pinged around and around as if she were drawing them on a spirograph, creating an orbital, atomic pinging mess of a scribble, but Tyler only thought the exact thing that he said, which was, "Maya. I'm glad you stopped by."

His mind, Maya realized as she zoomed in on him, was organized like a game piece in Trivial Pursuit, a wheel with empty pie-shaped holes where he could put thoughts and store them for contemplating later or responding to now. One thought never bled into another. Each thought stayed obediently in its compartment, and because it was penned-in, it could not grow so large from obsessive perseverating that it would take over the entire wheel.

Whoa, Maya thought. Was this nature or nurture? Were

men born this way or were their minds shaped by the patri-archy? Is this how a mind shapes itself if it does not have to constantly worry about survival? Predators? Poverty? Preg-nancy? Belittling? Gaslighting? Equality? Shame? Rape? Be-ing Seen? Being Heard? Being Liked? Is this just male-think or has meditation done this? And just like that, her spiro-graph brain was scribbling out of control.

"So, you try," Tyler said.

"Sounds pretty straightforward," she said. If she could learn this, she could shut everyone out. Maybe she could turn down the volume on everyone else and try to have a life.

"It's actually the hardest thing in the world, grasshopper. Here, take my pillow," he said, and swept his arm into his little meditation nook. "Okay. Close your eyes and begin breathing. Maybe use a little mantra. *I breathe in, I breathe out.* If you notice yourself thinking of anything other than *I breathe in,* then start again."

Tyler sat cross-legged in front of her, and she thought, *I breathe,* and she didn't even get to the word *in* before she thought, *Wow, he's really flexible. His knees just flopped open to the floor like a Venus flytrap.*

And she started again. *I brea,* but she didn't even get to the *th* sound before she saw Tyler thinking.

To occupy his mind, he was dreaming up the most ludi-crous promposal he could imagine, which involved a hang glider, a waterfall, a rainbow, and a soft landing on a heart-shaped bed of green tea mochi, which they could wallow around in for a while, before taking a hayride to a rustic sto-rybook farm where a Charlotte-like spider would spin the word "prom" in a giant web above the pigpen. He had to stop himself from laughing out loud. Maya zoomed in, but try as she might, she could not figure out who was lying on top of him in his zany, pretend promposal, horizontal hang-gliding sac thingy.

Did she wish it were her?

It was decidedly so.

He couldn't stop thinking about her. Which wasn't like him. He usually kept his crushes high-key under control. He had cultivated a certain perspective. He could compartmentalize. Have a good time with a girl, consensually, then stay at somewhat of a remove. He was famous for his cool. And the girls knew this about him. Knew what he was good for. A one-night stand. A fun time. He was not relationship material, and they knew not to count on him for anything. The rules were in place, and no one got hurt. What was it Lucy said? He was a Yoga Pants Play-a. He honored the light in a girl (or an occasional boy), she honored the light in him, and then they went their separate ways. Namaste.

But this girl had him in a spell. He could see multitudes, universes inside the smoky green of her irises. The smoke inside her eyes moved like weather. Like the crystalline cosmic clouds they were only now just discovering with the James Webb telescope, the ones that created the stars. She was enchanting. And even more so because she didn't yet realize her power. She was humble, vulnerable, funny, and smart. How was he supposed to stay cool about this girl? And the dimple in her right cheek. That just wasn't fair. *I breathe in,* he thought, trying to push Maya into a closed Maya box in his brain, but suddenly all the boxes melted into one. His brain was only "Maya," which he knew in certain eastern religions meant "illusion." Distraction. He needed to stay focused.

He ran faster around the track, a burst of speed shocking the long jumper on his right, who usually lapped him at every practice. *Simp!* he called himself. *Simp. Simp. Simp.* He needed to push her away because he had so much to learn before he could truly have a relationship. He had researched and found entire new religions for himself because his father's religion could only understand women using the two-Mary dichotomy.

And Mary Magdalene was not a whatever they said she was, btw. She was Jesus' partner. A disciple. An academic. She wrote a gospel. She was probably behind it all like Gwen Verdon was behind Fosse or Frida Kahlo was behind Diego Rivera or Camille Claudel was behind Rodin. Women were geniuses, and he wanted to be worthy enough to deserve the company of one before he committed.

In the meantime, he needed to honor his mother, who was also a genius. She sacrificed everything for him, and he was going to pay her back with his success and a condo in Boca. He'd already saved $10,000, but he needed to stay on the path.

He'd just finished two laps, and he did not think about Maya once. He had tried to build a fortress against her in his mind, but her name seeped beneath the cracks like a tantalizing vapor. It suffocated everything else and he was back to square one, wondering when it was he could see her again.

Aquafresh

"Bish. You owe me," Lucy said. She leaned against Maya's locker looking kinda cute in a half pony and a distressed Nirvana T-shirt dress that paired well with the day's selection of black Jordans. *Was that a trace of eyeliner?* Maya wondered. Lucy unpeeled a square of Aquafresh from her pack and popped it in her mouth. "Flavor burst?" she asked, tipping the pack to Maya.

"Even your gum is vintage?" Maya said, peeling off a piece. "What do I owe you for, again?" It was the end of the day and Maya rubbed her eyes. She was exhausted, but not as tired as usual because she had been practicing Tyler's strategy. Whenever a teacher thought *Why am I doing this?* or *I hope it's tuna day at the sandwich bar* or *I can't wait 'til 2:30 so I can rub up against Coach Jim's blond hairy legs in his stretchy polyester coachy shorts. . . . Who cares if he's married. YOLO!* she breathed these thoughts into a "Teacher Babble" part of her brain and tried to focus instead on the things they were saying out loud. PV = nRT and whatnot.

"You owe me for all that tutoring," Lucy answered.

"Yes, you were such a big help," Maya said sarcastically. Maya was the one who tapped out the code for all the answers to the oral exam in Pre-Calc and earned them an unprecedented (without-Tori) A minus. "What do you need?" Maya asked.

"A flavor flave. Just like a tiny favor fave." Lucy pretended to be coy, fake batting her eyelashes. "I just need a friend to come to my house for dinner."

"Dinner?"

"Yeah. My mom has a new boyfriend, and I don't want to face it alone."

"That sounds like a high price for friendship."

"It's going to be the most awkward dinner of your life," Lucy said. "He's a Libertarian."

"I don't even know what that means, but you're not really selling it."

"Please? I need your help. Libertarians are the ones who believe corporations are people and still use the terms 'handout' and 'welfare queens.' They love the Koch brothers. He's probably in the NRA and has like ten guns. To protect the white privilege that he refuses to acknowledge."

"Is he white?"

"I don't know. His name is Terry, though, so."

"Is he really a Libertarian?"

"Yes. My mom said Libertarian."

"That sounds bad."

"It is. Come on. My mom makes awesome mac and cheese. You'll be the perfect buffer."

....

Lucy was right about the mac and cheese. It was awesome. It had a sriracha swirl in it and was topped with a crispy panko breadcrumb concoction that you had to crack like a crème brûlée in order to get to the gooey center.

In just about every other sense, though, Lucy was way off base.

Terry, for example, was Black and not white. And he was not a *Libertarian*, but a *librarian*. He was a super tatted-up *librarian* who spent his free time bike racing on the cyclo-cross circuit, where he often found himself on the podium. He was fit as heck. And rode his bike everywhere, so he didn't use a lot of fossil fuels, out of his deep consideration for their z-generation and their pending necessity to grapple with the climate apocalypse. He was doing his part. Or else, he couldn't afford a car.

"I just fell in love with research," Terry said, describing his leap into librarianship. "It's like a treasure hunt."

Classic Terry.

Maya could think, *Classic Terry*, because she had spent a lot of time getting to know him, while Lucy spent her time either ignoring him or trying to sabotage the whole evening.

"So, you must get off on shushing, huh? Gives you a little power trip to shame people," she said, and then she slumped back and scrolled through her phone.

"It's actually not like that anymore. That's my least favorite part of the job."

"No phones at the table," Lucy's mom said.

"Since when? Oooohhh, since we're trying to impress Terry

the librarian," Lucy quipped. "Just doing a little research, Mom. Terry loves research," she said and looked back at her phone.

Lucy's mom, Jeanne, gave Terry an apologetic glance as she set the green beans down onto a trivet. The green beans were also panko encrusted, which Maya decided all food should be forever until the end of time. "You might be interested in what Terry does, Lucy. He's in the library's entrepreneurship department. He helps people do research for new startups."

"I'm sure he's an invaluable resource," Lucy mumbled.

"Lucy, come on," her mom said. *Can't she tell I'm try . . .* Maya caught herself reading a thought and tried to breathe it away. She was not going to engage. *I wish she'd just tell me about her girlfriends. It's crazy that she thinks I don't know. A mother knows her daughter. And as Margaret Cho's mother even says, "Everybody . . . little bit gay."*

I breathe out!!! Maya thought and she tried to put Jeanne's thought into a "Things Mothers Think" compartment, but she didn't understand why it shouldn't be cross-referenced into a million other parts of her brain. Coming out. Lesbians. Secrets. Margaret Cho. She knew if she were a boy, "Things Mothers Think" might just be locked away in an iron vault never to be considered again.

"Come on, what?" Lucy said to her mom. "Wasn't it just yesterday you stormed into my room and threatened to shut down my Etsy page if I didn't get my grades up? Terry, don't let her fool you. She's not very supportive of my business," Lucy said, looking Terry in the eye for the first time since dinner started.

It went on this way, Lucy acting out, Maya complimenting

Lucy's mom on the food and answering Terry's questions about her mom's record store, which was really Maya's only extracurricular she could discuss aside from room 143, until finally, they were excused.

Up in Lucy's room, Maya said, "Ugh. Now you owe me," then reluctantly added "Bish." Lucy's room looked like a shoe store. An entire wall was covered floor to ceiling with invisible plastic floating shelves on which she displayed every shoe she owned white to black, in ROYGBIV order from left to right. She had a rotating rack of T-shirts in one corner, a couple of mannequins missing different appendages that were arranged as if they were having sex.

"You'll never understand about Jeanne," Lucy said, and when she noticed Maya staring at the mannequins said, "Oh, meet Casey and Sydney. They, them pronouns."

"Pleased to meet you," Maya said to Casey and Sydney, and then, "Don't you want your mom to be happy, Lucy? Terry seems like a nice guy."

Maya tried to breathe away the onslaught of thoughts and emotions that pinged around Lucy's brain, which operated much like her own tangled spirograph, and she tried to focus instead on what she was saying.

"When your mom has a boyfriend," Lucy said, taking a deep breath, "you lose her as your main person. As much as you probably take your supercool mom for granted, she will always be your main person. She will always go to bat for you. Not so much with Jeanne. She is ripe and ready to throw me under the bus at the first sign of conflict because *Terry* is my mom's main person right now. Her main focus. His needs will always trump mine because she's trying to get in his pants and into his life and whatnot, and he will never have my best interests at heart, because he will never be my father. The unconditional love she's supposed to have for me suddenly has a giant condition, named Terry. Trust me. I'm on my own without a main person. Abandoned. So eff her. Did you see how she's suddenly pretending to be on my side with the business? Such bullshit. I hate her." *Plus, she would disown me if she knew I liked girls*, Lucy thought.

I breathe in! Maya thought, trying not to engage with Lucy's mind and fix the communication gap. *Your mom knows you like girls*, she was dying to say, but she would not engage. *I breathe out*, she thought and watched the issue of Lucy's coming out to her mom float away on a little cloud.

As she spoke, Lucy slid and scraped some T-shirt hangers around on the rack, picked one out, stood Casey up, and pulled it over their head. It was an authentic Pink Floyd concert T (the one with the prism) that had white baseball sleeves. Lucy had distressed and bedazzled it and then accessorized it with a ruffled white Peter Pan collar that you would think would be inharmonious, but actually made a statement about embracing the dark, mysterious side of femininity. It was genius. Signature Gilding the Monster.

Lucy was still fuming, but styling Casey seemed to calm her down. She headed to a second homemade rack against the wall and grabbed a vintage pink denim jacket that she had painted with SMASH THE PATRIARCHY on the back and then put on some lacy socks and Docs.

"They need pants," Maya said, and Lucy wrapped Casey's butt in a short pleated skirt.

"Lewks," Lucy said after she was satisfied with the look, and she took a photo for her Instagram.

"What about pockets?" Maya said. Men had pockets. Men kept all their stuff close to their bodies and could "draw" at any moment. If jumped, or challenged to a duel, or struck with an inspiration, they'd never have to go digging through their purse to find a weapon or a pen or their iPhones. Pockets were power, Maya thought.

"Oh, you're right, Storm. Good call," Lucy said as she wrapped a double-layered leather fanny pack around Casey's waist and a garter with a little pocket attached to it around Casey's thigh. "I want to do this instead of college, or at least study fashion merchandising," Lucy said. "But my mom says she won't send me to college to learn how to fold T-shirts at the Gap."

"Ouch."

"Yeah. I wish I could prove to her I can do this, but she doesn't believe in me, unless Terry's around of course. Maybe if I could show her the money, she'd believe me."

"Why don't you sell this stuff at my mom's store?" Maya asked. They could use a merch element of the business, and this was so cool and sustainable and perfect for their brand. Plus, it would be cool to work with a friend sometimes. Make the time pass faster. "I'll ask my mom," Maya said.

"I would love that," said Lucy, and then Jeanne knocked on Lucy's door.

By the way, she thought into Lucy's brain, *your mom loves you and she knows you're gay. And you only have so much time left together.* Then she set it all to "Landslide" by Stevie Nicks.

Lucy's face flushed for a second without knowing exactly why. She felt a sudden rush of affinity for this awkward new friend of hers standing in front of her wearing skinny jeans (*Oy, were they Abercrombie? Oh and smh . . . light wash.*) and Adidas Superstars as if she'd just portaled here through some middle school wormhole. *There's something about her, though,* Lucy thought.

"Maya, your mom is here," Jeanne said, and as Maya began to slip out the door feeling self-conscious about her mall-wear, Lucy said, "I'll pick you up tomorrow in the Toyota Corolla. Six forty-five. Be ready. Time is money."

Circus School or
Failure to Launch

"Maya, I like you," Lucy announced, the next day. "I'm not letting you become a 'failure to launch.'"

"What's that?" Maya asked. They sat in the din of the cafeteria, making a show of picking at their salads before shoving them aside in favor of Styrofoam bowls filled with Cap'n Crunch.

"It's the people who never move out of their parents' basements because they never learned the courage to live. Their parents protected them from life . . . just let them stay home from school and eat chicken nuggets for every meal. So now they are skinless amoeba people without membranes or coping mechanisms, and they have to live in the basement, so they don't get triggered. Their parents protected them to death. That's one theory, anyway. I just read about it in *The Atlantic*."

"*The Atlantic*? Are you sure you don't want to go to college? And. That's not me."

"It's not?" Lucy asked, but it sounded like "hits hot" because she was letting the Crunch melt a little bit in a pool of milk in her mouth before chewing. If you chewed it too soon, it would lacerate your bony palate.

"No," Maya said. "Why do we eat this stuff again? It's like razor blades."

"Because of the milk," Lucy said, and she unwrapped a straw and loudly slurped the milk dregs directly from the bowl. "You have to find a thing. . . . Like you have to just pretend to care about something. What's your hashtag? Your brand, your sob story, your cause, your purpose. What's the thing you write your college essay about?"

"It has to be just one thing? I think my purpose is to take an interdisciplinary approach." *I am the alpha and omega,* Maya thought. Wasn't she supposed to be concerned with all things at once? "Anyway, I'll probably go to a place that doesn't ask for all that."

"What kind of place is that?" Lucy asked.

"County . . . trade school . . . jail." *Bartender, Acrobat, God. Where does god go to college?* And then she said, "Bartending academy. Circus school. Seminary. Cult."

"Circus school is a thing, actually," Lucy said. "You have to have logged many hours on the silks to get in now. You know, those silks that hang from the ceiling. Plus, it's in Canada, so everyone wants to go to get out of this country before it's too late. Have you devised a new way of juggling?" she asked.

"There are new ways?" Maya asked.

"Yup. . . . Have you done Circus Smirkus? How long can you walk on your hands? Got any trapeze?"

"What is Circus Smirkus? I thought I could just run away and, like, feed the elephants."

"Nooo. No one has elephants anymore. PETA. Etcetera. Having elephants is the circus equivalent to wearing a fur coat to the Met Gala," Lucy quipped. "Cringey . . ."

"Oh," Maya said, and she couldn't tell if cringey described her behavior or if that had become her new nickname.

"You have one summer left. You can pack it all in," Lucy assured her.

"Pack what in?" Maya asked.

"The experiences. The leadership. The perceived empathy. Maybe you can design an app," Lucy listed.

Maya was beginning to agree. Maybe having one friend, a fake boyfriend, and a diploma wasn't enough. Maybe graduating just ahead of John Ackroyd and scuttling around like a crab on the bottom of the rankings just to climb out on the other side of high school and live forever coding from her parents' basement was not as noble a goal as she originally thought.

Maybe she should aim higher, just for show.

"Here, I'm going to help you," Lucy continued. She pulled up a photo-collage app on her phone. "We can vision-board it," she said. "What does your life look like in two years? What are your goals?"

"My goal is to blend in, right? Or, wait, is it to stand out? Maybe the goal is to stand out in order to blend? Or was it to blend in order to stand out?" Maya asked.

Lucy shook her head. "I'm like actually s-m-h-ing at you in real life right now."

"Wait," Maya said as Tyler strolled in, his loose pants hanging off his hip bones, his big feet making giant casual strides toward the courtyard where he aimed to spend lunch playing Smashball™ with a bunch of smashing, spinning, cartwheeling bros of the everloving broscape. "I think he might be aligned with my goals." Maya pointed at Tyler, who caught her in his peripheral vision and waved at her sweetly and utterly without self-consciousness. It's good to be king, she thought.

"Damn, Cringey," Lucy said, still disappointed. "Those are some shortsighted goals. Think bigger. I'll allow him one square in a nine-square grid." She pasted a pic of Tyler into the upper left corner of the collage. "What else?" she asked, but Lucy could sympathize. She glanced under her hair at Ruby sitting on the radiator behind the jock table and Maya could see her picture a photo grid filled with Ruby, Ruby, Ruby. She shook herself out if it and then started writing on a paper plate.

"Tyler can be part of it," she said. "He's part of step one. Like, as far as I can tell, here's the road map, although, mind you, I am eschewing it altogether for a different kind of life. But you need to know the rules before you can break them, right? So here are the rules. That is, if you can't get recruited for sports," she said and then scribbled:

1. Become popular. Get people to like you. Go to prom, etc.
2. Galvanize that popularity to champion some quirky, oddly specific cause. Save the world. Like Greta Thunberg (Here she drew a heart. She was a Greta-stan and had a powerful crush on Greta, which she

knew was a little weird. That's what Maya liked about Lucy. At least she was self-aware.)

3. Write about it for the Common App

"You also have to ace the SAT. People say it doesn't matter anymore, but it totally does. Unless you know someone on the board of directors at Brown. Do you know someone on the board of directors at Brown?"

Maya just gave her a knowing stare, like "Does it look like I know someone . . ."

"Right," said Lucy, but she thought, *You never know with white girls. Everything comes so easily to them. They just saunter in with all their milky milkmaidness and get all the milk,* she thought, slurping up the last of her cereal milk for emphasis. "You're welcome," she said out loud and folded the paper plate into a flower that she stuck in Maya's flannel pocket.

"Thank you so much."

"We'll continue working on the vision board."

"Ugh. You sound like my mother," Maya said.

Amanaplanacanalpanama
or Sportobot

"Did you know that up in Quebec, in the Gulf of St. Lawrence, little baby seal pups are drowning because the ice floes are now too thin for them to float around on until they have enough blubber to swim? They're falling through the melting ice and dying a blubberless baby death.

"It's like the end of the *Titanic* movie playing over and over up there. Little baby Kate Winslet seals are floating around on stuff that's too thin to share. And by the way, why didn't she share the door, anyway? Do you know? They could have taken turns on the door. Was she narcissistic? Borderline personality disorder?"

I think I'm just going to wait this out, Amy thought, so Maya would "hear" her. She'd learned she could just think things at Maya rather than speak everything out loud, and their sessions had become extremely efficient.

"Aren't you going to say something like, 'Do you feel like you're on thin ice, Maya?' I gave you the perfect in."

"Do you feel like you're on thin ice, Maya?" Amy said, and

then she got a little entrepreneurial for a second, which was unlike her, because Maya suspected Amy suffered, herself, from a little bit of the depresh. She was not oft inspired to take initiative as far as Maya could tell. She thought, *I should do a seminar on teens coping with the climate crisis. It seems to be weighing on these poor kids' minds.*

"You think, Amy? We basically have no future. Jeez. College. Who the heck cares? They have us distracted with this college industry bullshit when we should be learning how to live off the land. How to dig a well. Build a shelter and defend it with some kind of personal arsenal. It's going to be every person for themselves. And the women. The women are not going to fare very well, as is the fate of women in these kinds of situations. There's going to be all kinds of rapey shit going on, so yeah. Teach your kids some Tae Kwon Do."

"I'm hearing that you feel like it's you against the world. It sounds like you're struggling to find hope amidst the violence. And that you're intimidated by the college admissions process."

Hope is a thing with feathers, Maya thought, and the entire Emily Dickinson poem appeared in her mind without her actually having read it. Maya just ignored Amy and kept rambling, "I mean, if we do survive, and if we do still have things called toilets, and we're not pooping in a ditch, then who's even going to fix the toilets?"

"What do you mean?"

"I mean if EVERYONE has to go to college, then who's going to be a plumber? Some people would be happy making bank as plumbers, but they can't just plumb because they have to go study macroeconomics for some reason. If we do survive the climate apocalypse, there will be no one to unclog the toilets. Or build the decks. Which is a cool job, by the way. Carpenter. It was good enough for Jesus. Anyway. No one will build the decks because the entire generation is hell-bent on college. Maybe they'll all go to college and *build robots* to unclog the toilets? Maybe this is how the robot apocalypse begins. You know how to code? Because that's going to be your only defense in the robot apocalypse. You gotta be able to hack into the mainframe. I don't even know what I'm talking about."

Amy exhaled. "It sounds like you need to take a breath. Have you tried that? Breathwork? Meditation?"

"That won't work," Maya said. She'd tried it already with Tyler.

"Meaning . . . ?"

"Meaning, if I ignore people's thoughts, I can't control whether they like me."

"Hmm," Amy paused thoughtfully. "I'm not going to pretend that's not important. We as women are endowed with very little power, right, so what's the answer to women gaining power in a patriarchy?"

"Blow jobs?" Maya asked in all sincerity.

"God! No. To get any power, we try to be liked. Likability is our only path to success."

"Likability is our superpower?" Maya said.

"Yes, sadly. And in order to be liked, we have to care what people think. Other people's thoughts become unduly important to us. So," Amy said, feeling satisfied with her justification, "we all do what you do on a much smaller scale. You're not that weird. I don't think you're supernatural. You're just natural."

"You make me feel like a natural woman, Amy," Maya joked. Amy was right; she needed to stop thinking like a boy and start thinking like a girl. "Like you said, I think *all* girls can read minds. They have to in order to be liked. I can just do it better than other people. It's a matter of degree. Maybe it's evolution. Maybe all girls will be like me eventually. Maybe I can use it to my advantage."

"That's an interesting observation. But what makes you think you're unlikeable the way you are?"

"Well, I made some friends."

"Friends. That's awesome, Maya. Tell me more." And Maya told her about Lucy and Tyler while, despite herself, hope fluttered inside her, a thing with feathers. Then Amy said, "We can build on this Maya. What's next?"

Her mother had asked her that same question recently as they sat around the firepit for a newly instituted tradition, called "family time," that Stacy and Glen had read about in the parenting pamphlets. "What's the plan?" Stacy asked, encouraging Maya to build on her minor success. "What about joining a spring sport?" Stacy said obliviously, as if this were 1983 and you could just walk on to a team for fun in your short shorts and rainbow tube socks.

"Glen. You take that one," Maya had said, and then she sat back in her lawn chair, letting the charbroiled aroma of the campfire seep into her hair as she scrolled through social media trying to find any trace evidence of Tyler's activity in cyberspace. She was dusting for cyberprints. Trying to track him down, because her plan was to be liked. By Tyler.

She found him on Snapchat. Maya was a part of Tyler's streaks. He had sent out a sideways photo of his left eyebrow being pushed upward by the orange-striped paw of his tabby cat, so she sent back a pic of her chin and the right side of her collarbone.

In the periphery, she saw Glen acting out the extremes of what youth sports had become. He pantomimed muscular girls strapped to their ergs, half woman half machine, pulling madly at all hours of the day until they threw up in the tiny garbage cans set next to the machine for this purpose. On his fingers, he counted off the years of experience student athletes had devoted to their sports, lamented their lost childhoods, and drew his finger across his neck when he described how Maya would fare if she lackadaisically stepped onto the pitch with these finely honed sportobots. While team sports could be great for a person theoretically, at this point, for the dilettante like Maya, it was actually a dangerous proposition.

"Don't worry, I do have a plan," Maya said to Amy, now.

....

At home, she did a little more cyberstalking to figure out what likeable people wear to school, and the next day she put on a giant Champion sweatshirt that would completely cover denim shorts that were so short and threadbare, the pockets hung out from the bottom. The shorts had to be panty-like. They were so short, she might as well have gone full Winnie-the-Pooh and worn nothing at all underneath.

"Where are your pants?" Stacy asked when she came down for breakfast.

"I'm giving you what you want. You want me to be like other girls," Maya said.

"I never said that."

"You didn't have to." *Careful what you wish for, Stacy,* Maya thought.

"Other girls go to school pants-less? Is there no dress code?"

"Dress codes are body-shaming, Stace. Catch up. This drip is fire," she said, because she'd overheard Lucy describe her fit in that way, even though she knew Lucy would never think Maya's current drip was fire. This drip was super basic, which was what boys liked. Boys liked easy and basic. Right?

Maya strutted into school in her short shorts and decided to get a seat at the table with the perfect girls at lunch. She was trying to be "in the room where it happens," or whatever. As she approached them, one of them thought, *Incoming . . .* and looked to the queen bee, Olivia, for a clue about what to do. Olivia looked to Just Maddie, who kind of knew Maya, right, and Just Maddie gave a combination shrug-nod of resignation, as if to say "might as well give her a shot," and so Olivia moved her backpack off the table, where Maya sat down and said hello.

She tried to read their minds for something to say to break the awkwardness, as she unwrapped the sandwich Glen had made for her, but it was currently all, like, nail polish, matcha lattes, coconut bowls, and charcuterie boards in there, and she didn't know how to make conversation.

She had hoped Tyler would see her schmoozing with the elite, but he never came into the cafeteria. Lucy did, though, and while she joyfully and enthusiastically waved at Maya from across the room, Maya read the minds of the girls at the table, who looked at Lucy and thought one thing together, *Ew*, so Maya turned away and pretended not to see her.

She could feel Lucy, though.

She could feel Lucy's heart turn into a sleeping bat. Meaning that, before seeing Maya across the room eating lunch with the in-crowd, Lucy's heart had been flying and flapping and trying to stay afloat in the air, skittering through the sunset, celebrating being alive (even though her heart was a bat, and bats are kind of creepy).

. . . And now, after seeing Maya ignore her, it slowly closed its wings around itself, turned itself upside down and let gravity just pull its creepy dead weight toward her stomach. Lucy's bat-heart hung there, heavy, black, dangling, and asleep until she remembered to breathe.

Not again, she thought. Lucy thought about giving up, walking away, and crying a little over losing yet another friend to the bitchosphere, but instead, she took a breath and marched over to the hot girl table. Lucy was nothing if not courageous. Maya pulled out a binder and set it upright to try to hide behind it. Olivia thought, *She seems to have lost her way; her people eat in the center of the room*, while both the Ellas and all three Sophias thought, *For fuck's sake.*

"Ladies," Lucy said. "How's the matcha today? I hope it's organic. Did you know that tea is one of the most toxic crops? Drenched in pesticides, apparently."

"Really," one of them said, then thought, *These smart people do know science*, as she lifted her to-go cup and swirled it around. While the rest of them were distracted by sniffing their eight-dollar matchas and googling whether they were organic, Lucy turned to Maya, who continued to duck behind her binder, and said, "Cringe. What are you doing?"

"It's part of the plan. Part one," Maya mumbled. "Get people to like me."

"OMG, Cringe. You don't pander to the oligarchy; you go out there and get the populist popular vote. You appeal to regular people. You have to Bernie Sanders it. Go for the two-dollar donations, from the nerds and the theater kids and the robotics team. They add up."

Maya turned red.

"Cringe. It's okay. I gotchyou. I'll cause a distraction and you can walk away, ready? . . . OMG!" Lucy said. "It's time to BeReal!" All six girls pulled out their phones and Maya and Lucy slipped away to the bathroom where Maya could finally shimmy out of her shredded cutoffs and put on a pair of roomy mom jeans that Lucy had embroidered with wildflowers.

"This your work?" Maya asked.

Lucy nodded.

"I like it."

"I'm very talented," Lucy said, but what she thought was *What am I getting myself into with this one?*

Unbeknownst to anyone at school, Tori had written a secret song-book, an album, called *The Bobcat Blues,* in which she recorded, empathetically, she thought, the secret struggles of the students at New Town High. It wasn't anything she could drop until maybe some time long after graduation because people would see them-selves in it, and she didn't know if they'd become, like, all de-fensive about it. People could be thin-skinned. Especially if they didn't meditate, or sign up for therapy, or work the crystals and tarot. Self-actualization was hard work! And she didn't know if people could laugh at themselves. So, she had an entire sweet, knowing, empathetic album that she kept under wraps.

When Lucy came by the other night to rescue her from, well, the hellhole that was her home life, she felt moved to share some of it, mostly because Lucy asked, "What are you working on?"

She had wanted to distract Tori from, well, the hellhole that was her home life. She wanted to distract her from thinking about the empty prospects of a person raised in such a hellhole. How can you launch, right, if you have no footing—if beneath you is only a fiery pit of shame? You can't generate any *thrust.*

Lucy knew what to ask, because Lucy, as much as Tori hated to admit it, was chill, which was the highest compliment a person could pay a teenager. So up in Lucy's bedroom slash studio, after they styled themselves in some of Lucy's lewks and took some photos for her lewkbewk, Tori felt emboldened enough to crack open her laptop and pull up GarageBand.

"You should really learn to play an instrument," Lucy said. "It will lend you more gravitas. They always love it on *The Voice* when someone whips out a guitar."

"Can you not? I'm being vulnerable here."

"Oh. Right. I'm honored. Hit play."

The tunes that issued from the tight grip of the laptop speakers were sonorous, deep, and blue. Even better than Tori remembered them. The lyrics of "Just Maddie" were really about writing your dramatic college essay.

Just Maddie though she had no name
Found her trademark
When she met True Pain
Silver lining in the race for college
You can use your hurt in the quest for knowledge . . .

True enough. The lyrics were true. Tori was a true artist. Contrary to what people thought about her, she saw people and tapped into their shared humanity, which is what artists do. The *sound* was even more impressive, though.

"Oh my god," Lucy said after a song about Tyler called "Yoga Pants Play-a." And one about her mom called "Fucking Laurie Is a Karen" and one about Lucy called "Stonks." "It's like Bonnie Raitt and Adele and Tracy Chapman had a throuple baby! Your voice!"

"I've been working on it," Tori said.

"It shows."

"I'm working on one about that new girl."

"Maya?"

"Yeah. I'm worried about her. You can see it in her eyes. She knows too much. No innocence left in that one, if she ever had any at all. You should help her. She's headed for disaster. Needs to work some crystals."

"Meh. I have friends. You and I are friends. I like her, but I'm treading lightly. What do I want with disaster? You're not selling it," Lucy said as she scrolled through Tori's laptop, giggling at the different subjects of Tori's album. "Is this about Cauliflower Ears?"

"Eddie? He's sweet, actually," Tori said, filing her nail and blowing off the dust. "And you and I are not friends; we're fair-weather friends."

"No. We're friends in situations like this," Lucy said, swirling her finger around in a circle. "We're *bad*-weather friends, which means we'll be solid when the climate apocalypse hits for real."

"In the meantime, Maya needs you. Be there for her," she said, pulling up the sad song she wrote about Maya.

"This is very generous of you. Sharing my friendship. It doesn't fit the Sharpay archetype."

Tori pretended to fall asleep and then nodded awake in a faux nap-jerk. "I'm sorry. For a minute there you just bored me to death," she quoted from *High School Musical*.

"There she is," said Lucy with a smirk, as if all had become right with the universe.

Encyclopedia of World Problems

Maurice was on edge when Maya took him for a walk along the brook after dinner. He tried to enjoy his normal grunting and snuffling like a truffle pig along the forest floor, but he kept lifting his head and right paw as if trying to point to some invisible danger. He was about to bark, when a chunk of meat fell at his feet, seemingly out of nowhere.

"Hi, Scott," Maya said, looking up.

She saw the undersides of Scott's callused feet swinging above her head. Sometimes Scott ate in a tree to avoid attracting bears to his camp and to get a glimpse of the sunset, which currently brushed wildly to the west in strokes of golden pink.

"How's it going with the making of connections?" he asked, picking his teeth with a stick he'd whittled for this purpose.

"Funny you should ask," Maya said, remembering her disastrous stint at the hot girl table. "I think I fucked up." Lucy had come to her rescue, but Maya could sense that Lucy was losing faith in her as a potential friend. She was just so awkward. Cringey.

In her head, Maya pictured a certain scenario: Lucy, fed up, holding up her hand, walking away and ignoring her forever. Secretly gossiping about her to everyone. Turning people against her. Ostracizing her forever. That was what girls did to other girls at the first sign of awkwardness. There was no tolerance for it. She was afraid, without Lucy, she'd be thrust back into the basement, managing her hermetic life alone again.

"Thoughts are not the truth, you know."

"What?"

"I mean thoughts are sometimes just pitiful imaginary stories we tell ourselves and they are not the truth. So, like, you can tell yourself that you're awkward and can't connect with people. You can anticipate that people might be mean and cruel, but that's all just a poisonous story you're telling yourself. It's not the truth. Tell a different story."

"Like what?"

"Like, I am a good person trying to be good, and I deserve to be forgiven at least by my own damn self. Just rewrite the story. Thoughts are all just stories. You can't count on thoughts. You can only count on actions. Sometimes you just need to act," he said, swinging himself down from the tree and landing quietly in an alert crouch, prepared for whatever might come next. "Speaking of actions, how's it going with the bobcats?"

"What do you mean?" Maya asked, remembering vaguely the square of newspaper he'd handed her a week ago.

"Are you saving them?"

"Me?"

Scott took her in for a second, sizing her up, and said, "Did you know there's an *Encyclopedia of World Problems*? It has fifty-six thousand entries."

"That seems like a low estimate," Maya mumbled.

"You know what yours is?" he asked as he walked to the edge of the brook to rinse off his knife.

"My problem? What?"

"Complacency," he said as he picked up Maurice and let him lick him on the face.

"Wow. Seriously?" Maya said, taking in Scott's grease-stained sweatshirt and women's flowered leggings from the Goodwill. "You know what yours is, then?"

"What?"

"Hypocrisy."

"Ouch. Fair, I guess," he said, kind of self-consciously brushing some crumbs off his sweatshirt. "I'm just trying to help you, like, live your best life."

"I appreciate you," Maya said, as Maurice pulled her toward the brook.

SCOTT

Scott was in love once. Well, more than once if you counted the stuff before the age of twenty-five, but he didn't. Sex was not love. No man is really ready to love until after twenty-five, something about the frontal lobe and its inherent immaturity in the masculine half of the species. And it's rare that a man in America is ready to love at all. Because, in his experience, and he'd bunked with a lot of men in the army, American men are taught that love means being revered. When American men look at women, they want to see themselves reflected back. They honestly have no idea that women exist in their own right as separate people from themselves.

Scott learned to love overseas, away from America and all its buffoonery. He learned by getting spurned, over and over again, until his fat head discovered what women wanted. What women wanted was to be seen, and how could you see them if you'd never cultivated a curiosity about them aside from the different ways in which they could service you?

Scott learned, and he loved, and it was beautiful . . . and then she died. And it seemed impossible that the world could keep turning on its axis without her wild spirit nudging it forward. When she stopped, so did he.

So he knew what Sheila from the café on Main Street must have been feeling when her husband, Antonio, died, even though he couldn't imagine Antonio ever learning to love her in the way she was meant to be loved. But, hey, you never know what happens between two people behind closed doors. Maybe Antonio loved her proper, and maybe she just imagined he did, but either way, she must have been feeling that halting grief that stoppers your life force in your diaphragm and makes you feel like a corked bottle. It took a while to get uncorked and even so, it was never the same again, and so, even though it was against his entire hermit schtick to be seen in public cavorting with neighbors (god forbid), he decided to start mowing her lawn.

Then without asking, he cleaned her gutters, and patched her driveway, and even though she had some children somewhere who probably should have been taking care of things, they must have been busy, so he repointed the brick front and installed a new railing on the stairs and changed all the air filters and made sure her furnace was filled with oil for the winter.

And he didn't expect this to happen—his intention was just to be kind—but he started to cultivate a curiosity about Sheila. And Sheila turned out to be one of life's great surprises. But he wasn't here to kiss and tell, that was for sure. He was here to attest to the fact that people could surprise you and the universe was slippery. You never knew what you were going to get, but all things told, you were bound to see beauty in it if you opened your mind to wonder.

Nerd Face Emoji

The bobcat population in the neighboring woods around their town had been robust at the turn of the twentieth century, and then the bobcats, after first being pillaged for their pelts, began losing large swaths of their roaming habitats. Subdivisions and McMansions tore through the tristate area forests so quickly in the sixties and seventies and eighties, and bobcats had lost so much of their roaming territory; they had become almost extinct in New Jersey and Pennsylvania by 1984.

In the nineties, conservationists brought down some randy bobcats from Maine to repopulate, and it was working. Bobcats were returning and thriving because they were also getting all Darwinian on people's asses and, like, evolving. They had figured out that, if they were going to coexist with humans (and there wasn't enough empty space for them not to anymore), they couldn't also be reclusive and skittish. The shy, reticent individuals began to die out and the ones who survived were the extroverts who weren't afraid to go full-on raccoon with human garbage cans.

The irony of this was not lost on Maya. She, too, if she was going to survive, would have to stop hiding and being reclusive. If she was to survive, she would have to act. She'd have to very reluctantly force herself to go full-on racoon and start mixing with other humans and their garbage.

She'd start a club. Save the Bobcats! That would be her front. And it completely jibed with Lucy's foolproof three-part plan for achieving normal teenager status.

She'd trick the Common App into believing she was a Wildlife Conservationist™, all the while, as a side hustle, she'd be acting to save the human Bobcats at New Town High, because Bobcat was the school mascot, so they were all really Bobcats at heart. She'd cure them of their insecurities, which would make them kinder, and thus therefore save the actual world? Maybe from the ravages of an increasingly probable flood? But that was only a theory based on a loose correlation that hadn't been tested with any kind of real science. Still, it couldn't hurt to help.

After completing a rough draft of her Save the Bobcats! club recruitment flyer (it did feel good to Act!), she got texts from Bobby (who'd just been released) and Tyler at the same time. They both said, unsurprisingly, sup.

'Sup was the monosyllabic communication used by the male of the teen species to indicate emotional distress. Or romantic interest. Or boredom. Or feelings of inadequacy. It could mean anything beneath the surface (if anyone ever dug beneath the surface of the boy teen psyche, which no one really took the time to do because: Delusional Pride. Overestimation of Son's Abilities. Slight Disappointment. Forgiveness of All Transgressions. Boys Will Be Boys. Repeat).

'Sup was sort of like a crude mating call.

One had to think very carefully about how to respond to 'sup. She replied to Bobby first.

It had been about fifteen minutes since he'd texted. She thought this was enough time to wait so as not to seem desperate, but not so long that Bobby, with his tiny attention span and his penchant for immediate gratification, would have forgotten about her and moved on to some other shiny thing.

Not much she texted. And just to save time and not overthink it, she texted the same to Tyler.

OK, well, have a good night. (sleepy face emoji) Bobby texted back.

That was literally all he could think to say. This exchange of *nothingness* precisely exemplified why some sociologists were worried about the future of the human race. Maya had seen it in a TED Talk during her basement days. Teens were not communicating properly, said the TED Talk. They didn't date anymore, or hang out face-to-face at the mall, or make out in the backseat of cars, or hold hands at the movie theater, or dance at the sock hop, or have nearly as much sex. Even the prom was just an Instagram opportunity. They hung around taking pictures of one another and had nary a conversation. Danced hardly a dance. They just did not have the skills to connect with one another like previous generations did. Teen social exchanges were mostly virtual, often just strange pics of their eyebrows and nostrils sent to keep their "streaks" alive on Snapchat. Their communications could be so noncommittal and void of meaning, said the TED Talk, that scientists feared humans would stop procreating all together.

Bobby Maya tried. Do you need something? How's it going to be for you, blending back into the broscape? (winky face, flexed biceps emoji)

And he texted back:

BOBBY

(broken heart, confused face, black heart, flushed-face embarrassed emoji, giant teardrop)

> *On scale where 1 is despair and 10 is hope*
> *where are you right now?*

He sent an animated GIF of Atari Pong bouncing back and forth.

But when Maya tried to text back How can I help? she had somehow jumped to Tyler's thread and texted it to him instead. So then, panicked, she texted, Sorry! (grimacing face emoji) That was for someone else

Popular Tyler texted.

Jealous? Maya asked and then added (green face emoji).

You wish Tyler added.

Maybe I do she finished because, me-ow, a bobcat has to evolve and someone has to save the human race from all the noncommunication.

She rushed back to Bobby's thread and typed again How can I help, Bobby? She was worried about him. He was her first Bobcat and she had to follow through in saving him.

He texted: (person shrugging emoji)

Maybe you should get back in the saddle, girl-wise.
(cowboy emoji) What about Delia?

Boyfriend he texted back. And then after a pause he wrote
What about you?

CRAP. She could not let this wait. And she could not bubble tease him by starting to type and then changing her mind. She had to decide what to text and commit. Bobby was not in a state to be left high and dry without an answer. But she also couldn't twist the knife deeper into his heart by rejecting him outright. He was so fragile.

Tempting, but I, personally, am not ready for love so soon after our "release" she wrote, trying to rescue the mood with a running man and police officer to indicate escaping from the law, and then face-with-tears-of-joy emoji, because where were they if they could not laugh at themselves.

I get it he typed. (Yellow thumbs up) But she could sense from his tone that he might be spiraling into thoughts she'd thought she'd taken care of at Whispering Pines. They might be flaring again because of the world and its expectation for him to be tough, crude, careless, unemotional, detached, and always getting some. When in reality, boys are born the most delicate of all the delicate flowers in the rainforest, Maya thought. The toughness is all an act. Boys are born with certain sensitivities that are beaten out of them during the harsh threshing the patriarchy calls socialization.

I could face it with Eliza he texted, obviously still pining after his first girlfriend.

Bobby . . .

No answer. Shit, she thought. She thought she had taken care of this at Whispering Pines. What she thought was a permanent fix to his mind must only have been temporary. She really had no control of her powers.

Hello?

Yeah?

Come to my club, next week. And listen
to Into the Mystic by Van Morrison.

What's your club?

Save the Bobcats!

To which he replied:

(question mark, nerd face emoji, tree, unicorn, cat, peace symbol, three more nerd face emojis)

BOBBY

Bobby was no stranger to mania. When he received the counter-feit "box of fun" from the Sunshine Club on his last night in the hospital, he knew it had been entirely forged in one manic sitting by the frantic hand of a single person pulling an all-nighter. How did he know (aside from the handwriting having a similar slant and pressure against the paper, despite all attempts to make it look otherwise)? Because for a person to be the recipient of such genuine goodwill from the general populace, a person must ac-tually be good.

It's not that he wasn't good, per se. But he never really went out of his way. He did nothing to deserve a general outpouring of magnanimity.

And so, he knew it was one girl alone who made the box of fun. And when he pictured her surrounded by art supplies with glitter glue stuck to her fingers, sitting on some fuzzy rug in some girly bedroom, draped with tapestries, plastic ivy, and pots of succulents hanging in macramé nets, he wanted to cry. He wanted to feel the density of his pain, heavy as the collapsed core of a giant star, and he wanted to feel his tears inadequately trying to drain the sadness in hot magma streams down his face. He wanted to be angry that everyone knew where he was in spite of his trying to keep it a secret. He wanted to feel anything at all, but the meds took all that away from him. According to the world, it was wrong to feel things so deeply. According to western medicine, something about him was broken.

"Shouldn't everyone be crying?" he had asked his therapist once. "Isn't everything just so sad? And can't that also be beautiful?" he asked, rubbing his already chafed septum with the hard institutional tissues he carried around in his pocket like a shuffling, housebound grandma.

"Maybe you have the soul of an artist," his therapist responded. "Maybe you put all that to use, because when it comes to our emotions, we only have one choice in this life, pal. We can use them as a creative force or a destructive one. Create or destroy, my friend. It's up to you."

This seemed hopeful at the time. Either binary held some promise of joy. It was fun to build a tower of blocks and it was also thrilling to smash your sister's to the floor in a clattering cacophony and watch the look on her face. But now even that simple choice had been denied him. He'd been stripped entirely of the force of his emotions and left with cold hard chemically induced reason. Men were reasonable. He would be a man. He would go to law school or get an MBA and make cold hard dollars with his reasonable, calculated decisions, and maybe someday everything would come into balance.

In the meantime, he'd make lists of pros and cons. Weigh his options. Build his résumé, join legal coalitions, meet the right kind of people, fight for rights, and, ludicrously enough, maybe save the bobcats?

Shinrin-Yoku

Something Maya had never told anyone at school was that she did have a purpose once, before puberty hit, before the true repercussions of her powers started to weigh too heavily upon her psyche. At a very young age, her parents recognized she was happiest away from people. As much as they tried to get her to enjoy team sports, choir practice, and birthday parties, she'd always eventually gravitate to a private corner where she could be alone, and they would know it was time to extract her from the social situation. She'd never complain, which made it more heartbreaking for Glen and Stacy. She was never a brat about it; she'd just hit her limit and sort of migrate away from the group and sit by herself, holding her goody bag on her lap, party hat askew, chocolate icing etched in a line around her lips, waiting to go home, while the other kids chased one another around the room, running off their sugar highs. At two, she had a favorite chair in preschool she'd sit in, waiting for Stacy to pick her up. The kids would be toddling around in the back yard and Maya would be sitting in her tiny patio chair with her lunch box next to her, serenely waiting. In the car, Stacy would ask her how her day was, and because, even at two, Maya knew Stacy needed preschool to work out so that she could get a little work done, Maya would say, "School was fun, Mommy." But then Stacy would look in the rearview and she'd catch the chubby little preschool Maya strapped snuggly in her car seat with one giant tear sliding slowly down her face.

They didn't know why, of course, but they knew from a very young age that other people exhausted her. They thought she was just a Pisces. So, Glen would take her walking in the woods. He found she had a knack for identifying plants and an even keener instinct for tracking down animals. Nothing frightened her at that age. She'd track down salamanders, over-turn rocks to find colonies of potato bugs, and pick up garter snakes, letting them slither through her open fists. "Isn't she beautiful, Daddy?" she'd say, holding the snake's face right up to her own and watching its tiny ribbon tongue flutter straight toward her nose. And Glen would have to choke down his revulsion, dad up, and agree with her, stroking the thin striped back of the snake as a shiver shot through his spine.

Eventually, he bought her a real camera. And their adven-tures got even more treacherous. They'd climb up the tumbled-down black boulders of the Poconos or maneuver the sheer cliffs of the Delaware Water Gap, so that Maya could pho-tograph an eagle's nest or a fox's den. They'd march deep into the dark woods after sunset, silently tracking regurgitated owl pellets (the tiny bones of their prey balled up in a package of fur) so that Maya could get a moonlit shot of a snowy owl perched on a high branch. It made Maya feel safe knowing that something so beautiful was watching over everything at night and that she could relax, leaving it up to nature.

They subscribed to *National Geographic*, and Maya started entering photography contests. And, at the age of eleven, the age that most girls peaked before the weight of the patriarchy started getting them down, she started winning them. Her photos were published on the Web and in print. They wrote a little article about her in the local paper. She won one contest where the prize was to have her photo hung in the home of Vice President Biden, which seemed like a big deal, but Maya later found out that the photo was simply uploaded with a bunch of other kids' photos onto a digital frame that sat in the entryway of the Bidens' second beach house, which they most often rented to tourists on Airbnb.

Her mom was obsessed with this old children's book called *Misty of Chincoteague*, which told the story of a pretend wild horse on a real island of wild horses. She took Maya to Chincoteague so she could sit with her camera, nestled in the dunes at sunset, and wait for the herd to run past her as if they were wildly pulling the chariot of the sun across the pinkening sky. It was Maya's best day. The wild horses photograph, blown up to five feet by five feet, still hung above their couch in the living room.

It wasn't much, her photography, but Maya knew that things survived if you paid attention to them . . . that the greatest gift you could give to a thing was your attention. And so, she kept doing it for a while, paying attention. Until the hormones hit and mixed with other people's thoughts. The darkness began seeping into her brain like oozing slicks of black oil, and all she could see when she went into nature were the ways humans had given up on the world.

She came home with shots of plastic tampon applicators and syringes and rubber gloves floating in soft edges of the loamy, foamy tide, and entire schools of giant red jellyfish who'd beached themselves in a horrifying heap of slick, anemic pink lungs lying breathless on the sand. It stopped bringing her joy. Or maybe she had just grown up and needed to "put away childish things," like it said in the Bible.

Today at lunch, though, she was going into the woods and she was taking Bobby with her. It was his first day back and she was going to give him the gift of her attention, since he was the first test case in her Save the Bobcats initiative.

They were going to do a little *shinrin-yoku*, which meant "forest bathing" in Japanese. The Japanese had discovered that simply existing in the company of trees and absorbing their essence was enough to raise serotonin levels, especially if you bathed in the forest at least three times a week.

Shinrin-yoku was a way to give Bobby what he wanted, even though he didn't know he wanted it. Bobby could never have articulated his desire for *shinrin-yoku*. Here's what he did articulate: *Fuck.*

And Maya had to understand what that meant. It meant that Bobby wanted to feel tethered to the earth, part of something bigger than himself. He wanted to feel like he belonged, and forest bathing was good for that. It would remind him that his dark thoughts were simply that: fleeting temporary little devils that had no basis in truth. He was not a failure. He was not a loser. He was simply a guy doing the best he could in a world that could be beautiful if you paid attention to the right things. So, they were going to the woods to track down a bobcat and photograph it for the club.

They had to walk beyond the football field and climb the fence to get to the woodsy hills behind the school.

"Why are we doing this?" Bobby asked.

"I told you. I need some incentive for the club. We're going to find a bobcat. We have to be silent, though. They scare very easily."

They didn't get far before Maya noticed a tuft of rabbit hair floating in a tiny patch of melting snow still hanging on after the thaw.

"This way," she said. As she zigzagged up the steep incline, she grabbed some tightly closed, freshly budded milkweed pods to boil into a syrup to use as a contraceptive one day, as if she'd ever need that. She gingerly plucked a recently blossomed jack-in-the-pulpit to boil and grind up for headaches and acne. She didn't know how she knew these things. The medicinal uses of plants. It was just inside her brain, some sort of ancestral memory planted there in her DNA.

Bobby looked at her curiously, but he didn't speak or judge. The damp, wet cold of the forest was beginning to seep through his skin and oxidize him. The forest pumped you with oxygen like they seem to do at casinos to keep you awake and happy and gambling. She could sense Bobby relaxing and waking up at the same time. He was rejuvenating, pinkening up a little, absorbing some vitamin D from the sunlight that pierced haphazardly through the gaps in the branchy canopy above.

They climbed up and around a boulder, while Maya, unbeknownst to Bobby, was tracking more rabbit fur that she had assumed the bobcat had shaken from its kill as it carried it up the hill to its den. On the way, she grabbed a branch of a black willow tree and swung herself around to the other side of its massive trunk. She whipped out a pocket knife and peeled off some of its bark. She gave a couple of strips to Bobby and whispered, "Boil this later into a tea. Nature's aspirin."

She made the mistake of touching her finger to the center of his palm for a second as she handed it to him, though, which sparked Bobby's hair-trigger seventeen-year-old libido. The tiny graze of skin on skin was enough to start his fantasies of pinning Maya against a tree and having upright sex with her with his pants around his ankles. He imagined her enjoying it very much. At least he was thinking happy, for him, thoughts. The forest was doing its work.

She kept hiking upward alongside a tiny trickling stream that she knew the bobcat had recently drunk from; she could smell his musky odor, and she pointed out some bobcat scat to Bobby, which temporarily shut down his dreaming of sex.

Maya held her finger up to her lips and motioned for him to hide behind a tree and they waited there while Maya let out a strange, muffled yowl. Bobby looked at her, wide-eyed, like she was a crazy person. *What kind of Sasquatch, wildling shit is this?* he asked himself, starting to spiral down into negative thoughts about himself.

He could be at lunch with Tom and Dave at the football table yucking it up with some cheerleaders, trying to make Eliza jealous, and instead he was out here traipsing in the woods with some wildling, off-the-grid, mountain-woman Sasquatch he'd met at the mental hospital. He really was losing it, he thought. How low was he going to have to go? Would he ever be able to recover any of his popular-crowd street-cred? How many beers was he going to have to shotgun at the next party to prove he was back in the game? Already he'd mentioned the idea of joining this club to one of his team-mates, and he'd found out that some of his football friends were hunting and gun enthusiasts. They had taken his gym clothes out of his locker and tie-dyed them in protest of his potential new hippie pursuits.

You would think they could abstain from hazing a person right after his release from a mental hospital, Maya thought, reading his mind, but—only evil continually.

I shouldn't be here, Bobby thought. He got a little shifty and was about to head back out of the woods alone when Maya signaled for him to be quiet. She pointed to a barely visible hole in the rocks shrouded by a tangle of tree roots and wet brown leaves.

Then she pointed again above the enclosure, and Bobby saw it. The motionless cat was the size of a large dog, and it had been there the entire time. The brown decaying leaves that carpeted the upward slope behind the cat camouflaged his dappled golden-brown coat, but his amber eyes glowered at them. It was strange and unnatural, almost supernatural or, like, alien. *What's the link between cats and Egypt and aliens, again?* Bobby wondered for a second, which was a breakthrough because he had a moment of curiosity that did not involve Eliza or trying to impress his social milieu of bros.

The cat let out strange purring warning snarl, making sure to flash his left fang, and Bobby was terrified and thrilled and exhilarated. It was almost as good as catching a touchdown pass.

Maya slowly pulled out her phone and zoomed in to get a shot of the beast, then whispered that they should back away down the hill keeping their eyes on him the entire time. She did that thing where she used two fingers to point at her own eyes and then the bobcat's eyes.

They took two steps backward down the hill and joined hands when the cat did jump toward them in an impossible athletic leap, his giant-for-his-body paws softening his silent landing. Maya tightened her grip on Bobby's hand, and they kept taking slow giant steps down the hill, trying not to lose their footing and tumble backward. The cat could not really eat them, per se, like a lion or something, but he could definitely do some damage. The two of them holding hands made them seem like a larger, two-headed, more intimidating creature, so they stayed together backing up slowly, keeping him in their sight. The cat's shoulders hunched, his ugly black-tipped bobbed tail swung menacingly behind him, like a stubby field hockey stick, until finally as they got closer to the school, the cat slowed down a bit and looked away from them for a second.

"Run!" Maya said.

Maya knew when he recounted this story in the locker

room later, Bobby would say he was chivalrous and stayed between the cat and Maya the whole time they were being stalked, but the truth was, when she said run, he dropped everything and tore down the hill first, his heart thudding in his chest, and he didn't turn around to check on her until he was safely in the end zone of the football field.

She burst through the tree line a minute after him, vaulted over the fence, and caught up to him as he was catching his breath.

"My knight in shining armor," she said sarcastically.

"Oh my god! That was awesome," he said.

"Right?" Maya agreed.

"So cool. Did you get any shots?"

"A few, I think."

They walked around the track and then up the hill and right into the outdoor picnic table area of the cafeteria as they leaned in together and Maya showed him her pics of the wild cat. She even got one of him hissing at them. She explained to Bobby that they had less than five weeks.

"Less than five weeks for what?"

"To stop open season. They want to hunt them. There's a vote happening at the town hall."

"Why do they want to hunt them?" he asked, appreciating the sheen of the bobcat's coat in the photo Maya had taken.

"Just for sport, mostly. Taxidermy, I guess? But I also saw some recipes online for bobcat burritos."

"Seriously?" Bobby asked. "Isn't that how you get SARS or whatever? Eating cats."

"Maybe," Maya said and felt Bobby's contentment. The trees had done their work on him, and he was so content for a second. He was happy and Maya was happy. They made a little connection like the one Scott was talking about, and it felt good, and then Maya felt a drop.

"Let's go," she said. "It's starting to rain."

Max knew how Bobby felt. Their disabilities were different . . . his CP was more visible than Bobby's depression, but it was hard to be around normal people sometimes.

Sensitive folks would walk on eggshells around you, which was weird enough, but "bros" who felt uncomfortable around your disability became bombastically inclusive in a fake jock-y way. They too enthusiastically slapped you on the back and loudly repeated, like a slick corporate alpha dad in a fleece vest, "So how you been, dude?" without really wanting an answer. It was awkward.

But the bros were trying. When they heard Bobby was being released from the hospital, the twins created a group text of the elementary school "crew"—Aidan, Jacob, Eddie, Max, and Bobby—and invited Bobby over to the twins' basement for a night of video games (and project: Bobby Positivity). They were there to boost Bobby's self-esteem and get him back on the right track, mood-wise.

They chose Minecraft of all things because they knew it was nostalgic and calm enough for Max's slow twitching muscles, but it was awkward, because it made Max feel singled out in a way he didn't particularly want to feel. The upside was that he was really

good at Minecraft, netting $16,000 this year for building struc-
tures for other rich, kind of douchey enthusiasts, who couldn't
even be chill about their video games. They had to one-up everyone in every space they inhabited and so contracted him to build
them elaborate gothic castles or modern abodes reminiscent of
Frank Lloyd Wright's Fallingwater. *It's a living,* he thought. He'd
resigned himself to the lifelong pursuit of helping build up rich
people's egos, since he couldn't really invest a lot in his own.
Humility was sort of built into the package he was dealt life-wise.

Anyway, whatever meds the hospital had given Bobby seemed
to be working at first. He seemed relaxed and grateful to be included, flopping on the sectional and zooming right into the world
of the game, rather than talking, god forbid, about anything he'd
just been through. They traded obscenities and barbs and yo
momma jokes and killed ghosts and zombies, and in so doing
created a kind of bro bubble of intimacy, completely devoid of
actual intimate communication.

Everything was going fine, until Bobby's phone dinged and
it seemed to agitate him. He tossed the controller to Jacob and
moved to the corner, where he sat on a low ottoman in front
of Max's wheelchair and scrolled through his phone as if Max
couldn't see exactly what he was doing. For all intents and purposes, even in a room with his best friends, Max was less than
human and completely invisible. He was used to it, sort of.

Bobby sighed for a second and then stood up to grab his coat.
"I have to head out," he said.

"Why don't you stay?" Max begged him after reading the text
over his shoulder. But because of his slow, slurred speech, Bobby
was out the door before he could even finish his sentence.

Flash Flood

Only the woodland creatures saw it coming. It wasn't a *flash* flood for them. For them, the water rose slowly, saturating everything from the ground up, filling the rooms of their warrens and drowning the baby bunnies in their sleep.

The grieving older rabbits fled for higher ground, as did the snakes and the woodchucks and the porcupines, but they didn't wake Scott, who for some reason camped at sea level that night when authorities knew he knew better than that, especially these days, with all we know about the floodplain after the thaw.

It had been raining for five days. And the river, white at first, lashed and licked violently at the rocks, devils' tongues. But then it rose, jumping and flickering until it galvanized itself into a thick black lava, swallowing whole giant boulders in its wake. At dawn, the entire forest was a brown, churning lake filled with silt and floating debris . . . a swing set, a rogue kayak, a coyote floating by nervously on the roof of a shed.

Maya awoke to the sound of news choppers overhead. They had to get live footage for the old ladies who loved to catastrophize. That line from the Morrissey song came into her head. The one about not watching the news because of the news's secret plot to frighten us. She sang it out loud as a joke, the choppers practically drowning her out, as she came into the kitchen to get some coffee.

She thought her parents would laugh. The choppers always came when the river rose a little. Her parents always made fun of the newsertainment on local TV. But this time their faces were gray and grave. Their eyes rimmed in red, as if they'd been up all night.

She read it in their minds before they had to say it.

"NO!" Maya said. "No no no no no!" she cried.

"Maya," her mom finally said, looking up. "It's Scott."

They had found him still in his sleeping bag, battered and bruised from his violent trip down the rapids. The coroner promised that a blow to the head killed him instantly, and he didn't have to endure a death by drowning, which was apparently a worse way to go. This was supposed to be comforting.

But something was off about the whole scenario. Scott was a survivalist. He knew how to survive everything. Even a flash flood.

Maya's parents fretted. They thought this would be a setback for Maya, just when she was getting into a groove, so they tiptoed around her and let her mope, weep, and do whatever she wanted, even cut school that day, and what Maya wanted, needed really, was to talk to Sheila. Something compelled her to find Sheila, actually, so she pulled on her rain boots and left.

Sheila was at the café, and Maya could see her inside, but

it was already eleven o'clock, and she hadn't flipped the closed sign around. Big plastic pickle buckets formed an obstacle course around the shop, catching the drips that loudly and intermittently plopped from the leaking ceiling. "Sheil!" Maya yelled, knocking at the screen door, but Sheila didn't even lift her head. Maybe her son had gotten her some AirPods? Maybe she was listening to a podcast? But that didn't seem like Sheil.

"Sheila!" Maya finally yelled and then she forcefully shouldered the door open, cracking the doorjamb a little and Sheila didn't even look up. She was catatonic. "Can you look at me, Sheil?"

And that's when Maya saw it. Sheila's face, while normally shiny and taut, hung in elephantine bags around her eyes and cheekbones. Her normally lavender irises shone dead gray. "Oh Sheila," Maya said to her because she could see it all. Sheila and Scott. Their last chance at love, something neither of them ever expected but grew to cherish so deeply. A happy accident.

"We were having a situation-ship," Sheila tried to joke, a new tear falling into her lap.

They both laughed, for a quick second, but then Sheila's heart rate sped up and her face began to pinken. "I told him to sleep with me. He couldn't sleep in a bed anymore, but I begged him, after what happened."

"What do you mean, what happened?" Maya asked.

"Oh, it was nothing. He wouldn't want me to say," she said, new tears welling up. "He wanted to sleep on the cool mud. It was good for his back after what . . ."

"Sheil."

"Nothing."

"Come on."

"It was the drunken Proud Boy types, I guess. They do it every few years or so. They hunt him down. Wreck..." She stopped, trying to take a deep breath. "They wreck his shelter. Vandalize his stuff. Spray-paint terrible things. Like, what do those idiots say? Libtard? Deserter. When he was the one who served..."

"I know, Sheil," Maya said, rubbing her across the back.

"They roughed him up, and he had no camp, so he wanted to sleep on the cold mud."

"Why didn't he report it?"

"Oh, Maya. He was Scott. He just said, let them be. If they get their frustrations out on me, he said, then they won't hurt someone else. They won't do even more terrible things, he said, but how is this not the worst most terrible thing?"

"It is, Sheil. It is the worst most terrible thing." *Only Evil Continually*, Maya thought, and she squeezed Sheila until she stopped crying, then she and Stacy took her to her daughter's house in Jersey.

....

The record store was not a total loss. The three of them, the Storm family, decked out in wet suits, waders, and wellies with push brooms on their shoulders, like rubbery Teletubby chimney sweeps, sloshed through the two feet of water on Main Street and pushed against the water to open the door of The Flip Side.

The inflatable sparkle chair floated by them and did an ironic little twirl in the current. As did Maurice because they had outfitted him in his tiny orange life jacket, and he paddled around splashing at the surface of the water, which was about two feet high. It could have been worse. The albums, nested in their elevated bins, were still dry but beginning to warp with the humidity.

Glen strode to the back door and opened it, and because they were on a hill, the water started to funnel slowly out toward the back door. Their job was to use the brooms to push the water and silty sediment out the back. Stacy, who couldn't do anything without music, set up her Bluetooth speaker on a top shelf (she couldn't risk plugging in the record player), cued it to Bob Dylan's "Blowin' in the Wind," and started to cry.

She swept and wept and kept the rhythm of the music, and thereby purged herself of some of her sorrow. Maya felt waterlogged and heavy and too numb to cry anymore at the moment. Everything was so saturated that her tears had nowhere to go, atmospherically. She didn't even get to tell Scott that she had stopped being complacent and started to act. And she didn't understand why it wasn't working. She was acting. She was saving all the bobcats, or she intended to, and it was flooding anyway.

She'd Zoomed with Amy last night to talk a little about the losing him. "He was like me," she said. "He had something. Not just the tendency toward isolation. It was like, he could read *my* mind. He knew what I needed in a way that regular people don't. Sorry. I appreciate you. I know you're trying, but he . . . He was . . . I'm alone without him."

"You're not alone. People love you and you haven't even met all the people who were put on the planet to love you. So much love to discover."

"Fuck, is that a meme you saw on Instagram? The one with the balloon letters taped to a garage?" Maya sobbed for a second. No one could replace Scott. He knew she was whack but he was, too, almost like he was close to god. Some kind of angel. "I feel like I was supposed to learn more from him. He was helping me," Maya admitted.

"Well, what did he teach you while he was here? Maybe lean into that," Amy suggested, still blushing and trying to remember if the phrase she'd just quoted was from an Instagram meme.

"I don't know," Maya said, getting fed up with this therapy bs. "He told me to make connections."

"Like networking?"

"No. Amy, see. You don't get it. No. Networking. God. Networking is for finance bros. Real connections. With people."

"I think you should write about it," Amy said.

"That seems like a bad idea."

"No. It's not. Get a notebook, maybe a black notebook, and whenever you're feeling down, just unleash all the negativity into the notebook and then close the book on it, and move forward. Keep moving forward."

"Like a shark."

"Sure, Maya," Amy said, "like a shark." Which was apropos of a lot of things. Sharks seemed to be winning this here climate apocalypse. They chomped their way through the limbs of innocent bathers all along the eastern seaboard last summer, while the kindly whales and dolphins gave up and threw themselves upon the sand.

Umami

Maya looked up from her sweeping and saw in the basement window, at street level, a goofy set of legs jutting out of board shorts and stomping through the water in giant yellow Crocs. They disappeared for a moment and then reappeared right outside their door.

"Maya," someone said.

"Tyler?" Maya gasped.

"I brought a wet vac and plastic wrap, like to wrap the records or something? I don't know," he said sheepishly and then he went back up the stairs to drag down the cylindrical drum of the vacuum.

This made Maya choke for a second in gratitude. "Thank you!" she said. Stacy was too preoccupied to even notice Tyler. Glen seemed distracted, too, but then he stood up, looked around, and said, "Where's Maurice?"

They dropped their brooms and vacs and split up, clomping through town and the backwoods, shouting Maurice's name through the continuing drizzle. He shouldn't have been that difficult to find, given his bright orange life jacket, but they were distracted by all the colorful debris that still floated in puddles along the side streets. A stroller, a frisbee, plastic garden gnomes, a Hula-Hoop.

This couldn't be happening, Maya thought. She couldn't lose Scott and Maurice within twenty-four hours of each other. That would be too cruel, even for this world. "Maurice!" she screamed. They'd been at it for a half an hour already. Why would he do this? she wondered. The doors were open, but he never usually ran away. It wasn't his style. Was he jealous of Tyler? she wondered ludicrously after hearing Tyler's deep croaking voice call out and echo to the left of her. Could dogs even be jealous? "Maurice!" she screamed. She could not live without this dog.

Suddenly up in the woods to her left, she heard a trampling and tussling. She saw a flash of orange and then saw Tyler reach his long, lanky arm into a rushing stream where Maurice was floating backward, paddling frantically against the current. An innocent caught in the torrents of our bad behavior.

Tyler caught the dog by the strap of his jacket. "Got him!" he said, standing up and cradling Maurice like a loaf of bread while trying not to slip as he stepped down the embankment in his silly wet yellow Crocs.

"My hero," Maya felt compelled to say as she moved a piece of wet straggly hair from her eyes and he handed Maurice over to her. Tyler didn't have a ton of thoughts in that moment, but he was feeling pretty proud of himself.

Above him in the sky, the sun poked out from behind the clouds for the first time in two days. It surrounded him in an obnoxious glowing halo of shooting, sparkling sunrays. He looked like a saint on one of those candles you buy at the bodega.

Okay, I get it, Scott, Maya wanted to say, because it seemed as if Scott were sending a message from beyond.

"Well, I gotta go," Tyler said.

"You do?" May asked dejectedly. She hated to be on the nose like this, but she was seeing him in a new light. She had had her doubts about him, but he seemed perfect in that glowing moment. A Bobcat who needed no saving. He was already kind. She wanted to be with him. Like, be with him be with him.

Stacy and Glen stumbled over and took Maurice, too distracted by his return to notice the obvious, fated love connection happening right in front of them. "Thanks!" they said to Tyler as they ushered Maurice back to the store.

"Did you drive?" Maya asked. "Can I walk you back to your car?" And she scanned Tyler's brain and noticed he, too, was currently oblivious to the fact that she needed to kiss him right now. He was overwhelmed by all the commotion and needed a little break. Tyler took a breath and balled up all his thinking energy, then let it drift into a compartment made entirely of antimatter—a giant black hole in his cerebellum where he could go if he needed to shut down—and that's where Tyler went, experiencing an instant blissful calm.

Instead of overthinking, perseverating, panicking, and *feeling* things, like a girl might do, he, and other boys like him, Maya presumed, had a coping mechanism in their brains called The Nothing Box.

She witnessed it now.

Interesting, she thought. When you ask a boy what he's thinking, and he tells you, "Nothing," he's not lying or hiding his thoughts from you! He actually has the magical capacity to think *nothing at all* for hours on end. Which she imagined females could never do, evolutionarily, because they had to be on constant alert in order to protect the baby offspring from the predators, etc. Rude.

She followed him a block or two to where he'd parked on a dry street. He had a Hyundai and it reminded her of that "Debra" song by Beck that her mom was always raving about. It was from the album *Midnite Vultures*, which, in her mom's opinion, did not *mimic* the styles of Prince and Bowie, it commented on them and took them to a new level. It was post alt-soul—an intellectual exploration of what moves us and why.

"Lady, step inside my Hyundai," Tyler said. *He knows the song!* Maya thought. *It is another sign.* Then he opened the door for her because his mother had taught him that it was just good manners, and then he psychically kicked himself for thinking of his mother in this moment and took a microsecond break in the nothing box in order to regain his momentum.

He looked at her, and something about the funky musk smell of his Hyundai upholstery baking in the humid floodwaters of this side street, or the fact that everything was covered in soggy wet yellow pollen (which is really just sex from trees), just got both of them so immediately hot that they both tried meditating at the same time. *I breathe out,* they said to themselves, trying to exhale some of the steamy energy back into the universe.

Maya was close enough in the passenger seat to feel him emanating something she'd never experienced before. It was sort of a smell and a change in air pressure—an invisible aura wafting off him in silent waves. It was like the experience of "umami" that chefs tried to describe. (The five taste sensations included bitter, sweet, salty, sour, and the mysterious "umami." Maya watched a LOT of cooking shows when she was hibernating in the basement.) Tyler was emanating a mysterious umami force. It was something powerful and essential and earthy, yet indescribable, like umami.

"You're emanating," she said.

"What?"

"Never mind," she said. She touched the cleft of his chin with the pad of her forefinger and tilted his head toward hers. She was inside the umami force now. It sucked her in, and the only way out was to kiss her way out.

They kissed in the car until their faces were numb, and Maya broke off and said, "I should probably get back," even though she couldn't care less about the record store right now. She'd much rather continue kissing. There was something cosmic about the feeling she had in her body. She felt weighty and effervescent all at once, as if the matter and antimatter of the universe were coming together inside her. Was this love or sex? she wondered. And then she imagined Lucy saying, "Who cares, Cringey. Stop overthinking for once." So she kissed Tyler again and then broke free and said, "Thanks. I should go. Thanks so much for saving Maurice. I don't know what I would have done if we hadn't found him."

"Don't mention it," Tyler said but then he thought, *Is that what this is about? Is she just relieved about her dog?* So Maya kissed him again, with urgency and certainty to remove all his doubts and remind him that this was fated. They'd been on a crash course to whatever this was since the first time they'd met in the wellness center.

They poured themselves out of the car and struggled against the gravity of their attraction to each other to trudge up the street and back to the store. He kissed her again. Quickly, but publicly. Right on Main Street, which made it seem kind of official. Were they a thing? Maya didn't know why, but she had thought if she *did* hook up with Tyler, he would be inclined to keep it under wraps, because of his religion-of-no-attachment, his choosing freedom instead of love, but here they were kissing *out in the open*. And the only thing they were thinking about was each other.

....

She hated herself for being so cliché, but that kiss was the best thing that had ever happened to her and she practically floated into the dank, dark, sodden record store, a happy ghost of her former self. She drifted to the Bluetooth speakers and cued up both Anderson .Paak and Aretha Franklin. Her feelings were so powerful and large and confusing and celebratory, and beautiful and sad, that only that particular combination of artists could contain them.

Of course, this could be easily interpreted by Stacy. She heard the first note of the Aretha and rounded the corner with her push broom, and said, "Awwww. You kissed the boy!"

"Mom!"

"Sorry . . . or a man! Or. A person!!"

"A boy. But why?"

"Aww. Why what?" Stacy asked. She leaned the broom against the wall and scooped up some album covers that had fallen into the floodwaters and floated aimlessly around the store, then she hung them on a clothing line set up in front of a giant fan.

"Why does this make me so happy? Shouldn't I be more concerned about the flood? Going to college? Saving the world? Leveling up, like, career-wise? Smashing the patriarchy? I feel so guilty feeling happy right after Scott. I feel like . . . I just. Why do I care about kissing when there are so many more important things?"

"It's the propagation of the species, puppy. You study nature. In nature, kissing's the only thing that matters," her mom said. "There's like a primal primacy to it. It's unavoidable."

"Wow."

"The only thing I don't like is his name."

"Tyler?"

Stacy's lip turned up in disapproval.

"What?"

"I thought it would be like Bas or Bear or Dex. I don't know. Monosyllabic. Can I call him Ty?"

"Sure, Mom. You can call him Ty, but, wait! Maybe he should not be named?! Does naming him jinx it? OOOH, I need to take a deep breath," Maya said, bending over. "Slow my roll."

"Aw."

"Stop saying aw! This is not cute. I really like him. This was not supposed to happen."

"What's going on?" asked Glen, rounding the corner and cluelessly biting into an apple.

"Maya kissed a boy," Stacy said.

"Aw," said Glen and then Maya watched him go immediately into his nothing box. He wasn't going to contemplate that for another second.

"What do I do with this?" Stacy asked Glen, holding up the credit card machine that may or may not have been waterlogged. Maya could tell, addled as they already seemed, that they had moved on from the most momentous occasion of her life and refocused on their doddering, mundane, daily workaday pursuits.

Maya resumed sweeping. Most of the water had drained out the back, and the floor was covered in a soft brown silt. Over in the Folk section, a scattered mix of junk—papers and posters and old photos and CDs and magazines—had pasted themselves to the floor in a kind of rock-and-roll mosaic. There was even an old cassette tape with Stacy's name written on it with a Sharpie. Maya bent over and peeled a piece of magazine off the floor. "What's this?" she asked.

"Don't touch that!" Stacy said too quickly.

"Why?" Maya asked. She didn't have to ask, though, because she could sense her mother, suddenly aghast, remembering what was stored over there. It wasn't junk; it was memorabilia. Zines, flyers, song lyrics, album covers, news clippings, photos from what seemed to have been . . . a singing career? Her mother's singing career? Maya realized this as she peeled up a piece of handwritten notebook paper that looked like a set list. She could sense her mother remembering the exact scent of the stage curtains at John and Peter's place, the exact way the sawdust slid under her feet on the stage at The Playhouse. The transcendence she felt at the Waterloo Village Folk Festival where she opened for Little Feat. The day she almost passed out when she touched Jerry Garcia's shoulder backstage at The Fillmore.

"Whoops," Maya said, and she held the set list behind her back.

Her mom just sat, for a second, silently shaking her head. She visibly cringed remembering being reviewed in *Rolling Stone* and this tragic line that she could never rise above: *The eighties have thankfully killed the doormat song and have ushered in and coronated some pop rock queens: Joan Jett, Pat Benatar, Ann Wilson, even Cyndi Lauper and Stevie Nicks, whom Stacy Allen tries to approximate. Sadly, it seems all Allen can pull off is Nicks's bleating bah-bah without any of the brah-vah-do.*

Maya, who thought she knew everything about everything, was suddenly humbled. Her mother was a literal rock star and she didn't even know it. She was just like every other selfish kid, she thought. She assumed her mother existed For her and never BeFore her. Even she, with all her brouhaha, could not truly know her mother, apparently. She'd have to write about this in the notebook.

On the plus side, maybe she had another "bobcat" to save! She wasn't going to let her mother limp along running solely on the fumes of a tragic broken dream. She could fix this. She could resuscitate her mother's dream, since it was her birth that probably took the breath out of it. And plus, today she'd kissed a boy right in the middle of Main Street, which meant nothing was impossible.

The Paradox

Maya dreamed of the weather. Tornadoes. Hailstorms. Cloudbursts. Cyclones. Squalls. Bombogenesis. Monsoons. Tsunamis. April showers. Mist. And when she woke, she saw her dreams coming true right in front of her on the weather channel. "Can you turn that off?" she'd beg Glen. He derived some strange comfort in knowing what was out there, so that he could be prepared. But she felt all these pressure systems actually swirling in her body, pushing her to make a change, fast!

Kids at school felt it, too. Maya saw it in their thoughts. A lot of surface thinking was about Snapchat. Who opened what and whether to send one to whomever. There was also a certain emphasis on bodily functions. This one had to pee. That one was starving. This one had a headache. They were all secretly freezing. Some had shameful regrets about how they'd left things with their parents this morning. The reading of minds is never as sexy as one would think.

But beneath all that was a literal streaming flood of anxious thoughts about the end of the world. About living in the shadow of doom. The specter of it all. *Fossilfuelsplasticsgerrymander-ingco2electoralcollegepipelinesbulletproofbackpacksdeadchildren-starvingchildrenmigrantchildrenrapeyrepublicansregressiverepro-ductivehealthfooddesertsprisonindustrialcomplexpolicebrutality-transphobia2050pandemicbookbansputinwhitesupremacyfloods-foxnewsAR15s.*

But they tried to distract themselves with the day-to-day. Juicy secrets only popped up now and again. And where were the happy thoughts? Where was the joy? When they bonded, these teens, they seemed to bond over their mutual hatreds.

She had to kick it in gear if she was really going to save any Bobcats. The first thing she had to do was find a faculty advisor for Save the Bobcats!, the fake club, and the next was to start collecting data on Save the "Bobcats": the purpose.

Thing One was easy enough. She just had to survey the teachers' minds to find the ones who were the most broke and could most benefit from the $300 stipend that came with the job. A biology teacher would be ideal, of course, or the dude who teaches environmental history and manages the compost heap behind the baseball field, but he was surprisingly thrifty and financially savvy. Ultimately, she landed on Mr. Benson. A compulsive gambler who taught statistics and was always trying to use his math skills to hedge his bets. He had recently found himself in a losing streak that he was afraid to tell his wife about, so he signed the form Maya brought to his office hours without hesitation, and they were in business.

She went about Thing Two very methodically. She even used a Google spreadsheet. And created Charts! And Data. Everyone these days was talking about Data and Data Analysis and Telling a Data Story. So, she started by collecting data as she sat alone in the cafeteria and recorded thoughts and prayers on her spreadsheet.

Here were the Top categories of Bobcat requests:

Please let me get more sleep (there was a lot of energy around sleep hygiene).

Please don't let me/her be pregnant (this was infrequent, given that statistically, teenage canoodling was down, but it was the most powerful of the prayers).

Please don't let me be fat/ugly/unlovable in some other fill-in-the-blank physical way.

Please don't let me be awkward. I must uphold the illusion of cool (see also: nihilism).

Please don't let me be failing x class (and by failing they usually meant a C because of grade inflation, but some were actually getting real Fs because they had given up and stopped handing in any work, which brought her to the final prayers ...).

Please help, I'm in way over my head.

While she was organizing her data and planning approaches for saving Bobcats, she would tick off small requests here and there. The low-hanging fruit.

For example, Alexandra Collins, whom Maya happened

to sit next to in the library one day. Alexandra thought her life would completely change if she could just kiss a boy. She needed to get over that hurdle, so she could stop hating herself, because hating herself was perpetuating her non-kissable vibe.

She knew it was some whack law of the universe that if you *think* you're unkissable, you become, in fact, utterly unkissable. But if no one is kissing you, it's hard to think you deserve kissing . . . and therefore get kissed! It was a paradox! Not unlike the one where you can't get a job if you don't have any job experience.

Alexandra knew that her problem, at first, was aiming too high. Clueless freshman year, she targeted jocks, whom she didn't realize only ever kissed each other. (Duh.) But whom should she target?

Maya saw her run through some prospects in math league and robotics and band. She'd been waiting for some of them to glow up and discover shaving and deodorant, and some were getting there. A few even started lifting weights.

Ironically, the entire boy-photo slideshow Maya saw in Alexandra's mind did not once stop at Cooper, the boy from improv who liked *her*. This, Maya thought, was another paradox! Subconsciously ignoring the person who *would* kiss you, because you're actually secretly afraid of being kissed.

So. Maya opened her pre-calc book to the page Alexandra was studying and asked her a question about secants. When Alexandra looked up, Maya gazed into her eyes and, doing whatever it was she could do, replaced all the boys in her mind-carousel with Cooper, Cooper, Cooper. A boy who actually had "glowed up" and who could make her laugh, which was the only characteristic you should look for in a boy in Maya's opinion. (Not that she was an expert, having only just experienced her first kiss herself.) *Cooper is a snack!* she thought into Alexandra's brain.

Then she searched her mental files for a soundtrack to add to the Cooper slideshow.

Oy, Maya thought, she's a Swiftie, like everyone else these days. Maya added Swift's "Love Story" to the background of Alexandra's thoughts about Cooper, which would seal the deal and point her in the right direction.

Mission accomplished. Alexandra hadn't kissed Cooper yet, but it was only a matter of time. She closed her pre-calc book and headed to English. She took a moment to think-talk to Scott on her way down the hall. *This is what you meant, right? Am I doing it right? Saving the Bobcats?* But of course, she got no reply. And the rain continued to fall. It was nothing people recognized as a crisis. Basements got sodden, sump pumps got overworked, train tracks got washed away, backyards sunk underwater, and a few houses in the Poconos slid down the melting faces of the mountains. Everything smelled like damp clothes left too long in the washing machine.

Trophic Cascade

"The first meeting of Save the Bobcats will come to order," she said and pounded an actual gavel she'd found in the basement.

"You don't have to be so formal about it," Mr. Benson mumbled from the back of the room, where he sat filling out lottery tickets on his account on the lottery website. He was a season ticket holder.

Maya knew she probably didn't have to be formal about it, but this is how she'd practiced it over and over again in front of the mirror last night and she had to stick to her script or be waylaid by reading haters' harsh criticisms of her in their minds. She had to plow forward with her specific agenda, ignoring other people's thoughts. Amy had actually taught her this. To prepare her own remarks before every class. To rehearse them, so she wouldn't get thrown by the mental chatter around her.

"In front of you, you will find your agendas. And if you read the first paragraph, you will see what's at stake. In one month, the town council is voting on whether to reinstate open season on *lynx rufus,* the bobcat. It should pass easily because as of yet no one really knows about it, nor has anyone organized an opposition. Our job is to raise awareness. But in order to do that, we need to raise money. Put some ads on social and in the local newspaper. At least make people aware of what's at stake."

"What's at stake again? Aren't the bobcats doing pretty well?" Chloe asked. Maya had secretly invited her so that she could hook her up with Bobby, but it made sense, because she was also the head of the EcoReps and Maya was trying to cross-pollinate the clubs.

"The loss of a predator can result in what is called a 'trophic cascade.'" Maya was prepared for this question and projected a slide onto the whiteboard. "Which is an ecological phenomenon triggered by a predator's extinction. Once the predator goes, it causes an overpopulation of prey that affects the entire food chain," she said. "Plus, trophy killing is just a bad impulse to perpetuate, don't you think?" Here, for dramatic effect, Maya showed a slide of Eric Trump with a rifle, standing proudly next to the dead elephant he'd murdered.

The gasps were audible.

Then Maya switched to a slide with some footage she'd taken on her excursion with Bobby, of the bobcat giving himself a little bath. "This guy lives right behind the school."

"Whoa," said the club.

Then she clicked and the slide changed to a photo of Scott that she had forgotten she'd left in there. He was bent over holding a branch aside so Maya could get a shot of some bobkittens, asleep in their den.

"Aw," said the club, but for Maya, seeing Scott was a gut punch. She had to stop for a second and catch her breath. He'd asked for no big memorial, even though everyone in town kind of knew him or knew of him. They knew of his kindnesses because sometimes they'd wake up to find the gate of their garbage bin rebuilt, or their mailbox pole replaced, or some other little handiwork that they'd been putting off miraculously fixed on its own, and they knew it was him, keeping himself busy. So he could have had a huge memorial. An outpouring of grief and support, but he'd written it down in a document he kept in a safe deposit box in town. No Memorial. No Funeral. No Big Deal. And then he'd drawn a peace symbol and the symbol for aum, and Maya didn't know what to do with the missing of him.

"Are you okay?" asked the club.

She found her breath and looked out at the room. In attendance were: Chloe; two tiny, earnest bespectacled freshman boys who had yet to go through their growth spurts and so had yet to make any sports teams and so had yet to add anything to their extracurricular résumés (even robotics club wouldn't have them until they were sophomores, and unless the spring musical included elves, or dwarves, or townspeople's children, or unless the school suddenly started varsity esports, they would have nothing to do all spring. Stupid puberty was such a saucy minx); and that was it. Bobby hadn't shown up.

The freshmen blinked up at her like baby birds and she didn't know what else to feed them. She sent a little prayer into their brains. *Spencer and Sam, when you do grow into the patriarchy, and it opens its overflexed, protein powder biceps to*

you, may you remember this time when you were too small for it
and work to uplift those on the other side of power.

"Anyway. Ideas?" she asked. "For raising bobcat money and, like, awareness? We'll also have to get a petition going, and perhaps show up at the town council meeting."

The freshmen were surprisingly organized and efficient, and, when given permission, sprang into action. "I'll open a Google Doc," Sam said and started right in confidently blurting and typing his ideas completely void of self-consciousness.

"Should we write a letter to the editor of the local paper? Start a website? Get some social media happening," Spencer added. "I'll start the petition."

"All excellent ideas," Maya said. "What's something that could get more people on board? Like the performing arts crowd maybe?"

"We could have a concert like Live Aid. Or . . ."

Maya could read Mr. Benson suddenly tuning in and thinking, *How in the world can this kid know anything about Live Aid?* But Maya knew it was because of the weird Christmas song that came out of it. Everyone was mocking it on TikTok for being so eighties-style clueless and tone-deaf to the cause they were actually trying to champion. Spencer also had a strange obsession with the eighties because of Pac-Man, Dungeons & Dragons, and other nostalgic games of the past that he played with his father.

"Yes. A concert! What's something more intimate?" Maya asked.

"Like a poetry slam?" Chloe said.

"Yes, and . . . ," Maya goaded.

"A coffeehouse?" said someone in the doorway.

"Bingo!" Maya said and almost wept on the spot to see Tyler and Lucy standing there, leaning on opposite sides of the doorframe. She didn't realize how much she'd been craving their support. "I was also thinking a coffeehouse. I already have some talent lined up."

"Tori?" Lucy asked.

"Yes, Tori," Maya said, hoping that Tori, with her Spotify single and all, would deign to perform at the Bobcats coffeehouse event. But she was thinking of Stacy, too, of course.

"I have a magic act," Spencer chimed in.

Of course you do, Maya thought. "Perfect," she said.

"Maya, don't you have some circus tricks?" Tyler joked. Lucy had told him about her fake plan to run away with the circus.

Tyler stood fantasizing about Maya in a shiny unitard sliding down from the ceiling with a silk rope between her legs.

"In your dreams, Tyler."

"Indeed," he said and did not take his eyes off her until she had to look down to break the intensity of his stare.

"Anyway," Maya said, trying to snap herself back to reality. "A coffeehouse. I know the perfect venue."

The last time Maya was at Antonio's she could sense Sheila's anxiety about the waning business. She was so alone with it all, and now after Scott, she was thinking of throwing in the towel. If they had the coffeehouse event at Antonio's, Sheila could begin to siphon the teens away from Starbucks and their ridiculous sugar shakes disguised as "coffee." Maya would help her develop a signature BobCattuccino for the event to lure in the VSCO girls and keep them forever. She could save Sheila.

"I'll make the merch," Lucy said. "Can you give me a pop-up?"

"Of course."

She was going to save so many Bobcats in one fell swoop. If Bobby ever showed up (where was he? she wondered), he'd find purpose and maybe date Chloe, which would ease his anxiety and depression, and vice versa. Tori would show off her beautiful voice and finally get some validation for her art, which would make her less of a salty b. Sheila would get some exposure to a whole new market of caffeine addicts. Lucy would sell stuff on the side and build her brand, and the actual bobcats could be saved from bloodthirsty hunters.

Most important, though, her mother would sing again.

"Wake up, Mr. Benson. We're all set," Maya said after adjourning the meeting and shutting down the projector.

He sat up and wiped the drool from the side of his mouth with his sleeve. Then Maya helped him lug the heavy buckets filled with raindrops that were planted strategically beneath the leaks in each classroom nowadays. They dumped them down the utility sink in the janitor's closet before putting them back under the leaks.

"See you tomorrow," he said. He trudged slowly out the door fishimmeled, sort of regretting staying up 'til three playing online poker the night before, but also plotting a new strategy for winning tonight's jackpot. It involved complex formulas of linear algebra and some alien symbols she'd never seen before, but as she contemplated it for a second, it all seemed to make sense.

"Good night." Maya wished she could save Mr. Benson, but he hadn't yet hit a low-enough low to be wishing for the right things.

Half Glob of Slime

Lucy texted after the meeting.

We're in 143

Not going home?

Tyler has track later

Track?

Yeah. He's a high jumper

With the pole?

No that's something else.

I have my appointment.

Man how fucked up are you?

Rude. Do I need to sign you up for
Maddie's Mental Health Awareness Club?

Sorry. That wasn't cool. Just come here.

Fine. I'll be there in a second.

Maya found Lucy and Tyler in room 143 hard at work behind their laptops. They sat on inflatable beach rafts that the parents had provided since, with all the rain, the basement space continued to fill with an inch of water, especially in the corners. "Hey, we wanted to apologize for not showing up to your meeting," Lucy said. She wore a kids' pink flamingo inner tube around her neck and let her kombucha float around in an inflatable coaster.

"You did show up, eventually."

"Yeah, but we weren't going to, and then I thought, I've created this monster. I'm the one who told her to find a purpose. Get a crusade. We just didn't expect it to be so like . . . endangered species-y."

"Threw us for a loop. Sort of weird and unexpected," Tyler added.

"It's cool, though, we're going to make it cool," Lucy assured her.

"High jumping is sort of a niche, too, isn't it? Weird and unexpected? I mean, isn't the point to stand out?" She didn't like how they were making her second-guess the plan. Was it too weird? Now she didn't know.

"High jumping is not my purpose, it's just more filler for the Common App."

"I need filler, too?"

"Yup. Come sit. I've noodled up some flyers."

Maya sat next to Tyler on his raft, and he was emanating again.

"Here, look." He indicated that Maya come closer, but she was reluctant to be pulled into the umami force.

"I can see from here," she said, and she craned her neck awkwardly over his left shoulder like a dorky llama.

"Just come here," he insisted.

So, she scooched over and sunk in next to him, thigh to thigh on the raft. She was inside the force now and could think of nothing but sex thoughts. She shifted her gaze to his laptop and snapped out of it a little when she suddenly saw his true purpose. The origami T-Rex he'd made and hid in her locker was no accident. He may have been a black belt in origami, but that was just an offshoot of this other giant talent. In just ten minutes he had noodled up a masterpiece.

He had, in no time at all, drawn a realistic black-and-white bobcat mom sitting and holding a kit by the scruff, which he inserted into a raw graffiti / tribal-inspired poster background that immediately gave the impression of the bobcat being in distress without actually saying anything. The whole effect was kind of Banksy meets Basquiat. You couldn't *not* look at it.

"We can use this for social and email and we can also print and distribute, do some flyposting, an entire street art campaign. We're just going to have this little guy show up everywhere in town overnight. I'm going to tag him, and Lucy is making a sticker to slap on street signs and whatnot."

"Slap tagging," Lucy said from her raft on the floor.

"Sasha over there has begun her yarn-bombing operation."

Maya had been so sucked into the force of Tyler, she hadn't even noticed Sasha, a quiet brown-skinned girl with freckles, a curly red Afro pushed back off her face with a solid green headband. She sat in a thrift store armchair in the corner, knitting needles furiously click-clacking away, creating a sleeve of green and yellow that was eventually going to say "Save the Bobcats." She held it up for Maya to see her progress. It was to be slipped around a tree on Main Street. The plan was to wrap a lot of things, fence posts, parking meters, trees, bike racks, etc., in these yarn slogans. Sasha had mobilized her entire radical grandma-chic yarn-bombing team, who at this very moment were knitting slogans and bobcats while they watched old episodes of *Teen Wolf*.

Lucy looked at her laptop, scanning the globe for the perfect oversized, secondhand denim jackets that she would emblazon with the bobcat or some other environmental messages about sharing the planet.

"Do you have a time and place for the coffeehouse?" Tyler asked. He was designing his own font for the poster, a slanted, jagged yellow thing that was insistent, yet pleasantly legible. He felt the warmth of Maya's thigh next to him, and she saw him consciously decide to manspread, pressing his leg into hers.

Then he stopped thinking about her altogether and started obsessing about the shade of yellow to use for the lettering. He was thinking, *Glazed Corn or maybe Forsythia Blossom*. She pressed her leg back into his in a light enough way that could be interpreted as accidental but in a strong enough way to perhaps jolt him back to the other box of sex thoughts.

"So, next Saturday for the date," Maya said, taking a breath and trying to focus on the flyer. "And one thing I want you to include on there," she said, reaching over to point at his screen so that maybe her breast would graze his shoulder, "Featuring Stacy Allen from Pet Rock."

"Pet Rock. You know someone from Pet Rock?" Sasha said. Her knitting needles came to a screeching halt.

"My mom," Maya said. "How do you know Pet Rock?"

Maya had spent all weekend on music's deep Web secretly searching for old grainy vids of her mother performing, because she had to man up and get to know her mother.

Pet Rock was the missing link between the eighties and the riot grrrls. The band was three women, on guitar, bass, and drums, who built on the legacy they'd inherited from Heart and Blondie and Joan Jett and Patty Smyth and Chrissie Hynde and Ann Wilson. The women of eighties rock played *with* men but never, and this was an important transition, never *for* them. They were mature (buh bye Joni Mitchell's little-girl bangs), mystical, witchlike creatures who had refined their anger into a wailing cry for liberation, and women everywhere finally heard the voice of their sad, collective rage.

Like them, Pet Rock seemed to assert that their deepest regrets were much deeper than the men who got away. *Good riddance, assholes,* the lyrics seemed to say. *I fuckin' got this, so fuck off.* It was so quintessentially Stacy. Maya still couldn't believe that Stacy had buried this experience so deep in her consciousness that Maya knew nothing about it. Also impressive was how far she had stayed off the grid ever since. She wasn't even on Facebook.

Sasha kept blinking at Maya for a second. "Wait, Stacy is your mom?" she said, and then she wiped a fat drop of water from her cheek. She moved her chair over and put down a mug to catch the new leak. They'd all just begun to take the leaks for granted.

And Maya repeated, "Wait, how can you possibly know Pet Rock?"

"I have a band," Sasha whispered, as if she were ashamed of it. She looked away and scratched her head with her knitting needle. "It's called Peach. And I'm, like, a music connoisseur . . . a collector. If my band doesn't make it, I'm going to library school to become a music librarian and archivist. I started a website and blog. *The Island of Misfit Toys.* It's all one-hit wonders, forgotten bands, and deep cuts. I bring old songs to the surface and try to leak them back into Spotify. Pet Rock is one of my pet projects."

"Wow, you're really specializing there. Way to go for, like, the Common App," Maya said as she tallied up the elements of Sasha's brand. She had the yarn bombing and the music making and the music history chronicling. "Wait, so, my mom is on Spotify?"

"Yeah, but she doesn't get on many lists. Search specifically under 1989. That was their big year."

Weird to hear that her mom had a "big year" and yet Stacy never once thought about it. Stacy buried her memories so deeply that they never once surfaced during the times Maya and her mom spent together. Was that even possible? Was Pet Rock so traumatic for her that she repressed it entirely?

"Well, guess what, Sasha? I hope Peach has an opening in their schedule next Saturday. Because I just booked you to open for Pet Rock!" Maya said in a rock-and-roll voice, and then she tentatively held out heavy-metal hand horns. Lucy rolled her eyes and thought, *Oh my god, Cringey, what are we going to do with you?*

She pulled out her phone and entered Sasha on her spreadsheet. And all the members of Peach. She was going to make sure this gig became their big break.

Sasha was elated. "That would be epic. Do you think she'll play 'Popsicle'?"

"Um, is that a good one?"

"The best." Sasha got back to her knitting while at the same time planning her set list and exactly which suspenders/drumstick combo she was going to wear for the event. She would definitely wear two small ponytail buns to rep some adorable bobcat ears.

Tyler stood up and got ready to go, shaking Maya off like a bad case of fleas. At least that's what it felt like. "Gotta run," he said. "But I think we made some good progress."

"We did," Maya said, standing. "I'm so grateful. The bobcats thank you. Can we work on this again tomorrow?"

"Of course," Tyler said and he ducked out between the beaded macramé of room 143.

Maya—emboldened by talk of her mother's girl band, and the concept of *getting what you want* that so many women before her struggled to attain—followed him out. She didn't have to be at the mercy of his whims, she thought. "Tyler," she said.

He stopped and she reached out and stuck her finger in the

top of his jeans back pocket. She pulled him slightly toward her until he spun into her space, looked down at her, umami turned up to eleven, and kissed her on the forehead.

They kissed, lightly. The whole time lightly, toying with each other, their lips and tongues barely touching as they let the serpentine force of their attraction just loop in and out around their mouths, taunting themselves, making them yearn for each other.

She tried to avoid Tyler's thoughts but she couldn't. *It would be so easy with her*, he thought. *This would be good.*

It IS good, Maya thought and tried to send this affirmation into his mind. He lifted her up and she wrapped her legs around his waist. He leaned her lightly on the cement wall behind her and he pressed against her. *Were they breathing?* Maya wondered. They didn't have to breathe. They had become each other's breath.

I knew this would happen. I should have stayed away, but how? Look at her. And then he looked at her in a way that Maya knew would only happen a few times in your lifetime if you were lucky enough to have it happen to you at all. He laid himself bare in that look, offering himself up while at the same time taking her in.

Tyler loosened his grip and Maya slid down his body and stood. The ground was hard and cold. She never wanted to touch it again. Being "grounded" was for people who were miserable. Being grounded was for bad children and planes in a snowstorm.

He took a deep breath in and said, "Um. Thanks. That was nice. But I gotta go."

He turned and walked away, and it was like pulling apart two globs of slime, the umami force between them stretching and thinning out until it was an invisible thread, and then, at last, broken altogether. Maya slid her back down the wall and sat, the way one does when one is a broken half glob of slime.

Another fan would be ashamed to gush like this, but Sasha had done a lot of therapy and soul-searching and even, like, outward-bound bungee-jumping adventures to peel away the layers of her insecurities and learn to give freely of her love.

Of course, at first, she was ashamed of her infatuations. Were they crushes? Was she IN LOVE with fifty-year-old women who used to be rock stars? Was that WEIRD? Did she have a fetish? Was she gay because she watched Dolores O'Riordan's "Linger" video 250 times on repeat after she died? Maybe. Was wanting to BE someone the same as wanting to have sex with someone? No, Sasha decided. Especially when it came to Maya's mom! She still couldn't believe Stacy of Pet Rock was Maya's *mother*.

Anyway, she'd learned her lesson after Dolores from the Cranberries had died. She realized her fandom was a positive life force! And it should be expressed and not bottled up. Her fandom could have saved Dolores, she realized. If she had written to Dolores about the impact she'd had on one life, then maybe, just maybe, Dolores would have felt how important she was in the world. And maybe, she wouldn't have gotten so drunk that she accidentally (?) drowned.

After that, Sasha wrote tribute song after tribute song to Dolores, but it felt empty because it was too late, and so she vowed ever since then that when she loved a person, even a person she didn't know, she would express her love, because Celebrities are just like Us! They need to feel precious.

So, after learning where to find Stacy (how had she stayed off the grid for so long?), Sasha got to work. She combined her love of Pet Rock with her facility with the needle arts and felted lifelike little figures of the whole band; even the tiny drumsticks were made of felt. And then she made a stop-motion video to the song "Popsicle," of course, manipulating the figures in a little shoebox diorama. It was a masterpiece, which she then forwarded to Stacy, because you never know when someone could use a boost, and you couldn't let your stupid insecurities stop you from saving a life.

Liquor in the Front

After Tyler left, Lucy yelled, "I told you so" from inside room 143. She poked her head out of the doorframe and the macramé strings of the door dangled over her forehead like ropey ragdoll bangs.

"Shush," Maya said. "I thought you 'shipped' Myler?"

"Oh god, Cringey. Stop with the Urban Dictionary. I'm ambivalent about Myler." From inside room 143 Maya could hear her mom's voice wailing what must have been "Popsicle" because Sasha sang along to every word.

"How are things with Gilding the Monster and whatnot?" Maya said, changing the subject. She needed to stop thinking about Tyler. Put him in the Tyler box and instead concentrate on the Lucy box.

"Good. I created a line for you," Lucy said, pulling out her phone covered in a red Air Jordan case and scrolling through her camera roll.

"What do you mean, a line?"

"The New Vavniks. Here, look," she said, flipping the

phone. "It's a line of shoes with designs based on Malala and Greta," Lucy said.

On one of their rides to school Maya had confided in Lucy about the vavnik theory. "The only reason god stops themself from destroying the rest of us is because they want to protect the thirty-six vavniks," she explained. "Folks like, I don't know, like Mr. Rogers. Why would god destroy humanity if humanity included Mr. Rogers?"

Come to think of it, Mr. Rogers was the patron saint of this whole Save the Bobcats operation, Maya thought. Wasn't it he who said, "There are three ways to ultimate success: The first way is to be kind. The second way is to be kind. The third way is to be kind." If people had listened to him, maybe the world wouldn't be drowning in floodwaters.

Maya flashed on some classic Rogerian mythology, like the time in the Jim Crow sixties when people threw acid in a pool to keep Black people out of it, and so he responded by filming a scene where he shared his kiddie pool with his Black police officer friend. Or the time a blind girl wrote him a letter to tell him she couldn't see when he was feeding his fish on-screen, so forevermore, during each episode, Mr. Rogers remembered to say "I'm feeding the fish" when he was feeding the fish.

"God keeps all us putzes alive for the sake of Mr. Rogers or, like, Dolly Parton."

"Jeez, Cringey." Lucy sighed. "Are vavniks only white people? Can you even think of a brown vavnik?"

"No. Sorry. Of course. There are vavniks of every race, obviously. Martin Luther King Junior. Gandhi. Nelson Mandela.

Thich Nhat Hanh. Maya Angelou. It makes sense when you think about it. Everyone always wonders how there can even *be* a god when there's so much evil in the world, and this explains it. God has just completely given up on everyone but the thirty-six."

Lucy stared at Maya, thinking about it for a second. "Most of those vavniks you mentioned are dead," Lucy said.

Maya took a breath. "Right. So. It's a new generation of vavniks. I was thinking maybe god is saving the world for Malala Yousafzai and Greta Thunberg. Today's vavniks are all teenagers, I think, stepping into their power. It's inspiring. The rest of us can only aspire toward their selflessness."

Now, outside room 143, Lucy scrolled through her new shoe designs and Maya saw beautiful, determined faces painted on the top of white Vans. "This is the girl from Marjory Stoneman Douglas fighting against gun violence, the girl in Flint protesting for clean water." So many eco-vavnik girls finally fed up with the status quo. "Terry the librarian actually thinks I should do a pop-up to convince my mom to let me go to merchandising school."

"You and Terry are in cahoots?" Maya asked.

"Maybe."

"I told you he was nice."

"Shush. Say less."

"What does it take to do a pop-up?"

"Well, I found an empty space, but it costs some Benjamins to bling it out with my brand." *Plus I just want to take a gap year, but Jeanne would never go for that, so I'm not even going to wish it.*

And just like that Maya had a Bobcat to save.

"How many Benjamins?" she said.

Maya was excited. It would be fun to save a Bobcat who had a wish other than a love match or a grade change, which is most of what she'd been doing these days Bobcat-wise.

....

"At the next light, take a left." Lucy's Waze voice was set to Shaquille O'Neal, whose sneaker game she usually admired, but who had also recently been caught in public wearing *midis*, which was a crime against all sneakerdom, but she kept his voice for old times' sake.

Maya had punched an address into her phone, and Lucy tried not to hydroplane as she sloshed through the puddles along the winding roads beside the river. Eventually, Shaq had them turn into a parking lot of a Knights of Columbus.

"Why. Are. We. Here?" Lucy asked, suddenly creeped out by their surroundings.

"You need ten thousand dollars."

"What?" Lucy asked.

"For the pop-up thing. Sell the merch. Guap Stonks. And for the gap year."

"Stonks? What?"

"Just come on," Maya said. "Oh, and if I clear my throat or scratch my nose, you fold."

Lucy gaped at Maya, still trying to understand what was happening, so Maya gestured at Lucy, pulling her fingers together at the middle of her chest to get her centered. "Be. Cool."

"I'm not going in until you tell me where we are and what we are doing here. How did you know about the gap year? I know I have told *no one* about that. Are you some kind of plainclothes detective narc? Like *21 Jump Street?* You are barking up the wrong tree, old lady. I don't do drugs. How old are you? Are you thirty-five, like all the actors in *Riverdale?*"

They were walking toward an outbuilding behind the K of C, and Maya thought she saw someone move the curtain to look at them through the window. "Oh jeez. Come on." She grabbed Lucy by the sleeve and took her to the edge of the stream, whose babble would muffle the sound of their voices. They leapt to the top of a giant beige boulder struggling to keep its head above the rising water. She was running out of time. "I have a thing," Maya said to Lucy.

"A thing? What kind of thing? Herpes? Dyslexia? A tumor?"

Maybe I do have a tumor, Maya thought. Why had she never thought about that? Maybe this was all caused by a giant brain tumor pressing into the 90 percent of the brain we haven't figured out how to use yet. No, that would only happen on TV, she thought. She shook it off, and stared Lucy in the eye.

"What?" Lucy said. But what she thought was: *Why am I always attracted to friend drama? That must say something about me. I have some kind of complex . . . or personality disorder that makes me a disaster magnet. Why do I bring this crazy upon myself?*

"Maybe you're bored," Maya answered out loud and Lucy almost fell backward off the rock in surprise. Maya grabbed her wrist to pull her up and said, "And I'm not crazy."

"What. Are. You?" Lucy asked, her eyes widening and her heart beginning to race a little.

"I'm trying to figure that out actually, but in the meantime,

I think you should focus less on why you're attracted to disaster and focus more on why you're romantically attracted to people who are unavailable to you. But the answer to that is easy, too. We all do it because it's safe. If we focus our crushes on celebrities and people we can't have, then we'll never have to become vulnerable enough to get in a real relationship."

"Okay. Step back," Lucy said. "How did you go from my Cringey to this all-knowing thing?"

"Listen. I just sort of know things I don't want to know. I know what everyone is thinking. I want to get rid of it, but I don't know how, so I'm trying to embrace it as my purpose. I'm trying to use it to help people. Save the Bobcats, and you're the most important Bobcat to me. Well, aside from my mom, I guess."

"Aw."

"I'm going to win you ten thousand dollars at this poker game."

"We're at a poker game?" Lucy said, clapping her hands together and cheering up a bit.

"Affirmative. Mr. Benson was thinking about coming here at the bobcats meeting. So. That's how I know that this is a poker game."

"Mr. Benson," Lucy said, tsking and shaking her head.

"Yeah."

"They should pay teachers a living wage," Lucy said.

"Right? Come on. We've practiced this in Pre-Calc," Maya said. "You'll pick up my signals. They may need to evolve."

The man working the door was large. Maya and Lucy knocked a special knock. They opened the door and pushed aside a thick red velvet curtain to find him sitting potbellied on a stool, chewing on the end of a cigar.

"Ladies, can I be of assistance?" he said. What he thought was, *What in the Jezus H. Christ have we got here?*

Maya knew the secret password because she'd read it in Mr. Benson's mind. "We came straight from Broadway," she said, which she knew was a reference to a poker hand and not a geographical location. Then she pulled out a wad of cash from Gilding the Monster that Lucy had been planning to deposit and covertly paged the bills into a fan in front of her chest, so he could see her bankroll (and her cleavage).

"Let me. Um. We don't usually . . ."

"Is this not an equal opportunity criminal pursuit?" Lucy asked. "You going to discriminate against our dollars?"

"How old are you, though?"

"Twenty-one. She's twenty-five. Go ahead, quiz her. Ask her any question. She'll know the answer."

"Because twenty-five-year-olds know so much about the ways of the world?"

"Try her. She's especially good at music."

"Why don't I just check your IDs?"

"Aren't we all undercover here, Mac? Just ask her some old-person trivia. Some real boomer Watergate stuff. Ask her about Nixon. Or, like, Gary Cooper."

"How old do you think I am?"

"So ask her about Reagan."

"There you go."

"Ask her about the Talking Heads."

Tommy, which is of course what this person was named,

started thinking up some questions. They had to do with bad eighties rock ballad singers. "Okay," he said. "Who was the lead guitar for Foreigner?"

"Mick Jones," Maya said.

"Poison, lead singer."

"Bret Michaels."

"See. It's fun," Lucy said. "No one under twenty-five would know that."

"Okay. Table three," said Tommy a little warily and then he sent a text to the dealer of table three that said sending you a couple live ones.

As Lucy and Maya approached, the men at table three pretended not to be shocked by the admittance of females. The four men at the table barely nodded at them and tried to keep their poker faces as they thought, *What do we have here? Aw jeez, they're gonna mess with the flop. For fuck's sake. We gonna bring wives here now? These two took a wrong turn at the bake sale.*

At least their first thoughts were patronizing and not pornographic, Maya thought. It was only a matter of time before their thoughts switched to pornographic, though, somewhere around the fourth round of drinks. That was good advice to anyone, Maya thought. Get the fuck out before the fourth round of drinks. Nothing good happens after that. She wasn't sure how she knew that, but it didn't take a genius.

"Evening," Maya said as she straddled a stool on one end of the table and directed Lucy to take the last empty seat on the other end. She slid her cash to the dealer and, without talking too much (poker players (read: men) hate it when you talk too much), indicated he give half the chips to Lucy. She prayed that Lucy could keep her $1,000 bankroll organized in stacks and be able to play it cool.

By seating Lucy at the far end of the table, she had arranged it so Lucy would bet last and, by the time the play came around to her, Maya knew she'd have figured out what to do. She was stonks, super Wall Street savvy, so she would catch on quickly. Maya had seen her doing figures in her head during math class and in any sneaker or clothing online transaction. She would get it.

In the next hand Maya was dealt two aces in the hole. She of course knew what all these other gents were holding, sitting as they were in such close proximity. She knew what they were holding and what they were thinking; she could smell what they'd had for dinner and what lies they'd told their wives to get out of the house this evening. She knew that Harv hummed "Sweet Caroline" whenever he had a good hand (or a boner).

Lucy at the other end of the table was thriving, as they say. She thrived on danger, newness, and improvisation. Her face shone with an understated admiration for Maya and the hope that this plan would work. As she looked around and sized up her surroundings, she mused about what she was doing here. It validated for her that she really couldn't see herself institutionalized for four more years.

Does Jeanne really expect me to discuss Hamlet *again? How is discussing Hamlet's indecision at having to avenge his father's death going to help me build a stonks empire of sustainable clothing? Are they really going to make me sit in a room with "like"*

people in like, Champion sweatshirts who, like, love, like, Brandy
Melville and, like, Panic! At The Disco, who, like, straighten their
hair and, like, wear false, like, eyelashes? I need to be in the world.
Not in a giant fake simile of the "like" world. Don't they get that?
I need to save it. The world. Before it all comes to an end. And if
winning this money will convince them to let me be in the world,
then who cares how I procured it, right? It's a game. "All the world's
a stage / And all the men and women merely players." See? I know
my Shakespeare. I don't need college, she thought. And then she
thought, *Wait! No male playwright would say "men and women"*
at a time when only men mattered. Shakespeare was definitely a
chick. It would be interesting to investigate Shakespeare's pronouns.

That last thought, to Maya, was maybe evidence that Lucy
should go to college, but she just continued with the plan. They
were up. Way up.

Maya had tried to pace it so that they didn't win too
quickly, but at the same time, they needed to get out of there
before the fourth round of drinks. It was a tight squeeze.

To entertain herself, she'd begun saving all the Bobcats at the
table. She slipped Harv some of her winnings, so he wouldn't
be tempted to go even deeper into debt with the dealer. She
silently helped Jason recommit to his marriage. She convinced
Tommy to take guitar lessons, and the rain outside pattered a
little more softly on the roof.

Before she could get to Brian, a younger man in a plaid
button-up shirt from Target seated two seats to her left, he
was emboldened by the first sip of his fourth drink and began
to blurt skeptical questions at them. "So where are you two
from?" he asked, obviously fake smiling.

"Town," Maya said.

"What town?"

"This town."

"What do you do?"

"We're in imports and exports," Lucy added.

"Really. How come I've never seen you around before?" *They can count cards*, he thought, narrowing his eyes suspiciously.

"We don't run in the same circles, I guess," Lucy mumbled.

This, Maya knew, was their cue to skrrt. She felt the tension around the room and noted the four men who were carrying firearms. She looked slyly at the dealer and nodded at him, which indicated that they wanted to cash out.

The dealer slid Maya a stack of C-notes under the table. Without looking at Lucy, Maya used Harv's cigarette lighter to tap "Get Out. Gun." in her special pre-calc Morse code, and the two of them simultaneously pushed their stools away from the table.

"Wow, this was fun, but it's getting late," Lucy said, fake yawning. "Catch you high rollers on the flip side. Harv, Jason, it's been a pleasure," she said and then looked at Maya, who mouthed, *Run!*

"Really, Cringey? Are you seri . . . ?" Lucy asked out loud, stunned for a second, but then she saw Tommy put a hand on his gun, and she made a beeline for the kitchen, where she knew there must be a back door, because their generation was trained to look for every exit in the building in case of an active shooter event.

Maya followed behind her as Lucy screamed, "I forget what I'm supposed to do! All I remember from ALICE active shooter training is to throw a stapler at the shooter. Find a stapler!"

"Just run!" Maya said, catching up to her and pushing her into the kitchen.

"But there's no *R* in ALICE!" Lucy cried. It was such a stupid acronym.

"GO!"

They made it out the back door and into the Toyota Corolla, where they both pig piled into the driver seat and Lucy drove away with Maya still lying on her lap. "Liquor in the front, poker in the rear!" Lucy screamed as they peeled out of the driveway. "Oh my god, I feel so alive!" Lucy said. "Best night ever!"

"Really?" Maya asked, happy that she could deliver a save the Bobcat moment. The mission was supposed to be all about money, but madcap as it was, this was a night they would never forget. They shared secrets and made a memory together. They made a connection and it glowed inside her. She belonged to someone for a second and she gave a little wink to the heavens, acknowledging to Scott that he was right. This feeling was god.

"Do you think they took down my plates?" Lucy asked.

"I don't think so. Damn, we only won five thousand dollars," Maya said, disappointed that she hadn't reached the ten-thousand-dollar goal. She was still lying over Lucy's knees, and she held the wad of cash out over the passenger seat.

"Five thou . . . ! Cringey?!" Lucy said, and she slapped her on the butt with one hand while using the other to steer, the wheels squealing around the sharp curves of the country road as they made their getaway. "Hot damn! How are we going to celebrate?"

"We could go see Ruby," Maya said, using her acrobat skills to contort herself into a ball so that she could forward roll over the console and into the passenger seat.

"What the . . . ?" Lucy stopped the car.

"And we can get some Korean fried chicken," Maya continued, still upside down, struggling not to kick Lucy in the face while she was driving. "We could get the chicken and bring it to Ruby and see if she wants any. Hey, why are we stopped?"

"No one but me and my wet dreams knows about Ruby. Damn. I'm not sure I love you being all up in my brain."

"Okay, but we're trying to make a getaway here. We need to proceed in the getting of the away! Go!" Maya knew because she knows all things that the poker gangsters were making a feeble attempt to follow them, but they were too drunk to really be making much headway.

"Ugh." Lucy pulled back onto the dark and winding road. "I think we need some ground rules. Or like a safe word or something so that you're not so up in my head. Ruby!? How did you know that?"

"Well, you like her, don't you?"

"That's not the point. The point is I'm not ready for you or anyone to know about that. How do I protect my private thoughts from you? But then again, I guess if we're best friends, I would share everything with you anyway. Be, like, vulnerable. Isn't that the buzzword of the day?"

Best friends? Maya never thought she would have one of those.

"I do like her, though. A lot. But I'm not ready."

"Let's go to her house!" Maya suggested. She was feeling liberated a little. A lot. It was such a relief that someone else knew her situation. They could have fun with it ... question mark? It didn't have to be drudgery all the time, knowing people's thoughts. "We could go to Ruby's and I could Cyrano it. Like, I could tell you what to say, based on what she's thinking. All you have to do is send her a text that says "sup. Want some chicken?' And then I could take it from there."

"Someone's been reading too many teenager novels. And anyway, then she falls in love with You! I know how that Cyrano plot plays out."

"Well, let's at least get the chicken." Maya had never had Korean fried chicken, but she could see in Lucy's head what a flavor explosion it was. Salty, sweet, spicy, crispy, gooey goodness. "I'm hungry."

"Now you're talking."

On the way to the chicken joint, Maya cued up "The Gambler" by Kenny Rogers. Lucy originally protested (*Cringey, what the eff?*), but by the time they pulled up to the ordering window, they were scream-singing about knowing when to fold 'em because it was actually a perfect song that told a bittersweet story about the ways of the world. They sat in the Corolla licking their fingers, contented and sleepy after eating the chicken, fried twice and hand-brushed with tangy specialty chili sauce, when she got a text.

What does the text say? Lucy thought at her, realizing she could totally communicate with Maya without speaking. Maya just flashed her the phone. It said Hey, I'll pick you up Thursday at 6. Tyler had texted.

I don't trust it, Lucy thought.

"Girl. You have no faith. In my, like, wiles," said Maya. "I think he really likes me."

Lucy laughed and said, "No. Cringey. I don't have faith in your wiles. You just sang every word of a Kenny Rogers song."

"Well," Maya said, flashing the phone back at Lucy. "The proof is in the pudding."

". . . and you just said 'the proof is in the pudding.' So. Yeah. I'm not really confident in your charms," she said out loud.

What did you have in mind? Maya texted to Tyler.

It's a surprise.

Say no, Lucy thought.

"No? Why no?" Maya said.

Here is how you answer every proposition for a first date: "I'm sorry, I have plans that day." Say it.

"I'm sorry. I have plans that day," Maya said out loud.

"Now type it," Lucy said.

"But I want to go to the surprise," Maya said, pouting.

"He just texted you out of the blue and didn't even phrase it as a question. You need to get him to step it up."

"Fine," Maya said. And then she typed Oh, I'm sorry. I have plans that day.

And all she got from Tyler, then, was the three dots, and then nothing at all. Then finally, Is Lucy with you?

Say NO, Lucy thought at her.

"Lucy!" Maya screamed. "He's onto us."

"Just say no," Lucy said.

No Maya typed.

The three dots came back on Tyler's end and then they just faded away into the ether.

"He got away," Maya said dejectedly.

"Patience," Lucy said, but as Lucy drove away, Maya secretly texted Tyler behind her back.

I'll be ready Thursday at six! she said and boldly added a kissing face emoji.

Greatest Show on Earth

How it started: Maya lured two freshmen into a room with a sleeping math teacher and showed them a slideshow. How it was going: Save the Bobcats was so successful, it was even receiving death threats!

These days, receiving your first death threat meant you were coming up in the world. It used to be a rare occurrence. Maya had asked around. None of the adults in her life had ever once received one, but wickedness, etc., was great in the earth. The preponderance of death threats was just one more indication that whatever devastation climate change was about to foist upon humanity, humanity totally deserved.

Maya's first death threat was sent from proudgunner23457. And it was rated NC-17: containing graphic violence, language, sex, nudity, adult situations, so she deleted it right away.

On the bright side, these death threats (*only evil continually*) from the hunters in town were an indication that the campaign was working! Word had obviously gotten out about the budding opposition to Ordinance 582a, which would, if passed, hereby adopt an open season on bobcats in the county. The coffeehouse event was coming up and everything seemed to be in place. The campaign was building momentum.

Tyler had kept his promise and painted his iconic bobcat on some overpasses and on some abandoned train cars and on a couple of warehouses where he had gotten permission. They had snuck out last night together, camouflaged in oversized hoodies, and he'd taught her some tricks of the trade. He let her try her hand on a few on the back walls of grocery stores. He really upped the street art game in town, and Maya hoped it might invite some more talent, maybe encourage a dedicated place where folks could tag away to their heart's content. Maybe creating a "graffiti alley" in town would be her next #activist #purpose. And then of course she'd raise money for a skate park. They seemed to go hand in hand. She could just keep racking up purposes for her Common App brand.

In addition to Tyler's baller mini murals, Lucy had slapped the sticker everywhere she went, especially on the backs of street signs. Sasha's yarn-bombing team had wrapped knitted SAVE THE BOBCAT sleeves around every cylindrical surface. It brought new hope to the town, except to the people who considered it vandalism. A lot of those people, though, were brought back on board by the wholesomeness of the yarn bombing.

Sam and Spencer had started a phone bank to encourage citizens to call their town representatives and save the bobcats. They had gotten some hang-ups and some scary NRA people shouting at them, but overall, the response was positive. Why kill bobcats? No one could think of a good reason.

Maya had also assigned them the task of creating a fact sheet to help folks know what the talking points were if they went to the town meeting, but they got lost in a tittering fit of hilarity after researching the mating rituals of bobcats and finding out that when bobcats mate, they do it sixteen times in one hour. "OMG, respect," Spencer said. And then they started wondering who the person was who sat there and counted. "One ... Two. Who was that guy?" they wondered, cackling, and they couldn't get back on task, so Maya had Chloe make the fact sheet in addition to booking and managing the acts for the coffeehouse.

The other Save the Bobcats mission was doing okay. Her spreadsheet now had thirty-six rows, the same number as vavniks, which wasn't terrible, but given the dismal state of humanity, and the continuation of rising floodwaters everywhere, Maya thought she could be doing better.

Some of her best work included helping Sophie P. develop better "sleep hygiene" by sneaking a lavender bath bomb and CBD oil care package into her locker, helping Lauren J. clear up her acne by suggesting she go gluten-free and add probiotics to her supplement routine, helping Arjun with his video game addiction by sending him an anonymous text that said Make Work Your Favorite every hour on the hour from 7:00 P.M. to 11:00 P.M. It was a line from the movie *Elf*, which he loved. So, she had saved a few Bobcats. She even anonymously sent the English teacher some links about getting her doctorate, since she seemed to be so resentful about where she had ended up in life.

She was proud of herself for finding a way to dovetail all

of her Life Plans. Amy said it was important to step back and reflect on what was going well. So she thought about it for a second. Save the B(b)obcats combined

1. the urgent plan to address the (albeit hypothetical) correlation between the wickedness in the earth and the insipient flooding of said earth;
2. Lucy's three-step plan for instant success as a teenager: get people to like you / pretend to save the world / write about it for the Common App; and
3. Scott's advice: make connections, stop overthinking, and Do something.

Things were going swimmingly, as they say. The only thing that gnawed at her was Bobby's absence. She hadn't seen him around, and he was ghosting her. She just had to assume he was doing okay. The forest bathing probably grounded him. And he went off to find his own purpose to write about for the Common App.

Save the Bobcats was moving forward little by little, and at the coffeehouse, she'd save her very own mom!

Stacy pretended to be annoyed about having to prepare for the coffeehouse, but she was secretly overjoyed by finally getting the feel of her guitar again. As a joke, Maya told her she'd have to audition with Tori and Peach tomorrow, but that was just to add a level of urgency to the experience. Stacy was a Taurus and prone to next-level procrastination and laziness if she didn't have a hard deadline. Either that or she was lost in a driven frenzy of ambition. She only had two modes.

At least her practice was distracting her from getting all "Stacy" about this other thing that was happening: Maya's actual first date.

At six o'clock the Hyundai rolled up their stone driveway, which of course ignited the protective impulse in Maurice to bark, yowl, yap, and jump four feet into the air, slamming his body against the front door, making it impossible for Maya to slip out unnoticed.

"Bye," she said.

"Where are you . . ." she heard Stacy stammer as the door was closing and she ran to the Hyundai to make her getaway.

"Peel!" she said to Tyler, who just went with it, stomped on the gas, and squealed backward out of the driveway, his tires spitting white stones everywhere into the periphery, like a popcorn popper without the lid.

"Wow. That was the most hillbilly pickup I've ever executed. Shouldn't I have, like, shown my face? Met your dad or something? So they know you're safe? Why are we Dukes of Hazzarding this?"

"No reason. Just go." She couldn't stomach seeing the look in Stacy's eye when she found out Maya was going on an actual date. She couldn't stand to see Stacy's glimmer of hope, the thing with feathers, her dream that Maya could perhaps become a normal person in the world—the daughter she'd always wanted. Seeing that glimmer would only reinforce Maya's knowledge of what a disappointment she might always be. This dating Tyler thing was probably not going to last, right? Why get anyone's hopes up? Hopes would always be dashed. Maya was a dasher of all hopes, which made sense if you thought about it. Bartender. Acrobat. God. God was always dashing hopes, weren't they?

"Where are we going?" she asked.

"Informational interview."

"What?"

"Lucy said you wanted to join the circus, and the circus is in town. It's a traditional circus, too. High wire, trapeze, strong men. None of the weird, creepy French cirque du so-lame stuff. Just straight-up old-timey three-ring goodness. With no elephants. Cats, though. They trained cats."

"No one can train cats," Maya said.

"You'll be shocked and amazed," Tyler said, smiling broadly, but keeping his eyes on the road, so that Maya could appreciate him from a different angle. He had a square chin and a wide smile that creased in a double parenthesis in the corner of his mouth. In profile, his nose seemed stronger and more chiseled than it did from the front of his face, and Maya could imagine him when he came into his power in middle age and trimmed the black curls that looped up sloppily now above his ears. He'd be forever handsome with this bone structure. No Mitch McConnell chins in his future, thank goodness.

She tried to get a read on Tyler and realized she was currently the only girl in his brain. *I love how perfect her ears are . . . the way she pronounces "water," how her eyes crinkle in consideration before she lets herself laugh. I love how her jeans are judiciously ripped in all the right places.*

She boldly put her hand on top of his. He was keeping it outstretched on the gearshift and hoping she'd do so. She was surprised by how hairy and masculine the back of his hand was. How adult. He spread his fingers out and she traced them one by one as if she were making a hand turkey, which got her really hot and, hence, sullied the experience of making hand turkeys for the rest of time.

They vibed like this the whole evening, discovering that they had a shared sense of humor. Tyler asked her questions about what she liked, and what she thought. And she realized she'd been spending so much time trying to figure out other people, she'd forgotten to figure out herself. Tyler picked up on this a little when she came up with vague answers to some of his questions. Favorite book? Favorite movie? So he backed it up. "Chocolate or vanilla?" he asked. "Cats or dogs?" And in this way, she started to fall in love with him. Because he was the first person who seemed genuinely interested in the inner workings of her mixed-up mind.

At intermission, he unwrapped a granola bar in his hand that promised to provide his body with complete nutrition. He snuck a photo of it to add to his "What I eat in a day" TikTok. It was a thing all cute seventeen-year-old boys were doing, sometimes to encourage healthy eating and sometimes to brag about the obscene amounts a seventeen-year-old can eat with their supercharged nuclear-reactor metabolism.

Maya read his mind as he looked at the wrapper. . . . *Creatine for the mitochondria*, he thought to himself.

"Powerhouse of the cell," Maya said quietly, spinning her finger around his thigh.

"Yeah, whoa," Tyler said. "I was just thinking that same thing," he said and stared confidently and unwaveringly straight into her eyes until she had to turn away.

She was suddenly terrified of herself. This was new territory. It had never even occurred to her to use someone else's thoughts to manipulate them before. Man-ipulate. Man-handle. These were things that men usually did. And she'd tried to keep it at a minimum in this relationship.

They fed each other popcorn, tossing kernels into the sky and leaning over each other to catch them. He let her bury her head in his chest during the high-wire act. She couldn't watch as a whole family stupidly climbed on top of one another and balanced up there on a sideways tilted-back chair. And when the clowns came around spraying water out of old-timey seltzer bottles and slamming pies in the faces of innocent audience members, they both hid behind Tyler's jacket and snuck a kiss.

Of course, when they rolled back into the driveway, they caught Stacy and Glen in the glare of their headlights. There they sat, red-eyed and white-faced like old possums, having cute pretend cocktails on the stoop, which they never did in real life at 10:00 P.M. This was a farce, a pretense, a front, a sham. They usually just watched TV and then dragged themselves to bed to read a few pages before sleeping the addled half sleep of the cash-strapped American midlife crisis. But tonight, here they were, chipper and alert, eager to catch another glimpse of this Tyler. They sat on either side of a cooler with a cheese board between them, as if Maya's first date were an occasion for tailgating.

"Oh man, I should have introduced myself," Tyler said, putting the car in park. *I gotta get out in front of this*, he thought, and he sprang from the car using the alacrity of his quick-twitch, high-jumping quadriceps and opened the door for Maya. They strode toward the stoop, Maya holding a bag of congealing cotton candy in one hand and a spinning flashlight circus souvenir in the other; Tyler's arm was around her waist.

Hands where I can see 'em, buster. Come out with your hands up. Show me your hands, Glen thought. He was obsessed with the whereabouts of Tyler's hands and stared daggers into the poor boy as if he were going to cuff him and instantly read him his rights. This wasn't like Glen. He was so instantly filled with a primeval hatred. For Tyler, the innocent. Maya spun away from Tyler's embrace, putting some distance between them until Glen could regain his composure. Tyler shook hands with them both and said, "Pleased to meet you, I'm Tyler. I'm sorry I didn't introduce myself before we left. We were running a little late."

"No problem," Stacy said. "Did you have a nice time?" For once, she was the normal half of this shit show. Glen was still losing it. To distract himself from his unjustified hatred, he couldn't stop making dad jokes to himself about Tyler's name. *Hey, what do you call it when Tyler's caught in a storm? A typhoon. What do you call it when Tyler makes a lot of money? A tycoon. What's Ty's favorite dinosaur? Tyrannosaurus Rex. How does Tyler write his papers? A ty-pewriter.* Thank god he didn't say them out loud, but *Poor Glen,* thought Maya. This was so hard for him, and now it was her turn to think, *Aw.*

"Dad, Tyler is an artist," Maya said, appealing to Glen's appreciation of anyone devoted to the arts. He himself still designed a few album covers as a side gig.

"I want to be a working artist, though. A designer. Everything needs to be designed, right? Even this thing," Tyler said, pointing at Maya's ludicrous spinning toy.

"Excuse me," Maya said. "This is a thing of beauty."

"Indeed," Stacy said. "And speaking of beauty, I need to get some beauty sleep. It's a school night. So nice to meet you, Tyler," she said. She winked at Maya and did a secret celebratory happy dance that Tyler couldn't see, and then grabbed Glen by the shoulders to guide him into the house, thinking something about leaving them alone so they could kiss good night, which, ew, after seeing this display would sadly be downgraded to a measly peck on the cheek.

Parents. The ultimate cockblock.

Frances McDormand

The night of the coffeehouse event had finally arrived. "Mom, are you ready?" Maya yelled down the stairs. "We have to get there early to set up. Oh, and Sasha still wants to know if you're playing 'Popsicle.'" It seemed oddly quiet downstairs and Maya got no response. "Mom," she said again.

She found Stacy in her bathroom in her underwear. The underwear part wasn't weird. Stacy was always traipsing around unclothed because she was trying to encourage body positivity and was trying to be all European about it. Stacy was often in her underwear. But she was never like this, sitting, legs splayed on the bathroom floor, leaning against the tub.

"Oh, hi, Maya. Have you tried this? This feels nice and cold on my back," Stacy slurred and let her head loll backward and side to side on the edge of the tub.

"Mom?"

"Hi," her mom said and smiled a dopey ear-to-ear grin.

"What are you doing?"

"Just, like, sitting here, cooling my back. It's nice."

"Mom, what did you take?"

"Nothing."

"Mom." Maya frowned.

Stacy tried to mimic her, frowning back an exaggerated frown, and she almost tipped over from the effort. "It's okay. I'm okay," Stacy said as she tried to clamber to a standing position, but then fell back and sat in a heap on the toilet seat.

"Did you take something?"

"Define take something."

"Did you swallow pills?"

"Like swallow down my throat?" she said, swaying a little with her eyes closed and trying to point to her neck.

"Yes."

"Nope," Stacy said, seemingly proud of herself. "And I didn't do it the French way either. Boop up the bum."

"Mom!"

"You keep saying that . . . Maya! There, how do you like it?" she replied, wiping the side of her mouth with the back of her wrist. "If you must know," she said, trying to keep her eyes wide open while looking at Maya's face, "I took some airplane medicine. It just melts under my tongue. Little sugary dissolving pills that are prescribed to *me*." Stacy pointed at herself. "For situations like *this*," she said, pointing to the toilet seat. As if having a prescription justified her ruining Maya's only stab at life.

"You are not getting on an airplane."

"Thank god for that. I hate airplanes."

"How many did you take?"

"I thought I should take extra. And it wasn't kicking in, so I took one more. So, like, three." She held up three fingers of her wiry, gnarled strumming hand, stared at it for a second, and then added another finger.

"Four! Mom! We have to leave now and you're headlining."

"Can't you let little Plum do it? Or the scary girl from math class?"

"It's Peach. People are coming to see you. Haven't you been getting fan mail all week?" Maya saw her mom tenderly remember the adorable, heartfelt video Sasha had sent her and a tear slid out of the corner of her eye. Then she shook it off and let out a sound like a whoopee cushion deflating.

"Mom, what happened? Why have you never told anyone about what happened to Pet Rock?" *Why don't you ever even think about it?* Maya wondered.

"You want the 'Behind the Music: Pet Rock' story where we all get too full of ourselves and do too many drugs and sleep with each other's boyfriends until we break up the band? Well. Whatever. It didn't happen exactly like that. They broke us up."

"Who?"

"The execs. All those Phil Spector creeps. And I sold out and trusted them like a stupid ingenue. I gave them the copyright to all my lyrics, and then because I didn't give enough blow jobs or because I gained a little weight or something, they canceled our record deal and signed Alanis Morissette. They booked her in all our venues and canceled our tour and then hired Laura and Susan to play in her band. I was already thirty, which was old for a rock star. This tour was our one break, and they gave it to Alanis, who was twenty-one." It took a lot for her mother to get all those words out and she took a big sigh and almost fell asleep on the spot, but then she opened her eyes and started again.

"I didn't sing after that, not even in the shower, because singing comes from the heart and my heart was pulverized. I hope you never feel that." She pointed to Maya's chest. "Heart pulverization," she slurred. "I practically forced your father to impregnate me. Give me new life. But it took us some years. Fuck them. I have you. We have each other. We have the store. What does Alanis have?"

Maya suddenly realized there were *zero* Alanis Morissette albums in their entire record store. Not even *Jagged Little Pill*, which was considered a feminist classic. They didn't even have the cast recording of the Broadway show, and they had the cast recordings of every Broadway show. "Um, I think she has three adorable children and access to private jets and whatnot?" Maya said.

"Fuck. Isn't it Ironic?"

"No," Maya said.

"Well, nothing in that stupid song was ironic, either. Here, help me get dressed, I'm going to do this thing."

"Mom, you don't have to do this thing. I thought this was what you wanted. Another chance at music," Maya said.

In the weeks after Maya had accidentally discovered the Pet Rock memorabilia, singing was almost all that Stacy could think about. She'd played the fan video that Sasha sent her almost a thousand times, still in awe of the fact that she had a fan who was younger than forty. She had a fan!

Maya would find her tucked behind the register at the store just ruminating about what it felt like to make something that actually moved people. She would luxuriate in the memory of hitting the perfect note—one with a cylindrical clarity that could actually permeate a person and vibrate at their very core. Finally, she had taken her guitar out, something Maya'd only ever seen Glen do, never Stacy, and she'd pluck away at her old songs, trying to put them back in her brain.

"I'm doing it because I thought it's what *you* wanted," she said.

"Well, that is ironic," Maya answered.

"She's not better than me. Alanis."

"I know. She's not. But like you tell me all the time, it's not a meritocracy."

"It's a patriarchy, I guess," Stacy said.

"You're just figuring that out now?"

"No, obvioushly," she slurred. "But maybe the implications of it. Yes. I mean we have never, and now, after the event-that-should-not-be-named, we *will* never have a female president. We are and always will be second-class citizens. It's so inthidious we don't even realize we've been groomed to eat shit our entire lives. There's no getting outside it. And if you are outside it, then nobody ever sees you. And I think I'm anxious all the time, because I'm trying to help you fit into it, because it's the path of least resistance. And then that makes me angry and there's rage. It's so confusing."

"Disappointment. Disapproval. Dismay. The occasional Pride and then maybe Envy," Maya mumbled.

"What? Yes. If I express disapproval, it's because I'm trying to protect you from other people's disapproval. I don't want you to get hurt by the mean people of the patriarchy, but empirically I approve. I approve of everything you do . . ."

"So how do I escape it?"

"Only Frances McDormand has escaped," she said, waving her sloppy hand that did not look like it could control the strings of a guitar right now. "Meh. I'm feeling petty about the patriarchy. Write that down. Actually, that's terrible. See. I just don't have it, Maya. My brain doesn't work that way anymore. You can't make art with a pulverized heart. Write that down. No, don't." She puckered her lips, then pointed to them and said, "Do me lipstick."

"You can't go on like this."

"The show must go on, Maya. Do you think I haven't performed in worse states?"

"Like Alabama? That's the worst state."

"Rim shot," Stacy said.

"Maybe your state is why they canceled your tour and hired the sober, spry Alanis Morissette," Maya said.

"Pffft. She wasn't sober. She was singing about all those jagged pills," Stacy slurred.

Glen was already at the venue. It was just Antonio's, but Maya liked how official it sounded calling it "the venue." He had hooked up the sound system and rigged Maya's laptop up to a projector so she could play some cute bobcat footage to open the show and encourage folks to show up for the town council meeting in three weeks.

So far, from their polling, they had found out that it was

going to be a close vote. Three of the council members were avid hunters/anglers and three were Green Party sustainability freaks. The swing vote would be Mayor Randy McBride, who was a townie, but with a heart. He gave to animal charities, but Maya couldn't tell if it was just to keep them alive so he could hunt them down himself. If they could put enough pressure on the mayor, they could obstruct the ordinance. Concerning fun fact, though: He had a cat named Trigger.

When Maya arrived with Stacy, Sheila was behind the espresso machine pre-pulling shots for the signature drinks they'd dreamed up for the event. Maya had shown her the secret menu from Starbucks—a bunch of rainbow-colored chemical concoctions—and Sheila figured out how to make similar things with healthier ingredients. Her own homemade strawberry compote, for example, or honey from the local apiary, lavender sauce, and sweet potato powder. They figured out that if they frothed the milk enough, they could suspend boba pearls throughout the drink and make it look like it had spots. That one was called "The Boba-Cat."

The plain "BobCattuccino" was a cappuccino with a dolce caramel swirl that Sheila made herself, and "The Kitten" was a decaf vanilla steamed milk with honey drizzle, honey sticks, and chocolate chips. Maya was reluctant to include anything with food coloring, but she knew she had to include something colorful for the freshmen. She also wanted to keep it woodland themed, so they created "The Easter Bunny," which was half all-natural strawberry milk and half purple sweet potato latte. Topped with two floating jelly beans and a homemade Peep.

"And this is coffee, how?" Sheila had wondered.

"I don't know. Just trust me," Maya said. The point was to make it photogenic for TikTok. It didn't have to be coffee, per se.

Now, Maya walked in with her arm around her mother's shoulder and guided her toward the kitchen behind Sheila. She plopped her on a stool and let her slump there.

"Caffeine, stat," Maya said to Sheila.

"What's wrong with her?" Sheila asked, wiping her hands on her apron.

"I'm fine, Sheil. I'm just relaxed," Stacy said, and she tried to cross her legs, but couldn't quite manage getting one leg to lift on top of the other. She finally gave up, sat knock-kneed, and said, "Hi."

Sheila grabbed Stacy by the cheeks with one hand so she could get a better look at her. Sheila looked at Maya with sad eyes and just thought, *Oh amore mio. Not tonight.*

"She took airplane medicine," Maya said.

"Does this look like an airplane to you?" Sheila asked.

"Scary," Stacy said, and Maya couldn't tell if she was referring to Sheila, airplanes, or performing at the coffeehouse, because all three of those things were swirling around in her mother's drunken thought tornado.

"Don't let her have any signature drinks. Just espresso and some water. Maybe a little bread."

At this age, Stacy was supposed to have a platform. A voice, a platform, a foundation, a nonprofit . . . a 501(c)(3), a place to rest on her laurels and put them to use for the betterment of other people. She was supposed to be recycling the fucking LAURELS. She was supposed to be on boards of trustees, for Christ's sake. At the last PTA meeting they asked her what boards she was on, and she almost choked on her seltzer water. "I, um, own a record store, sort of," she mumbled (the bank owned most of it). "Sometimes I teach Zumba." She had $857 in her checking account.

It was Psych 101. Erikson's stages. She was stuck languishing in the seventh stage and couldn't help reminding herself about it. Stage Seven: Generativity or Stagnation. If she failed to *generate* goodwill for the next *generation*, she would stagnate. It was true; fucking Erikson, he was right. She was dead inside, living beneath the weight of a pathetic broken dream. Langston Hughes knew what she felt. When you ceased to dream, or when your dream was deferred, he wrote so famously, "life is a broken-winged bird / That cannot fly."

Tiny violins, she thought. Boo fucking hoo. You couldn't be a Rock Star. Wahhh.

It was not even that she felt entitled to her preposterous dream;

it was just that she had gotten so close; she was playing the big stages; and she didn't know how to do anything else. She couldn't "job." She could barely add. Spreadsheets were beyond her. She wasn't good at keeping track of things and wasn't that what jobs were about? And now when she saw Dolly Parton saving the world, or Joni Mitchell, or Stevie Nicks, or Cyndi Lauper out there rocking their generativity stages, she was just reminded of all her unfulfilled potential gone to waste. She was supposed to be giving back.

Her blackbird was struggling, too. Maya was her blackbird. She'd sung the Beatles' "Blackbird" as a lullaby to Maya every night in the womb. "That's life, baby," she would think. "You need to learn to fly, even though you're inheriting all the brokenness. Even though all conditions conspire against it, you need to learn to fly. No one else can do it for you." And she knew Maya would fly. She knew she would, but first she needed to set a better example. She needed to fly herself. So she googled "How do you give back, when you have nothing left to give?" And she asked the universe, "How do I give back, when I have nothing left to give?" And she waited for an answer.

She could teach music at a nursing home; she could play music at a nursing home; she could be a Big Sister; she could teach people to read; she could read books to blind people; she could walk dogs at the shelter. But Google didn't know how low a person like her could get. Google didn't know how little confidence she had. People in nursing homes had been successful once. What could they learn from her? Little Sisters needed someone successful to show them paths to success. She felt like an impostor, trying to help. But then the universe responded, too. The universe said, "Do it anyway."

So now she had a schedule. Nursing home Monday, literacy tutoring Wednesday, and Friday reading books to the blind. She even started writing a fucking song for the first time in fucking forever. It was called "Life Is a Broken-Winged Bird."

Pounce

Tori opened with a smooth, mellow alto jazz number reminiscent of Adele, but with more gravelly undertones and without Adele's meandering anticlimax. Tori's song, "Bae," actually went somewhere. It had a funky breakdown and a big finish. Even Stacy noticed, and, reaching a new manic state of intoxication, probably from the espresso, she stood up whistling loudly through her fingers and then held up a lighter for an encore.

Everyone turned around to look at her and thought: *What the? Wow. Obnoxious. Who is that? Crazy. The apple doesn't fall far from the tree.* Maya pictured herself physically pushing these thoughts out of her mind with a snow shovel (a tactic Amy had taught her) so that she could take the stage and show her bobcat video. It was well received and elicited a few golf claps, except, again, for Maya's mother, who stood up in the kitchen, whistled and screamed, "Woooo! Save the bobcats!"

Maya gave Glen a look, like, "Deal with her." And he left his sound mixing post to talk Stacy down a bit.

"And now back to the music," Maya announced. Peach set up with Sam acting as roadie and, with their adorable bops, had everyone fixated. The side conversations just came to an immediate halt. Sasha played the bongos and a whole host of other miscellaneous percussion, like windchimes and cowbell and even triangle, which all added layers to the joyful if sarcastic lyrics belted out by Snow and Jackson. Their final tune, "Gap Year Girlfriend," was kind of the Bangles meets Suzanne Vega meets Rex Orange County meets *Sesame Street*. It was retro-bop *Sesame Street* soul. They had their own sound.

Lucy, who was game enough to wear a cat ears headband and a leopard print money belt for making change, had set up her merch table next to the stage because that was the only place it would fit. The bobcat socks were getting some play, but Maya hoped more things would sell at the next break. She gave Lucy a thumbs-up. And Lucy thought, *OMG, Cringey. Thumbs-up back, I guess.*

The plans for saving Lucy, the Bobcat, were moving in the right direction. She shared her poker winnings with Terry. Terry did some research and hired a marketing consultant for her pop-up, which was happening soon at an as yet undisclosed supercool location. At first, Terry gave pause when Lucy showed him her cash winnings for her investment, but then she said, "Don't ask me about my business," and Terry decided not to pry. Lucy's mom was thrilled that the two of them were getting along. They were a great little team. Dare she say, family? And in one fell swoop Maya had saved an entire pounce of Bobcats, which was what a group of bobcats were called when not called a clowder or a clutter.

Maya climbed up to the stage to tell people about the

merch table and announce the next act—Spencer and his magic.

Spencer, dressed in satiny pants, a white shirt, and a yellow kerchief, asked for a brave volunteer from the audience and the room quieted to a muted hush. The audience just stared back at him in silence as if he were an eighth-grade science teacher who had just told a joke. Tyler, who had snuck in through the back door, tried to rescue the whole operation by leaping to the stage in a single bound with his taut high-jumping thighs, volunteering for Spencer's card trick.

Maya almost choked on a boba. Seeing Tyler rush in, bounding to the stage and smiling to the audience and waving at them using his big, knuckly drawing hand that had such a fine sense of line, seemed to have paralyzed all her autonomic systems that were supposed to function on their own without thinking. Breathing, Swallowing, Blinking, all those things suddenly locked up and became impossible.

"You need the Heimlich over there, Storm? Can you speak?" Lucy asked her.

But Maya was in deep. It had been a few days since their date, and she and Tyler saw each other or FaceTimed every night between ten and midnight. It became intimate quickly because Maya knew the workings of Tyler's mind, and contrary to popular opinion, a teenage boy mind could be beautiful and generous and true and naive and curious and funny, which her parents told her was the most important thing for a mind to be, because laughter could heal you when everything else turned to despair.

"Maya!" Lucy said and nodded toward the front. She had been in such reverie about Tyler that she didn't see Spencer wrap up his magic act or witness her mother taking the stage.

"Taking" was sort of an overstatement, though. She was . . . What was she doing? Wooing the stage? Stalking the stage? Teasing the stage? She crept toward it like a drunken bobcat, sort of interpretive dancing, but then as she got to the three small steps that would take her to her destination, she'd spin around and dance the other way.

The crowd began playing into it. Cheering mockingly when she got close to the steps and then letting out a collective "Awww" when she spun away. Finally, they started chanting, "Rock, rock, rock, rock" (short for Pet Rock, Maya guessed), and her mother did it, bounding spryly up the steps and waving at them, but never really looking up from the ground. She was timid, shy, reticent, exactly like a bobcat or Chrissie Hynde.

Stacy plugged in and made some final adjustments, tuning the guitar she called "Madge." Maya had recently learned all her mother's guitars had names. There was Madge, Mr. Stinky, Big Red, Slippery Devil, and Saucy Minx. Maya'd never known about them until this week, when her mother began creepily referring to them as her "siblings." Until now, her "siblings" had been packed away in a storage unit in Trenton so as not to provoke a single memory, thought, or inkling of the rock star career. Madge was her mother's first guitar and the one who was most dear to her—a well-oiled extension of her own body and mind. Stacy and Madge were symbiotically connected at one point, giving each other life . . . each feeding off the other. Intimately related as if they shared DNA.

Anyway, her mom made some final tuning adjustments on Madge, and without even introducing herself, began strumming with some intermittent percussive taps on Madge's body like Ani DiFranco, another of her mom's contemporaries. It was super impressive how much sound she was getting out of this old acoustic—hard to believe all the sound was coming from one person. People in the audience stopped thinking, *Who is this washed-up Boomer Grandma?* In fact, if she hadn't taken the stage when she did, some teens were preparing to start chanting "Boom-er! Boom-er!" Because wickedness was great in the earth.

But her mother's sound disarmed them. Her mother's sound—her fingers now flying up and down Madge's neck, in a display of her classical and flamenco training, which set her apart from the other rock stars in her milieu—was the sound of the universe itself. Her mother's sound was her purpose. And hearing it now, Maya thought it was the purpose to beat all other purposes. Nothing could take the evil out of the humans like music could. Especially this music.

Other rock stars tried, but other rock stars only had three chords, her mother often complained. Current rock stars had no chords. No one played instruments anymore, and it drove her mother crazy, because look at what you could do if you *played* music rather than imitated it with a computer program like Tori did.

Peach collectively looked up at her, their chubby teen faces stretched tight, their eyes glassy and joyful. Sasha posted Snap after Snap to her story, with stickers that read #inspoforever #petrock #imdead #rolemodel #womeninrock #fangirling. But Stacy seemed to appeal to more than just her existing fan base. At the end of "Popsicle" (which Maya pretended had nothing to do with oral sex), the entire house stood and held up their iPhone flashlights for an encore.

At the end of the night, Glen sat with his laptop open, reconciling the receipts. Lucy's merch pulled in $500. Sheila had sold $400 worth of signature drinks and handed out coupons to solicit return customers. Ticket sales brought in another $400. Save the Bobcats! was rolling in dough. They could begin to print legitimate yard signs. Place ads on Facebook where the geezers lived. Maybe even create a radio spot. But best of all, Stacy had sobered up and stood in the corner like the rock star she was, signing autographs and reveling in her renewed personhood. She answered interview questions for Sasha's blog post about her first album, called *Carnage*, which she didn't think anyone remembered anymore. Sasha also promised to TikTok or TikRok about Pet Rock, which, because of her fan base, could cause Stacy's plays on Spotify to skyrocket.

Stacy thanked her but then called Tori over. She whispered something to Tori, which Maya couldn't immediately hear, but which she knew because she knew all things was "I'll introduce you to my agent."

Outside on the lawn, Maya took some breaths and tried to remain present in this moment. The rain had stopped, and the teens poured out of the venue and let themselves feel joy. The music had worked its magic on them; they checked their nihilism for a second and took goofy, jumping selfies in front of the double rainbow that now arched across the river.

The rainbow, Maya thought, could not be a coincidence. She remembered back to her very short stint as a biblical scholar (lol). And right after God explains why they flooded the earth the first time, God says this in Genesis, chapter 9, verses 11–13:

> *Never again will all life be destroyed by the waters of a flood; never again will there be a flood to destroy the earth. . . . I have set my rainbow in the clouds, and it will be the sign of the covenant between me and the earth.*

Maya still wasn't sure about "never again," but for the first time in a long time, she allowed herself to hope.

Shoulder Angel

Maya had been thinking a lot about sex lately. As one does? Probably because of Tyler, not that he'd brought it up or anything. It was just a way that things progressed. Eventually you'd have to approach the idea of sex, wouldn't you? But even her all-knowing whatever-she-was was a little nervous about the whole prospect.

According to popular fiction, she thought, sex was only considered sufficiently "sexy" for women if it flirted dangerously between the boundaries of pleasure and pain. This was the big takeaway if you learned about sex from the sex novels that different generations of mothers left lying around the house. At thirteen, poor Stacy was strongly impacted by the book her mother's generation was reading, which was about a well-endowed caveman who meets a cavewoman raised by Neanderthals.

Maya was similarly troubled by the vampire books her mother left around the house in which a Mormon writer described how a vampire was afraid of injuring his human lover with his supernatural strength, which, while in the throes of passion, would become utterly unrestrained. The bruises left on her body after they finally consummated their love bruised Maya's psyche for a long time.

What would sex be like with whatever *she* was? Maya wondered.

She and Lucy now sat on her bed printing out images for their vision boards. Lucy cut out endless pics of sneakers as well as some runways at fashion week, storefronts on Rodeo Drive, a tasteful gold tooth in a grill, some ideas for tattoos, palm trees, a beach, and a sticker that said WEST COAST. Maya just cut out a picture of Tyler and a bobcat. She was distracted.

Maybe you're, like, an angel, Lucy thought at her out of the blue, as she dipped her finger into her tiny trial-sized Vaseline and swabbed some on her lips, then tilted it toward Maya.

"I'm all set. Angel is unlikely. You've met me, right?"

"No. For real, though," Lucy said out loud. "Maybe you're an angel like my mom used to tell us about. Sent here to keep an eye on folks. My mom's personal interpretation of her Korean Christianity preaches that angels live among us. Maybe you're that. And . . . if you want to stop being an angel, you just have to sin. And usually, sin in whacky Christianity means sex, so maybe if you have sex with a human, you can become, like, a *fallen angel* and lose your power and live among us nasty regular folk and just be nasty."

"That is a preposterous theory."

"It would be fun to try. Just have sex with Tyler, and then maybe you can be free from all this. It must be annoying. Feeling responsible for everyone."

"You have no idea. And what do you mean, 'just'? Tyler is a mystery even when I know everything he's thinking."

Maybe it was true that having sex would finally make her human, Maya thought. Maybe whatever supernatural force that was connecting her to this supernatural knowing would just give up on her and let her walk the earth in ignorant bliss. Maybe she could swap her omniscience for carnal knowledge. It made sense. Sex got rid of a lot of things if you were old enough and in the right mindset. Acne. Neurosis. Anxiety. Insomnia. Maybe all those endorphins people talk about could cure her affliction.

Lucy then thought, *You have to get it over with anyway at some point. We shouldn't go to college like this.* She circled her finger above her nethers.

"Like what?" Maya asked, nervously munching at a handful of Smart Pop and then letting Maurice lick the nasty cheeze from her fingers.

All, like, virginal. So, you might as well.

"I thought you weren't going to college. And we still have a whole year."

Oh yeah. I'm not. You shouldn't go to college like this.

"I'm also not going to college." *Bartender, Acrobat, God . . .*

"Then I'd get to work on that vision board, Cringey," she said and held up a Toyota ad she had just cut out that said: *You don't need to be amazing to start, but you need to start to be amazing.*

"Deep," Maya said sarcastically, and then back to the topic at hand, "Maybe I should do it at prom."

Cringe! That's so cliché, though! Lucy thought, as she visibly cringed this time and sucked the last of the boba up her Bob-Cattuccino straw. *Sheila's getting better at these.*

"Right?"

When Maya walked into her next therapy session with Amy, she found her sitting in her chair in a cap and gown, swaying back and forth to "Pomp and Circumstance," and blowing on a child's party noisemaker. There were even tiny party hats on the elephant tchotchkes.

"What's all this?" Maya asked.

"Congratulations, Maya. You've graduated therapy!" Amy joked and then blew again on the obnoxious noisemaker. "I feel like my work is done here."

"Really? Or is it just that my insurance is running out?"

"Well. Maybe the latter," Amy admitted sheepishly. Her parents' crappy insurance only paid for so many visits a year. "But I feel like you're ready! Don't you? I mean. You've come full circle in understanding the importance of mindfulness, the importance of making connections. And the importance of belonging. And you've figured out how to do those things. You're developmentally right where you should be. Kissing boys, starting clubs, making friends, passing classes. There's nothing more I can do for you until you start to screw up your marriage someday."

"I appreciate your honesty."

"Well. It behooves me to be honest since you can read right through me."

"We didn't really land on a diagnosis for that."

"I don't think that matters. I think you have power and you're using it for good. You're learning to be more positive. How's it going with emptying all your negative thoughts into your negativity journal?"

"I excel at that," Maya joked. "I'm going to need a new one because it's almost full."

"It's good, right?" Amy said, hopefully. "You get it out of your system and then close the book on it. Start fresh in a new day."

"Sure. It's fine."

"What's the matter? This is a joyous occasion," Amy said, giving a sad, meager blow to the noisemaker.

"Well, I mean, you're rejecting me. Abandoning me. I feel unmoored. I got a little accustomed to this," Maya said, picking the baby elephant up off the coffee table and stroking its back.

"You're not unmoored, Maya. You've done the work to build supports. And I'm only a phone call away."

"What if I'm an angel," Maya said. She wasn't ready to say goodbye, so she tried to start up another discussion. "You know, just hanging around down here in some sort of purgatorial existence watching out for humankind, but, like, I'm not really supposed to get involved, per se, because my power is to know and to witness or something weird."

Here we go again with the supernatural identities, Amy thought.

"There's one sect that thinks the purpose of angels is to lead each person to good, by directing their own thoughts.

You know. Like those cartoons where the character has an an-gel and devil on each shoulder. That could be me. I could be a shoulder angel trying to help people follow their consciences and make the right decisions. But how does a teenage girl know what the right decision is? I can't even decide what to have for breakfast in the morning. I'd rather just get rid of this. . . . And I think I have a way out."

"Meaning?" In her line of business, Amy didn't love people talking about ways out.

"No, Amy, not the ultimate out. A way out of this predic-ament. My friend Lucy says that angels can lose their powers by having sex with humans, so if I am an angel, I just need to have sex, right? And then poof, god will forsake me and let me be. I really can't stand it anymore."

"That seems like an oversimplification of a mythological process that doesn't actually happen in the world. . . . Maya, are you trying to tell me that you want to have sex?"

"Oh, you silly psychologist humans," Maya joked. "You misunderstand. I'm trying to tell you that living this way is still sometimes unbearable. What other people think, espe-cially what other people think about me, is not supposed to be any of my business."

Can't argue with that, Amy thought, empathizing, imag-ining for a second what even her best friends thought about her in their free time and then shaking it off. She really didn't want to know.

"I think I might do it, though. And I'll have no one to talk to after it's done."

"Do what?"

"It, Amy. The deed. The, um, nasty, as they say."

"Ew. Who says that? You want to have sex? With Tyler?"

"Yes."

"Then that, too, is developmentally appropriate. As long as it's your decision and you feel supported in it by your partner. And, like I said, you use birth control, for god's sake. You're using birth control, right? Because I can hook you up with . . ."

"Got it covered. Ha. Pun intended." Maya laughed. "But, do you think it will cure me?" Maya asked, feeling ridiculous. Hope is a thing with feathers.

"Again. I don't think you have a disease. You have a talent that you're learning to use and manage in the world," Amy said, but in her head, she was calculating recidivism rates for hospitalized juveniles.

"You make it sound like I'm freakishly good at crossword puzzles or something. It's a little more than that," Maya said.

"To answer your question . . . I don't know if it will help with your situation. I doubt it, but if that's the only reason you're doing it," Amy put "it" in finger quotes, "then I think that's a bad idea."

"No. I like him a lot."

"Aw."

"Why does everyone keep saying that?! It's infantilizing."

"Sorry. I know this is very serious," Amy said, trying to wipe the smile off her face. "Anyway, Maya. That's time." Maya could see that Amy was caught off guard by her emotions. *I really loved this one*, Amy thought.

"Love you, too, Amy," Maya said. "And hey. Do you know how many species of tigers are now endangered because of deforestation? Your kids are going to think of tigers as mythical animals like dragons or unicorns or griffins. They're not going to believe they were real creatures that roamed the actual earth. Eat vegetarian."

"Will do, Maya. I'm here if you need me."

Awards Season

Maya thought he'd forgotten about it, but the next day after school, Glen did decide to go ahead with the annual Stormies. Maya could tell because Maurice—as he tumbled across the lawn in his normal exuberant greeting that afternoon—was decked out in his white bow tie.

A red shag carpet remnant lay awkwardly across the sidewalk pathway. It looked like Glen had tried to cut it into a runner shape to fit the path, but it was too difficult to cut, so he just covered one giant rectangle of the sidewalk with it and called it a day.

"Do we have to do this?" Maya said. She came into the house holding Maurice as he wriggled and licked her entire face, and her father offered her some champagne from a silver tray. "It's been a long day."

"We can't put it off any longer. We need to uphold our annual traditions, creating bonding opportunities and fond memories of family togetherness so that you can go out into the world feeling like you're grounded and special and have somewhere to belong."

There's that word again, Maya thought. Belong. "Couldn't we just go to the Jersey Shore like most families?" she asked, and then, "Wait, are *you* reading from a manual, now?"

"No," Glen said, as he slid a parenting book beneath the console table with his foot. "I have great parenting instincts." Maya could sense him second-guessing himself, though. He had some parenting regrets. *Why didn't I volunteer as soccer coach, or build sets for the school play, or let things slide instead of starting so many petty arguments? She'll be gone in a year or so and I think I messed it up,* he thought. *I could have stepped up to the plate. Dadded up.*

Maya could actually feel his heart darken and sink. He did dad up. He was the one who took her to the woods and helped her find some temporary purpose. So, she rubbed his upper arm and said, "You're a great parent, Dad, I agree."

Stacy came down the stairs, then, wearing an aquamarine sequined gown. Thin rectangles of sequin stretched vertically toward her neck, stopping at different heights as if they were measuring some statistic in a bar graph across her chest. The whole thing was held together with a "nude" mesh body stocking two shades darker than her natural skin tone. It was like a bad ice-skating outfit; the sleeves even ended in a point with an elastic ring that looped around her middle finger to keep it all in place.

Her father catcalled and dropped his tray of champagne to get his phone and take pics. "Ms. Storm, over here!" he yelled like a fake paparazzo.

"Where did you get that thing?" Maya asked.

"It's a rental," her mom said, posing on the last stair for a glamour shot. "They do that now on the internet. Like tuxes. Yours is on your bed."

Hers. Great. Hers was a whole different kind of nightmare. A completely unforgiving copper silk number with a plunging neckline to her diaphragm. Her mother had even sprung for a rented wristlet bag in faux white fur, a white fur wrap, and some chandelier earrings that hung to her shoulders. There was no way in hell she was going to let them see her in this getup. But she knew how relentless they could be, so she was going to have to compromise.

She sausaged herself into the dress, whose high slits up the side thankfully let her thigh meat burst out of the seams a little, so she could walk. It fit her like a floor-length loincloth, she thought. She didn't dare attempt the heels, opting instead for Doc Martens, and then she topped the whole thing off with an oversized gray sweatshirt that said, simply, COLLEGE. To appease her mother, she swept her long bangs to the side of her forehead and clipped them back with a fancy rhinestoned barrette.

Her parents were playing some John Williams hits compilation as she came down the stairs. Glen took pictures while Stacy swung a flashlight back and forth over the ceiling to mimic a movie premiere spotlight.

"Ooo, I love how you improvised," Stacy said when she saw the sweatshirt, and she actually stopped herself from any critical thinking for once, even though Maya knew she must have hated the sweatshirt.

The "dais" was set up in front of the fireplace (a couple of cardboard boxes topped with a TV tray, held together with duct tape). On the mantel, Glen had lined up about seven or eight Stormie "trophies" (Maya's old Bratz dolls spray-painted copper and Gorilla-glued to some of Glen's old hockey pucks). Each hockey puck had a label stuck to the front on which you could write the category of your impromptu "award" in Sharpie.

"How long are these ceremonies?" Maya asked. "I have a lot of homework." As if she would actually do homework, especially on a Friday night. She actually had a lot of Bobcats to save. Ella B. did not get invited to prom. Kira M. did not get invited to the prom pregame, which was a fate even worse, apparently. Jack B. just got his scatterplot back from the college counselor and his college prospects were not at all what he'd thought they would be. Nearly everything was a "reach." Etc. Etc. She was in the business of adjusting expectations.

And she hadn't heard from Bobby in a while. Plus, she had to check with the printer about the lawn signs for the actual bobcats, because the town council meeting was coming up fast.

"Ah, well then, we'll forgo the monologue," Glen said, tossing aside the remarks he'd scribbled on some notebook paper. "Welcome to the annual Stormie Awards," and he paused for a second, staring at Stacy, waiting for her to pick up on his cue.

"Oh!" she said, and then she fumbled with her phone and pressed some button that played fake applause.

"You guys really, really have too much time on your hands," Maya said.

Maya's phone buzzed from inside her fur pouch. It was a Snap from Lucy. My mom just threatened to shut down my whole business enterprise because I got a B on my history paper. How's your day going? (This, Maya had learned, was sarcastic and rhetorical teen-speak that did not require a response, so instead of writing something sincere about her day, she just snapped a photo of her barrette.)

Whoa, Lucy snapped back. What's happening over there?

Save Me, Maya wrote.

That looks like a good prom barrette. Excited for prom? Lucy snapped.

Maya couldn't decide which meme to send back. Obama Face Palm or *Home Alone* Kid Aftershave Face that said, *What have I gotten myself into?*

"And a friendly reminder," Glen announced from the dais, "for the enjoyment of all who have come to the show, please turn off your cell phones, and there is no flash photography."

He glared at Maya, so she quickly chose the Obama and hoped it wasn't too cultural appropriation-y, because she sincerely loved Obama so freaking much and wanted to be able to use his meme always.

Lucy shot back the standard You Got This meme . . . the toddler in the green sleeves holding his fist in front of his face.

Only if you're styling me, Maya wrote back.

To which Lucy replied with: {photo of Awkwafina at the Met Gala}

Glen loudly cleared his throat, so Maya tucked her phone back into her bag.

"Our first category for the evening is Best Hill to Die On," he said as he wrote the name of the category on the first Stormie. "This award goes to the most stubborn holding of one's ground, and the nominees are . . . Stacy for that time in December when she refused to do the dishes for fourteen whole days because she was tired of being the one who most often did the dishes. Or team Maya-and-Glen for refusing to wash dishes during those fourteen days and instead going to the supermarket to buy paper plates and utensils to use until the standoff was over. And the winner is . . ." Glen pretended to open an envelope. "Stacy Storm! Because of her tenacity, we now have a functional system for KP and dishes never sit overnight in the sink." He pressed his applause button on his phone and Stacy shuffled forward in her awkward gown. The mini train gathered up a dog toy, a balled-up sock, and a kernel of popcorn, and dragged them behind her to the dais.

"Boo." Maya laughed. "You're always on her side," she joked, and because Stacy won, it was her turn to award someone.

"The next category is Best Second Effort. This award goes to the person or animal who despite all odds against them decided to try again and not completely give up, even though trying is so fucking hard." Her mom choked up for a second, and it was a rare moment when Maya felt seen. Like her mom saw how difficult it was for her to be in the world, even though she didn't know exactly why. "The nominees are Maurice," she looked into Maya's eyes and thought, simply, *I love you.* "Maurice," she repeated, "for the time when he couldn't decide where to hide his bone for about thirty minutes. He almost just gave up and dropped his bone on the floor, but then, in a moment of divine inspiration, decided to place it in the umbrella urn in the entryway, where it remains to this day, covered in a giant dust bunny. . . . Or Maya, for persevering through her therapies and playing by the rules and getting herself through high school one day at a time. And the winner is Maya."

Her mom rushed this big reveal because she seemed to suddenly realize she was onstage and vulnerable and feeling emotions and she wanted to put an end to it. She was actually having stage fright at the Stormies.

"Speech, speech," her dad said, but Maya declined and instead gave the next award for Best Song Parody Created on the Fly to Glen and his version of "All I Want for Christmas Is You," which in his rendition was about trying to get through Christmas as a Jewish person. (I don't care that much for Christmas / That's because I am a Jew . . . etc.)

For the entertainment portion of the evening, Stacy played a little thing she'd been working on since the coffeehouse and Glen told a few terrible jokes. In spite of herself, Maya felt safe and at home. Even though she had to witness her parents' constant, nagging self-doubt—their anxieties, and quirks, and criticisms—they were her weirdos, and if she had the opportunity to choose her parents from a bargain bin of parents, she'd choose her weirdos all over again.

Maximalism

Lucy had come prepared. Out of the Toyota Corolla she pulled sacks and sacks of clothing and embellishments.

"We're going maximalist," she said, as she spread her wares on the old, scratchy plaid sleeper sofa in the living room. "Does this have bedbugs?" she said, pausing.

"There's no telling," Maya said, and Lucy just shrugged and continued her busy work.

She laid out two stretch velvet gowns in different shades of neon leopard print, one pink and one blue. Next to them, she plopped two cropped denim jackets with shearling sleeves and slogans painted on the back panels. One said I DO CARE, DON'T YOU? and the other, of course, SAVE THE BOBCATS.

"Are you sure Tyler is okay with this?"

"Hundred Percent," Maya said. Maya had explained to Tyler that she was *going* to prom with him but *entering* the prom with Lucy. Lucy needed some backup and didn't want to walk in alone, and since it was Junior Prom, they didn't feel the pressure to have photo shoots at each other's houses and whatnot. Maya would walk in with Lucy. Plus it was sort of a publicity moment. They would be wearing all Gilding the Monster designs and needed to strut in together.

"It will be a buddy operation," Lucy said. "We're going to Bonnie and Clyde the prom, or Thelma and Louise it, or iCarly and Sam it. Take it by Storm, or whatever. Get it? And then you can do your pathetic straight cisgender slow dance with Tyler."

After conceding to a quick photo shoot where Stacy, Glen, Jeanne, and Terry clucked around them like chickens with cameras in Maya's front yard, they climbed into the Corolla and descended upon the venue, which was their high school. They de-Corollaed and stomped kind of slow motion, breeze through their hair, in their bedazzled platform sneakers painted with the faces of the new vavniks, Malala and Greta. They were doing it. Taking the Junior Prom by proverbial storm. Creating a moment for Lucy's brand. Their hi-lo street couture seemed to be just what everyone needed right now. As they strutted, Maya read the thoughts. The "basics" were seething with envy, and she tried not to let this bring her joy. *I breathe in*, she thought.

They made it through the balloon arches that led to the school gym and stood in front of the photographer's back-drop in ironic eighties poses: Maya behind Lucy with her hands looped around Lucy's waist, Lucy pretending to pin a boutonniere on Maya's jacket, a *Charlie's Angels* back-to-back shot holding pretend guns in their outstretched arms, and a looking-over-their-shoulders, finally, backs-to-the-camera shot so they could capture the slogans on their jackets.

Then Tyler, in a perfectly fitted royal blue skinny suit that must have been Italian and tailored exquisitely to his measurements, approached the backdrop, extended his hand, and said, "May I have this dance?"

As he took Maya in, most of what was going on in his head was just white-hot desire, but then when a thought did sneak through, it was a Lisa Simpson quote. "She's not plain, she's beautiful!" It was a line where the writers of *The Simpsons* mocked the predictable transformation a woman made in a nineties rom-com. Maya knew Tyler meant it as both a joke to himself and a compliment. He had never thought of her as plain.

"You're beautiful," he said.

"You clean up pretty well yourself," she said back.

They danced a little. Slowly at first. She was close enough to smell his aftershave, feel his rough five-o'clock shadow graze against her cheek. The umami was powerful. Then thankfully, because they either needed to get a room or get a break from the umami, everyone started dancing for real. Everyone danced because the prom committee, led by Sasha, resident music historian, had come to their senses and realized that disco had never sucked! So they revived it at prom with a disco theme. Some folks even zoomed by on roller skates. Maya bopped with Lucy, keeping her eyes closed and letting the music wash over her. She let the music drown out other people's thoughts.

Then she opened her eyes and realized she was bopping alone for a second, but she tried not to panic. She scanned the sea of glistening hair products until she zoomed in on Lucy holding hands with a tall girl in a black silk tuxedo with no top underneath. They all had their phones out on the dance floor because they couldn't just "be here now," so Maya shot Lucy a bulging eyes emoji along with a smiley face with star eyes, to which Lucy responded: (eggplant emoji).

Maya tingled with happiness for Lucy, who was, for the first time, taking an actual risk and testing out a crush that was not on an eco-celebrity. She was basking in her happiness for Lucy when Tyler scooped her up from behind and carried her out the door to the parking lot.

....

Maybe it was because it happened in the Hyundai, but the first time Maya and Tyler finally had sex, it was awkward and terrible and irritating.

They embarked upon their normal kissing and fondling routine, which Maya couldn't enjoy because she kept hearing Lucy jokingly refer to it as "heavy petting," a term that the seventy-year-old librarian who got roped into teaching their sex ed class last marking period kept using as a euphemism for hand jobs.

Have fun heavy petting Lucy had texted when she saw them leave the gymnasium.

Remember about the pre-ejaculate that resides in the meatus she texted, again quoting the Librarian.

Quiz: True or False you can get pregnant just from the pre-ejaculate that resides in the meatus she texted, just to drive the point home.

Stop saying meatus! Maya managed to text back as they

drove to the woods, which is where Maya had requested that it happen. The woods. In nature.

Tyler parked in the Delaware Canal State Park lot in a forested section of the river upon Maya's request. She hoped hearing and breathing in the rapid tumbling water would charge her with negative ions and render her energized and with a sense of well-being. The many health benefits of running water were a thing she knew about because of knowing all the things.

She did feel pretty relaxed and alive in the beginning. Her bra was unhooked, and her breasts were sprung free from their padded foam fortresses. Then as Tyler shimmied his pants down, his penis sprung forth from the confines of his tight, skinny tux pants. It was an exciting moment. The springing forth of the penis. Everything was sprung and out in the open. And the textures of things were different from what Maya expected. Some things unexpectedly soft. The inside of his forearms. The taut skin between his hip bones. Others impossibly hard. His chin. His knuckles that bent into different creases of her body. His knee. And the obvious insistence of his erection. How was there no bone in there? They shuddered as they caressed each other and eventually took different body parts into their mouths. She felt that thing: the light tingling effervescence mixed with the heavy weight of their combined life forces. Matter and antimatter colliding.

The gushing tumbling water did little to drown out Tyler's thoughts, however. She knew his every move, and everything seemed to be going as planned according to the porn sequences that Maya had seen flash through all the boy brains in the hallways. There was a certain predictable sequence. And Tyler followed it to a T, even while sometimes stopping to ask her what felt good, which kind of embarrassed Maya because she didn't know yet, and also because she was anxious to get it over with.

Could she really join the ranks of humanity by engaging in this base, most human of acts? Could intercourse tame her brain? Could it make her a better dancer? Could it increase her breast size? Could it finally, finally quiet her mind? Why didn't she know this? Would she bask quietly in a flushed and contented afterglow? Would she need a cigarette?

A little prematurely Maya climbed on top of Tyler in the driver's seat, and he reached over her head to grab a condom that was held to the visor by a rubber band. He ripped it open with his teeth and rolled it on just in time for Maya to grab him and try to plunge on top of him.

She wasn't ready, or he was too big like the caveman in the caveman sex novels. It wasn't working, so Tyler suggested they climb into the hatchback and lie down. He was nervous about making this a memorable experience for her. He was regretting abiding by her request to be outdoors in nature. He should have gotten them a room at the Times Square Marriott or something.

She saw this in his mind and said out loud, "Oh god no. This is perfect, Tyler. I love the Hyundai." But it was the wrong thing to say because he thought she was being facetious, and she saw him fret about losing steam.

She stuck her tongue into his ear and then blew into it and

whispered, "We got this." She lay back on the cheap, scratchy trunk upholstery. The hatch was open and the cool spring rushing river air with all its negative ions swirled around them. She grabbed him and put him in the right spot, then saw him think only of her as he slid inside her and tried to squeakily move in and out.

When he was finished, and he lay curled beside her with his lips pressed against the back of her head, she could detect none of his thoughts. She listened (or whatever the verb was for what she could do with people's thoughts) and she detected nothing but the crickets and the rushing water and the breeze crackling a bit through the trees. It was quiet. She heard crickets. An owl. Cars passing above them on the road. None of Tyler's thoughts. Maybe Jeanne's whacky Christianity was right.

Was she cured? She had sinned and was forsaken. Her stint as an angel of god was over and she could fully join the ranks of blissfully ignorant humans who had no idea what horrific havoc they were wreaking upon themselves. How joyous not to understand the consequences of human behavior. How liberating to become an asshole among assholes. What a relief! She could stop knowing what old men wanted to do to her. She could stop hearing what young boys presumed about her lack of intelligence. She could stop feeling the jealous spite of women her age who had no path to power other than trying desperately to be liked. She could stop seeing the wickedness that was great in the earth.

She unfurled herself from inside Tyler's loose embrace and ran to the river to baptize herself into her new existence. She needed a ceremony (and she'd heard that you should always pee after sex). She dunked herself and then rose in a pool of slowly moving water between the rocks. She stood with one arm draped across her breasts and a hand instinctively covering her vag, her wavy strawberry hair snaked around her shoulders, when Tyler appeared at the bank of the river. A quiet shadow. He said nothing at all, but then she heard (or whatever the verb was for what she could do with people's thoughts), *Holy shit! Botticelli.* The Birth of Venus.

"Fuck," Maya whispered.

Turns out that some boys think *nothing at all* for about twenty minutes after they finish . . .

In these twenty minutes Maya assumed she was cured, but Tyler was, in fact, simply marinating blissfully in the nothing box of his brain. And now here he was using the art box of his artist brain, making references to art that Maya could unfortunately hear and see and identify. *Fuck*, she thought.

She didn't know if she was more upset about her body looking to him like the well-fed early Renaissance ideal . . . the pale glow, the smallish breasts, the thick thighs, the slightly rounded stomach and hips . . . or the fact that she was doomed forever to continue hearing all the thoughts from all the people all the time. Sex didn't work.

She climbed out of the water clumsily, stumbling, stomping and bruising her feet on the rocks, mumbling "shit, shit, shit," and Tyler stopped idealizing her and thinking of her as a Renaissance icon goddess. He wrapped her in his flannel shirt.

"What's the matter?" he asked. But what he thought was

Oh shit. I heard this can happen. You deflower them and they go off the deep end. Ophelia, etcetera. To stop him, Maya kissed him hard on the mouth in a powerful, almost bruising kiss, his sandpapery new beard scratching her face a little raw. It was different but it was all still powered by the umami force. It felt right and necessary.

He looked down at her with that way of looking that he had, and she swung her wet finger beneath the definition of his bare pectoral muscles. A drop of the river water ran down his stomach and she knelt in front of him and caught it with her tongue, which she continued looping and kissing around his abs.

They ended up back at the Hyundai because she wanted to try again. It was easier this time and they found rhythm and moved through all the different "styles." Doggie, missionary, Harry, etc. She almost laughed out loud when that word came to her head.

"What?" he asked.

"Nothing. Proceed," she said, kissing him.

And so he did. He never grabbed her menacingly by the hair or the throat, which is what she saw a lot of boys fantasize about. He began to follow her lead, because she suddenly seemed to be getting a feeling for what she wanted. She lost track of his thoughts. He touched her with his knuckly fingers while at the same time finding places deep inside her she hadn't discovered on her own. She came to that place where she realized what all the fuss was about. The little death. Maybe *this* had to happen. Maybe now she could be freed from other people's thinking. She'd have to wait twenty minutes to find out.

But Tyler in his final throes had a thought that she heard. It was a beautiful thought. He thought, *I love this girl.*

He lay, slumped on top of her, his head turned to the side on her chest. A little lump caught in her throat as she combed her fingers through his thick black hair.

"I thought you would be happier. Did I do anything wrong?" And the hope in Maya's heart—the hope she could get rid of her affliction and stop being such a weirdo—that hope, like the last shriveled brown and battered leaf that clung desperately to the branch in late November, gave up then, and broke away for good.

The sadness mixed with the euphoria of feeling Tyler's head, a heavy grounding weight on her chest. She wasn't alone. It was all so bittersweet, which is what life should feel like if you can take it all in at once. Maya was living life.

He let her keep his flannel as they drove through the black dark of the woods and he tried to cross the deep chasm of disconnect that inexplicably, to him, cracked open between them. "You're okay, right?" he asked. "We're okay? I mean, that was good, right? We shared a good thing?"

"Yes," Maya said. "It was totally consensual, obviously, if you're worried about that. I wanted to drink the tea."

"The tea?"

"Didn't they show you that consent video in seventh grade? About how you wouldn't pour tea down someone's throat if they didn't want tea?"

"I went to public school, Maya."

"Okay, well. Tonight was great, thank you! I'm happy. I am. It might not seem like it, but this is the happiest I've ever been," she said, and she hugged him around his bicep and put her head down on his shoulder.

The Life Rafts

She wasn't *regretting* losing her virginity to Tyler. That was definitely the move. *I mean. Look at him,* she thought. But she was still regretting that it hadn't had the desired side effect of eliminating her weirdness. Which was a message for girls everywhere, she thought. Doing "it" will never eliminate your weirdness. You're stuck with your own weird. Embrace it; your weirdness makes you, you.

In the car, after they had gotten dressed, Maya's phone had buzzed with a text from Lucy.

GET BACK HERE. THE PARTY'S MOVED TO THE BRIDGE AND IT'S HIGH-KEY OFF THE HOOK! NEXT-LEVEL HEDONISM. {photo of flushed-faced Lucy and Ruby, prom hair akimbo, glistening with sweat and swinging maniacally from a rope swing over the river}

They reached the dugout near the river, beneath the bridge, a little beach, where the bass of someone's car speakers shook the ground and echoed out over the water, rippling the current.

It was cool and damp and clammy and cleansing to be near the river. There was a richness and mineral clarity to the smell of the water, filtered as it was around rocks and through soft bright green vegetal funk, mermaid hair. It was Maya's happy place.

She looked under the intersecting riveted steel girders of the rusted bridge and noticed Tyler had tagged two bobcats here! Which was a great spot to bring their message to the fisherpeople, but how did he get up there?

She sauntered into the mix of teens, looking like some harlot from a saloon in a movie about the Wild West, bouncing every now and then off Tyler's shoulder. "You okay?" he asked. "I'm keeping my eye on you," he said to her as they crested a small hill and saw Lucy still swinging from the rope.

"Cringe!" Lucy said, as she swung toward them on the rope swing. She said something else, but they couldn't hear her as the pendulum swung her away. She dismounted across the way, and then ran to Maya, hugging her and then holding her at arm's distance, taking her in like a big sister. "How was it? I mean spare me the details. But tell me everything. But. Yeah. Never mind. I don't really want to know."

"I'll go get us a drink," Tyler said. "But I'll be right back." He did that thing where he used his peace fingers to point at his eyes and then Maya's eyes, to reiterate that he was keeping an eye on her.

"It didn't work," Maya said.

"The sex?" Lucy asked. Someone's red bra had just sling-shotted onto Lucy's head and she removed it nonchalantly and dropped it to the ground.

"No, the sex was, like, um, really good. Especially the second time," Maya said, taking a step forward before a sweaty shirtless boy, still in his bow tie, almost landed on her vavnik sneaker.

"Hey! Watch the kicks!" Lucy screamed at him. "Second! time! You are my queen," Lucy said, bowing. "What didn't work?"

"I thought it would like, quiet my mind or something. But it's almost made it sharper."

Ah. A woman's intuition, since you're a woman now, Lucy thought at her and then nodded knowingly.

"Shut up."

"You do look a little more womanly. You're glowing," she said, curling a loop of Maya's sex-bedraggled hair around her finger.

"You said it might make me fall from grace if I, like, sinned," Maya said, blushing.

"In whacky Christianity! That shit is not real. Sex is not a sin. Well, I wasn't exactly sure, since I was raised on that stuff, but now you've proven it! It's not a sin."

"And I'm not an angel."

"No, you're a dirty girl. Come on."

"Come on what?"

"Let's dance!"

Maya closed her eyes and tried to feel the music and avoid getting trampled by the people jumping up and down, which was the only move some people had aside from some weird hokeypokey hand gestures they learned on TikTok. But the jumping up and down worked. It was cathartic enough and this here debauchery was all about catharsis. They may as well enjoy it as much as they could because the cops would probably break it up soon, so they had to cathart quickly. Leave it all on the dirt dance floor.

At first, Maya's cheeks hurt from smiling so much, but then something happened to her. She could feel the alcohol she'd drunk in the car with Tyler slowly leeching through all her cell membranes, relaxing her and making her movements heavy and slow.

"You okay?" Tyler asked her.

Maya bent over and tried to breathe. *I breathe in. I breathe out,* she said to herself, but she was bombarded with dark thoughts.

Mean girls aimed specific thoughts directly at her. *Slut,* mostly. And *What does he see in her?* And *Who does she think she is?* They brought back her old nickname *Maya the Pariah.* Thoughts are not the truth, she reminded herself, but then other more vague thoughts joined together and pulsed inside her body: *Help me. Help me. Help me.* She pulled up an image of her spreadsheet and tried to mentally add people to her list, but it was too much.

"Let's go get some water," Tyler said, and thought, *Shit. I was just starting to have a good time. Chicks cannot hold their smoke.* It was a line he stole from *The Breakfast Club,* which his mother made him watch with her once in a pathetic attempt at mother-son bonding.

Maya straightened up. "You stay here, Tyler. I'll be right back, promise. I just need a second," she said. A terrible thing was happening, but she couldn't pinpoint what. She couldn't just sense the thoughts. Because of the alcohol or the recent loss of her virginity, becoming a woman with full-on women's intuition, she could Feel the thoughts inside her. She ran to the top of a hill to get air, and all the sadness and badness that people were trying to hide by jumping mindlessly up and down on the dance floor balled up inside her solar plexus and she thought she might puke.

She drifted farther away from the cavorting teens, and something drew her to an unlit corner of the woods where she found it. The source of her nausea and anxiety.

She didn't scream, because she was good in an emergency.

She sobered up, went into crisis mode, and *handled* it. She grabbed the cat's back paws, his oversized toe beans still warm, and dragged him deeper into the woods, then covered him with leaves and sticks. Who would do this? she wondered. When the shock wore off, she realized she was crying, anointing him with her tears. But what good was that going to do? He laid still: a muscular golden bobcat, seemingly in the prime of life, still thick with his winter coat . . . a bullet hole shot directly through his head.

This is not real, she told herself. She shook it off, wiped away her tears, and focused on the warm glow of the bonfire and sounds of celebration still emanating from the water's edge. She locked this trauma in a special part of her brain, like Tyler would do. A place where it would not get out. She shivered and twirled and did some karate chops and a high kick to purge the horror out of her body.

Then, on some kind of instinct, she looked up and noticed Bobby. He had climbed up under the bridge in the same way Tyler must have, because he stood precariously on a tiny ledge twenty feet above them right next to the bobcat graffiti. Every once in a while he leaned out over the water, gripping tightly to the edges of a girder, and then pulled himself back in as if he were dancing with it.

"Bobby!" Maya screamed, but there was no way he could hear her over the rush of the water and the din of their reveling classmates. "Fuck," she said, and she sent a little silent apology to Lucy as she ripped the entire side seam of her skirt and tied the dress together in a big knot below her waist, then started climbing.

Adrenaline is such a flex, she thought, because it pumped through her veins, destroyed her fear of heights, and brought about a singular focus: Get Bobby off the Bridge. She didn't even feel her legs as they powered up the side of a giant piece of infrastructure like Spider-Man. And like Spider-Man, she was responsible for this shit, right? Great power. Great responsibility. She didn't know what was bothering him right now, but she had been the one who convinced Bobby he was okay on the outside. She had been the one who was egotistical enough to think she could cure him. She had spun this fucking web of Spidey disaster.

She tried to be casual about it as she got closer and called up to him, "Hey, Bobby! What's happening? How's the weather up there? Want some company?" But then the breeze blew a barrette out of her hair, and she looked down, watching it fall and fall until it finally plopped into the water. She let out a little gaspy scream, and held on tighter as her hands began to sweat.

"Maya, hey. Um. I'm fine. Just need some alone time," he said, but he was slurring and swaying and so close to slipping and falling. She could tell he had been crying again. His face was red and splotchy like it was when she'd met him, and it was entirely wet with tears.

"Bobby, look at me. You feel so much. That's such a good thing. Hold on," she said, "I'm coming up!" She kept climbing, her Greta Thunberg vavnik sneaker finding footholds on the cross rails, and she kept talking as she climbed. "It's okay to have feelings."

Maya suddenly realized what the patriarchy tried to do to you. If you existed outside the binary, it refused to even see you, for one thing. But it was detrimental and dehumanizing even to the boys who seemed to benefit from it. While girls are told they're hysterical and therefore *become* hysterical, boys are told they are tough and unfeeling, and therefore that's what they sometimes become. Numb to their own emotions. Angry and impatient with others. Walking around in a kind of shell-shocked Frankenstein-monster fugue. If a feeling does leak into their consciousness, like a curl of smoke seeping beneath the door of a house on fire, the adolescent male, having no framework with which to deal with it, becomes ashamed for having it at all. He tries to stomp it out. "It's okay to have feelings," Maya repeated to Bobby.

Even now, other people's thoughts drifted up above the woods, innocently at first, like little blinking fireflies, and then buzzing furiously around her head in a swarm. She couldn't escape them. The sex didn't work. The alcohol made it worse. She was suddenly so tired. Bobby was right. Nothing changed. It was all too overwhelming. Hope drained from her body.

But not all of it, dammit. Just like in the Emily Dickinson poem that haunted her recently, a tiny bit of hope remained. Even in "the chillest land" and "on the strangest sea," even when she never fed it a crumb, there was still hope. She tried again. With a final surge and a gymnastic flair from her secret acrobat capabilities, Maya hoisted herself to Bobby's ledge and stood next to him, back to the giant bridge support.

"I promised to be your friend. I let you down." She continued to send a message to his brain, *Wait for me.* "Bobby," Maya said and was overcome with a feeling of powerlessness. Bobby was her OB Original Bobcat, and she had to save him. Another tear dropped from his chin and fell fell fell to the water below.

"Listen, I just figured something out," she said, taking baby steps.

"What?" he said, blinking his eyes, trying to get the tears to stop. "What did you figure out?"

"Having hope is more important than getting what you hope for," she said, and as she said it, she realized it was true.

"You can't just have hope," Bobby complained.

"It's always there, Bobby, you just have to stop turning away from it. Look down," she said.

Beneath them, Eddie had rallied the troops. Drunken teens, suddenly sober, gathered around the base of the bridge and listened to Eddie as he barked the commands of his rescue operation. A gaggle of swimmers dove into the river and tread in the current as they held in place the three impossibly giant inflatable rafts people had hauled to the celebration . . . a unicorn, a flamingo, and a sprinkle doughnut with a bite taken out of the side. Tyler was already halfway up the pillar screaming her name.

Counterintuitively, Maya relaxed! They could all relax because people were good to one another in a crisis. God wasn't a single being who could prevent bad things from happening. God was the best in people. God was ever-present in the way that we help one another when bad things happen. It was not about preventing the flood, it was about cleaning it up. Or something. She was working on it.

"Look at me," she said, hoping she could pull off another healing by staring into his eyes. She did it once; she could do it again. She could ease his pain about Eliza and fitting in to the broscape or whatever he was worried about. She could show him that the world needed his magic. She had this.

He looked at her kind of sideways and ashamed. It was difficult at this angle, but she finally caught his sideways glare, and she gasped.

Wait. What? Maya thought. She watched his face curl in on itself, weeping as he remembered it. He didn't want to do it, he thought. They dared him. He had no choice. He was weak. Why couldn't he say no to them? They made him send the death threat from proudgunner23457. They suggested he kill the bobcat. And, she gasped for a second and grabbed his giant wrist. *Oh my god.*

She watched him replay it in his mind. He was in a group. A gaggle, or what do you call a drunken crowd of football players? A squad. A brawl. An offense. He was in an offense of mean football players trampling through the woods, carrying cases of beer on their shoulders and tossing the empties behind them as they went as if they were scattering seed. They suddenly reached a clearing and handed Bobby, who was up for team captain next year, a crowbar.

"No," he'd said, when he realized where they were. But they were drunk and insistent and, frankly, bigger than him. They smeared his face with camo paint. They told him it was tradition. A football initiation. And then they watched and egged him on as he trashed Scott's camp. He swung the crowbar, screaming like an animal so he wouldn't cry, leaving Scott homeless on the night of the flood.

He wasn't supposed to die, Bobby thought. *I'm sorry, Maya.* Maya felt his heart split open and send a throbbing ache to his throat. A new tear dropped onto Maya's hand. When she looked at it in a daze, she began to sway.

It was too much to process, and grappling with her shock, she accidentally let go.

Big Misunderstanding

She hadn't imagined the afterlife to be so institutional-looking. She always pictured it would be kind of trippy and colorful and surreal, like Wonderland or Hogwarts or like the beach in *Teen Beach Movie*. But when she awoke, she found herself staring at a cream-painted cinder block wall and a window covered with cream venetian blinds, and she thought that god, whoever they were (she, herself, never would have approved this), could have totally stepped it up, design-wise.

She hoped beyond hope that she'd get to see Scott, to tell him that she'd tried.

She wanted to reach out and slide her finger in the groove between the cinder blocks, a thing she'd done as a kid to soothe herself, at the doctor's office, but she couldn't lift her arm. She tried again, and realized she'd been tied down to a hospital bed with leather restraints. She breathed in and squeezed her hand together to make it as tiny as possible, then tried to slip it up and out of the loop. Still no dice. She wanted to avoid the obvious pathetic choice: thrashing, but there seemed no other way.

She thrashed. Which alerted whoever was in charge and made her realize her other arm was in excruciating pain.

"Ow," she said as some young people in scrubs charged in the door, followed by her mother.

"I thought I was dead. Am I dead?" she asked her mom. As one of the eager interns lifted her eyelid and flashed a penlight into her pupil.

"No. Maya. Thank goodness!" she said. "I'm so glad to see you awake. You scared us," she said, hugging her and kissing her all over her face that was bruised and streaked with different layers of prom makeup: Smeary streaks of black, blue, red, and purple dripped down her face like a bad art project on 5-Minute Crafts.

"Why am I not dead?" Maya asked.

"The Lord works in mysterious ways," one of the older nurses mumbled as she scooted a cart over to take her vitals.

The lord, Maya now knew, had nothing to do with it. She was saved by the giant flamingo that broke her fall and she was fine, but her right arm was likely broken.

"Am I a flight risk?" Maya asked. "Do people think I'm going to flee to my tax shelter in the Cayman Islands? What's with the restraints? You really need to free me or I'm going to lose my mind," she said, with a tiny final thrash for emphasis.

The intern looked over at Stacy, who nodded, and they unbuckled her from the bed.

"This was your idea?" Maya asked, feeling suddenly, sharply betrayed. "Why would you do this to me?" Stacy had never restrained her. Even as a toddler, when Maya threw giant, supernatural-sized tantrums, Stacy would talk things out with Maya, try to reason with her, rather than shut her away in a time-out. "Did I hurt someone?"

"Isn't the answer to that obvious? You hurt yourself, Maya."

"You think I did this on purpose? Oh my god. You think I jumped?!" Maya said, suddenly realizing what it looked like, especially if Bobby hadn't told them the truth. "Mom. I know what it looks like, but this was an accident."

"Why were you up there, Maya? Your blood alcohol level was through the roof, and we found this."

Out of her bag, Stacy pulled her black negativity journal plastered on the cover with stickers Maya'd found on the internet. A crying earth, a burning earth, a melting earth, a tornado, a Statue of Liberty, also crying, and then, on the spine, simply the word "hopeless."

"I can explain," Maya said as her mom paged through the black journal.

"There's stuff in here about thinking you can save people. And knowing people's thoughts. Like, a god complex or something? Isn't that schizophrenia? Why didn't Amy address this? And there's rage. And sadness. Maya. It's so heavy—a black hole of dark thoughts. I'm surprised I can still pick it up . . . so much gravity. I didn't know you were still living like this."

"I'm not, really. I . . ." The hospital had given her something in her IV and she was too tired and confused to untangle it all and set the record straight.

Instead, she tried to infiltrate her mother's mind. Reassure her. But her mother's mind was a dark, swampy morass. She couldn't find a way to rewire it. Stacy was so happy one day ago. She'd rediscovered music. She was thinking of doing some open mics. Maybe contacting her agent. Her daughter was going to prom. It was subtle, but even Glen seemed a little less "glen" and more, like, "crag," regaining his rugged complexity. Everything was straightening out. Stacy'd parented herself out of a dark spot, and now this. "I don't feel like I'm good enough at this to keep you safe," Stacy said, welling up with tears, admitting defeat.

"Okay," Maya said.

"Okay, what?"

"I'll stay here," Maya said.

"I'm sorry," her mother said. "I can't think of another way." She sighed, sniffled, sobbed, and tossed Maya's phone onto the bed. "Text your friends," she said. "They're worried about you."

LUCY

Cringey, Are you ok? !!!! {Boomerang video of Maya falling from the bridge, her prom dress flowing upward like a human drop of fire}

I'm falling backward, Maya was about to say to her mom. It was obviously an accident, but she didn't have the energy to argue. She could be resigned to it. People did good work in mental institutions. The artist Yayoi Kusama, the one with the spots and the giant pumpkins, made it work. She got sick of the patriarchy abusing her. Stealing her ideas (fucking Andy Warhol and Claes Oldenburg). Diminishing her powers. She literally held a mirror up to the world. She showed them the truth, and the world didn't like it.

There was no pleasure in it, being a truth teller. So Yayoi

retreated. Now the world's most famous popular visual artist, she still made art but from her studio in a mental institution. Maybe Maya, too, could just live here forever, painting dots.

Speaking of dots, just then her messaging app lit up with three dots from Bobby for a second, and then he texted I'm sorry. I'm going to make it right. But Maya knew that the power of a teenager telling the truth to adults only went so far. She couldn't rely on Bobby. She couldn't rely on anyone.

The text from Tyler was too difficult to read, so she didn't.

······················

"Maya, welcome back," Matt the shrinktern said as he pushed the button on the wall that activated the giant high-security lead-filled doors. The craning raptor head of the security camera arced toward her and she winked at it and secretly gave it the finger with the hand sticking out of her pink cast.

"Um thanks?" Maya said. She outwardly tried to keep it together for Stacy and Glen. They were just barely functioning, trudging in like executioners, feeling not that they had failed, but that they had failed Maya, who was the only person who ever mattered. They were feeling so awful, she couldn't show them how torn apart she was that she'd have to live again like a prisoner. The prospect of being trapped in with everyone else's neuroses, stripped of all fundamental freedoms, lorded over by petty, mean-spirited cretins who pumped her with all kinds of unnecessary (for her) psychotropics. This made her actually want to jump off a cliff. But she didn't see any other way. She wasn't going back to school. And she was depressed. Not about her symptom, but the fact that she could do nothing at all to harness it, or even keep it at bay and live in the world. How many times could you fail and try again?

She knew the answer was: infinity times! But she didn't want to hear that from her better self right now. She was done trying. She couldn't stop the evil. Her whole body shuddered, though, as the door sealed shut behind them.

Jumping off a two-story bridge was on a whole different level than jumping into a swimming pool (her nickname went from Cannonball to Freebird), so Maya was prescribed a whole different level of therapeutic residency, not quite akin to the kind you see in the movies—patients in hospital johnnies, shuffling back from electroshock therapy and staring mindlessly at the TV in the featureless rec room that housed nothing but uncomfortable chairs, a TV, and a Ping-Pong table no one had the motivation to use—but close.

"Can't I go back to my old room?" Maya asked, wondering if Jenna was still there, reading Sylvia Plath and giving herself paper cuts with the pages.

And Matt said, "This is only temporary, 'til we get a handle on your diagnosis."

"This is all only very temporary, Maya," said Glen. "We're not abandoning you." He was never on board with this draconian measure and was having trouble supporting Stacy in a united front. All the parenting books emphasized the importance of a "United Front," so he conceded, in the end, to give it a try. He didn't have any better ideas for what to do when your daughter kind of thought she was god.

Her room was stark and bare, and she was only allowed

to bring one thing to remind her of home, so she brought a picture of Maurice and asked for some tape to tape it to the wall next to her bed. The staff went through her clothing and confiscated her toiletries in case she tried to smuggle drugs or razor blades in with them. They also took her shoelaces and the drawstrings to her hoodies and sweatpants.

Her parents, also putting up a brave front, avoided tears as they hugged her goodbye. Maya, knowing that they needed to hear this, said, "I'll be okay. I'll see you soon. We'll talk tomorrow."

Her parents shuffled out together, bent and broken as if they'd suddenly aged thirty years, and Maya, scared and alone, finally exhaled and let the tears stream down her face. She was worried about Stacy, but Stacy would be okay. She had developed a lifelong *practice* of being kind of ashamed and disappointed and heartbroken. Like yoga or meditation or piano, shame was something you never completely mastered; you practiced living with it, and you got better at it with time. Stacy would stay in bed for two days until her hair began to mat like a mangy dog and it felt like her teeth were wearing a suede jacket, and then she would get up, take a long shower, and brush her teeth. She would spend one day drinking coffee, staring out the window. And on the fourth day, she would open the record store and go back to work.

Amy finally visited her on the third day.

"Took you long enough," Maya said.

"I'm sorry, they have special protocols in place and I wasn't allowed to come until now. Why didn't you tell them the truth, Maya? At least about the journal. You could have told them what that was for." *And you need to tell me what else went on that night.*

"I guess this is a cry for help."

"Well, you got it. This is an overcorrection, though. Too much help. I'm working to get you out of here," she said and then thought, *Unless you actually . . .*

"No, Amy. I fell. But you know what? Don't bother."

"Wait, what?"

"I think I've had enough of the back and forth. We tried, you and I, but it didn't work. I don't want to get my hopes up again. You didn't know how to help me. Which is fine. People need to help themselves, right? Self-Reliance. Bootstraps and whatnot. Libertarian ideals. Thanks for trying, but I no longer need your services."

Cute. Is she seriously firing me right now? "Maya, no path to wellness is a straight line. We could keep working . . ."

"It's fine. Just go. You did the best you could." When they locked these big doors behind her, she realized that maybe she wasn't built for life on the outside. Bobby had broken her heart. She was tired of disappointing Amy. She needed to set her free, but her breath caught for a second right in that little divot between her collarbones and she forced an exhale so she wouldn't cry, and she stared at Amy kind of side-eyed.

"You know what. Fine. Maya. You need some time. But know that I'm not giving up on you." And because this visit was supervised by some creepy higher-ups on The Staff, Amy thought the following at her: *You need to know your secret is safe with me, and you need to know I'm not going to give up. You were getting better. This was just a hitch.*

"Right," Maya said dismissively as Amy packed up her purple shearling oversized fanny pack and slung it around one shoulder so it hung jauntily under her left boob. Lucy would have loved that bag. That bag was fire and Amy's little fashion moment almost convinced Maya to change her mind and beg Amy to get her out so they could continue working in the room with the little elephants, but she needed to stop dragging other people into her mess.

Tyler came to visit the next day. It was during visiting hours, and Tyler sat across from her in the common room.

He held Maya's healthy hand, and the feeling of his rough and calloused boy fingers melted her, and she almost lost her resolve. Tyler seemed shaken. *I did this*, he thought. *Look what I've done.*

"So, it's not your fault," Maya said, employing a little of the uptalk and vocal fry she'd heard other girls use so that she didn't sound so serious. "Let's get that out of the way. I didn't go off the deep end because you deflowered me. Think about it. That would be giving yourself too much credit, wouldn't it? Like, that would be making it all about you. When it really wasn't about you, Tyler. I don't mean to be callous. I only mean to let you off the hook."

"I was so scared, Maya. I thought you were going to die. . . . I just. It was traumatizing." She saw him think of the splat when she hit the flamingo and the splash when she rolled into the water, the too many seconds it took for her to surface, the blue tint of her skin as the EMTs strapped her into a stretcher. He was so alone with all of it.

"That word is a little overused these days, don't you think?"

Maya said, looking at her fingernails colored with Sharpie. She had to keep her heart closed in order to proceed. "Everything can't be trauma. And if everything is trauma then nothing is."

"Maya! This was! I care so much about you. And I saw you falling from the sky. Why aren't you telling them that you were helping him? This was an accident!"

"Maybe it was an accident," she conceded. "But listen. Remember who you were when I met you?" she asked, squeezing his hand and looking him in those eyes, deep and brown and sad and feral all at once. Wolf-like. He was a wounded wolf. She'd wounded him and she had to stop. "Your religion of no attachments, remember? Maybe you need to meditate a little and detach from all this. I mean, look around. This would be a good time to enact your detachment protocols. Breathe me away."

"I don't want to, Maya. You're the first person to make me want to engage. To attach. For real." *I love you. I think about you all the time.*

She breathed in and physically tried to shake it off. She could not fold. She tried to convince herself that it wasn't love, it was just infatuation.

"Tyler," she finally said. "You must know what my name means, right?" Maya tried again, exhaling.

"No," Tyler said.

"I wish you did, because then you'd know what I was going to say to you right now and I wouldn't have to say it, because I don't want to have to say it."

Tyler knew what "maya" meant, and he knew what she was about to say. He was just stalling. *"Maya" is a word for "illusion,"* he thought. *In the sense that everything . . . all material reality . . .*

every sensory perception related to the material world is an illu-sion. Every tempting thing in the physical world is maya: a dis-traction from the spiritual path.

"You need to stay on the spiritual path." Maya nodded at him, and he didn't realize she'd read his mind; he just thought they were connected in a special way. On the same wavelength, so to speak.

"Other girls are maya," he said. "You, ironically, are not. You are the real deal," he said, standing up. "But I'm not going to argue with you if this is what you want."

"It's not you; it's me," she joked. "We can still be friends." Tyler didn't think it was funny. He took her in his arms, chest to chest, their hearts beating in time with each other, and Maya could feel the sadness permeating through his body. It yanked at his heart-throat and all his extremities. It just yanked and pulled everything toward the center, like the centrifugal whorl in the middle of the smoothie blender. She had created in Tyler a deep, smoothie-blender whirlpool of sadness, a vortex, a swirling toilet, but it had to be done.

Maya felt a tiny sob catch in her throat. For her, it felt like thunder slowly rolling inside her chest, where it suddenly clapped and then rained inside her body. It wasn't a nour-ishing rain, though. It was the kind of rain that dampens the stone walls of tunnels, coating them with thick black vegetal muck. The kind of rain that creates acute swelling in old la-dies' joints. The kind of rain that makes you lose hope in ever again seeing a rainbow.

Tough Love

Upon her release, she retreated back to her basement "hidey-hole" and, in between blankly staring at cooking shows on an infinite loop, where chefs over and over again tried to describe what umami was (come on, did anyone really know what they were talking about when they used the word "umami"? No, Maya concluded. They didn't), she thought about the past few weeks. Who did she think she was? How did she ever think she could save people?

She should have just left well enough alone. And realized that if she were to pursue the only careers suited to her— Bartender, Acrobat, God—it wasn't ever part of the job to save anyone. It was only incumbent upon bartenders and gods to LISTEN to them. So, her purpose, she guessed, was *not* to take away people's pain, but to sit here and absorb it. And that she could do from her basement. Save the Bobcats was canceled. The Bobcats could actually save themselves.

She got on the internet and ordered the Comfy wearable blanket in seven colors, one for every day of the week. She loaded up on snacks and subscribed to a fruit farm share delivery service #supportlocalfarms, and she bookmarked some HIIT workouts and Yoga with Adriene on YouTube to stay fit. She made a schedule for *RuPaul's Drag Race* so she didn't burn through too many episodes at once and leave herself stranded without Dragnificence in her life. She also ordered some vitamin D, because she really didn't care when she would next see the light of day, and she got herself some new blue light–blocking glasses in four different styles because screen time was going to be the only kind of time. She created a few "hidey-hole" playlists on Spotify and named them Black Light Waterbed and Surf the Poke Bowl and Umami Dreaming. She downloaded a few audiobooks she could listen to if she took a rare walk in the woods with Maurice. She also checked out some free online courses she could pursue by herself. Maybe something in carpentry. Like Jesus. Maybe she could build an ark.

She was completely prepared and could learn to love the solitary life. Scott had done so for more than thirty years, and that was without the internet. It was decided. She would live in her basement forever. Remove herself from humanity before she could do any more harm.

But wait, was it Sartre who said, "Hell is other people"?

Because "other people" had different ideas. Other people (read: Glen) were suddenly making her life hell. Other people were suddenly very invested in her #resilience, which was shocking because it was usually Stacy who would insinuate herself into a situation like this and try to pry Maya's fingers off the emergency brake of life.

After day five of Maya's quarantine, he turned off the cable.

After day six, he shut off the Wi-Fi. He slipped notes under the locked door that said things such as: *if u want cable, u need to go back to school.* (When would boomers realize that "u" was not even a thing anymore? It was not cute. *U are pathetic,* Maya thought about writing back, but she was too kind.)

He discontinued her phone service on day eight. On day nine he showed her a picture of *cringe* a mustache he was growing that he wouldn't shave until she came out of the basement. He was pulling out all the stops. He made a T-shirt that said MAYA'S DAD that he threatened to wear to his meeting at school with her guidance counselor. But Maya just dug in deeper. He could cut off the electricity, for all she cared.

And then he cut off the heat and electricity. But that didn't matter. She just doubled up on her wearable blankets. She had survival skills. Her preparedness kit included lots of jerky meat sticks and tuna fish, seeds and dried fruit, and powdered milk. She could hunker down there for months. He couldn't smoke her out.

And then he literally tried to smoke her out. With giant burning pyramids of Nag Champa incense that he somehow blew through the ducts. But she was in the basement. Where everything was stored. Even the gas mask her mother bought in a moment of paranoia after September 11. She put that on, opened the two tiny basement windows, and waved a piece of a giant cardboard box at the smoke, wafting it toward the windows until she just became accustomed to the sickeningly sweet aroma of the stuff.

On day twelve, he sent in the troops.

Maya heard some voices in the backyard. She knew it was

day twelve because she'd used a white rock to mark off the days with tally marks on the cinder block wall. She rushed to the tiny rectangular window at her eye level, but it was ground level for the house, and her view was mostly obscured by the stems of some budding young daffodils. Then she caught a glimpse of some Air Jordan 1 Retro Highs in University Blue tiptoeing among the tulips. A five-hundred-dollar shoe. Lucy.

"Here we are," said Glen, bending over to grab one of the door handles and lift it open. The basement door, from the outside, was one of those sloping metal horizontal double doors built into the ground that a person had to creak open, like the flaps of a giant picnic basket. Maya had spray-painted a skull and crossbones on them and in puerile kindergarten lettering painted *Keep Out*, and Glen had included *repainting the basement doors* as a line item in an invoice he had slipped to her yesterday #ToughLove. It also included rent, which, because she was barely seventeen, seemed illegal and desperate.

"This is the point in the horror movie where the whole audience is telling me to run," Lucy joked.

Maya contemplated finding a place to hide, but it was too late. The two of them ducked down the cement stairs and found her there, gas mask dangling around her neck, giant furry sweatshirt bound to her body by crisscrossing bungee cords across her chest. Strapped to the bungees were her essential tools: two flashlights, a pocketknife, a can opener, a lighter. She shielded her eyes from the sunlight as if they had just rescued her from falling into a well. Maurice, who had been her trusty companion of the dark, barked at them.

"Cringey. What the fuck?" Lucy asked and then said, "Oh sorry, Mr. Storm."

"No, that's okay. I've been thinking the same thing myself," Glen said. "I'll, um, just leave you guys to it then." Glen trudged back up the stairs, hands in pockets, and Maya heard him think, *I hope this works. I can't put her back in that hospital, but I will, I guess.*

"Nice mustache," Lucy called after him and then she thought at Maya, *What is up with the mustache?*

"Hey. Yeah. I don't know," Maya said as she picked up Maurice and offered him a piece of bacon she'd pulled from the giant marsupial pocket of her Comfy.

Crap. The girl keeps bacon in her sweatshirt. That's fire. "Hey. So I see you have some survivalist skills," Lucy said aloud. "Impressive." She walked deeper into the basement and surveyed some of the contraptions Maya had built for cooking since Glen had turned off her electricity. A few logs and sticks propped up so that her old soup pot could dangle over a trio of Sterno candles from their old fondue set. In the far corner she was using her mom's old stationary bike, previously relegated for use as a drying rack for laundry, to create a human-powered generator to try to start up her laptop. "This is good, like, Eagle Scout shit to put on the Common App."

"Speaking of that," Maya said.

"Why should we speak of that? We should never speak of it."

"But you are always speaking of it."

"I know. That's what they've done to me. It's a conspiracy."

"You sound crazier than me right now."

"Really?" Lucy asked, holding up a book called *The Self-Sufficient Life and How to Live It*, and pointing to the old couch that was scattered with *Prepper's Long-Term Survival Guide* and a copy of *Walden* by Henry David Thoreau. "You know Thoreau was only a mile from home and his mommy used to make his dinner, right?"

Maya saw Lucy glance at the wall where she had been crudely ticking off the days, thinking, *This is a little above my pay grade.*

"I screwed everything up. People. I screwed people up," Maya said.

"Huh?" said Lucy. "I mean. What?"

"Bobby. Stuff happened with Bobby. I, like, interfered, and I should have just trusted the universe. Because people are god. All of us. There is no one being who has any power to make things better."

"Um, okay. Good revelation. Valid. But you did not screw up. You made everything better. Bobby came clean because of you. We all know what happened. He fessed up about everything, got his community service for the vandalism. He wrote letters to get you out of the hospital. He started a blog called *Soul of an Artist* and he got a tattoo that says *Create*, to remind himself what to do with his emotions. He built a memorial in the woods. It's a process, but he's turning over a new leaf. Joined a million clubs. He's doing TED Talks about bullying. Constant fixture in the wellness center. Tries to give thirty compliments a day. He's practically Mr. Rogers."

"That doesn't bring Scott back," Maya said. The pain of

losing him still caught her breath, weighed on her chest like asthma.

"Well. I think he knows that. He has to live with that. And he's trying. It was sort of an accident. Kind of. Come on," Lucy said, as she uncharacteristically gave Maya an awkward hug. "We . . . I need you out there," she said, pointing out the window.

"What would be my next move?" Maya asked, sniffling a little and pointing to the crumpled paper plate she had hung on the wall, the one on which Lucy had drafted her three-step life strategy.

"Well, have you even looked at your vision board?" she asked. Lucy pulled out her phone and flashed it at her. All the squares were still filled with Tyler. "Your next move is to get back on the horse. And by horse, I mean you. Get. Back. On. This. Horse," she said, as she made a crude gesture with her hips to punctuate each word. And then she thought at her, *Sex heals all wounds, right? It's good for what ails you?*

"Time heals all wounds."

"Time's boring," she said, and she threw her arm around Maya and escorted her out of the basement and into the real world. "Also, do you know what day it is? I mean of course you know, because, you just know," Lucy said.

"I'm not going," Maya said.

"Please? For me?" Lucy begged.

Participatory Democracy

The town hall meeting was being called to order. Someone even said "Hear ye! Hear ye!" and then pounded a gavel down onto the desk.

Participatory democracy! Lucy thought. Even Lucy, prone as she was toward nihilism, was a little in awe of the process. Then she whispered manically, "I can smell the founding fathers. Can you smell the founding fathers?" She looked at Maya, who was preparing to answer, and thought, *Please don't answer that.* So Maya didn't.

Maya was here at the town hall, enjoying the culminating moment of her efforts to become a teen in the world (with a purpose that can get you into college!) because Lucy had come back to her house, stripped her of her wearable blanket, sprayed her with some Abercrombie perfume, and forced her hair into a ponytail, then pushed her into the Corolla.

"I smell like the mall," Maya had said.

"Shut up, Cringey. We're going."

It turned out that Save the Bobcats! was not just a whim,

but a #movement that had carried on without her while she was distracted by her #situationship with Tyler and recovering from a #freefall.

Tonight, in the town hall, Spencer and Sam and Chloe were already seated in the front row of seats, their notes in hand, looking up at the wood-paneled half circle of raised desks where the town council sat. They rustled their notes, eager to get it on their résumés that they had participated in the political process as active citizens and won an initiative to save wildlife.

Flanking them on either side were some other faces Maya recognized from the coffeehouse audience. Sasha was even there. They each wore Tyler's bobcat icon on Save the Bobcats! T-shirts expertly screen-printed by Lucy. And right behind Chloe, dressed in a button up and suit pants, holding a clipboard and whispering some last-minute strategy in her ear, was Bobby. He seemed serious and insistent and engaged, and when he heard that Maya and Lucy had snuck in the back, he turned and gave them a little salute.

The stage was set, but the person in charge of the town hall docket must have been a hunter/angler, gun-toting, NRA-funding person, because he or she made sure the students would be last to speak. An awesome strategy in Maya's opinion, because with each complaint brought to the council ... this citizen needing a variance for his toolshed, and that person complaining about his neighbor's hedge encroaching upon his property line, and the next person wanting to build a fence, and the next person arguing for speed bumps on his street ...

each complaint chipped away at the chippy youngins' enthusiasm for participatory democracy. Participatory democracy was SO Boring.

Maya could read their thoughts and by 9:00 P.M. knew that most of the teens were considering just bailing before they even got to the bobcats. They had homework after all and hadn't known that they could have just brought their laptops with them. They had assumed, as they usually do, that this would be all about them. They didn't realize they'd have to share the limelight.

Finally, the gavel dropped and Ordinance 582a was called to vote.

"We now turn to the consideration of Ordinance 582a in which the county of Bucks would establish an open season on *lynx rufus*, the common bobcat. Do we have any cause for opposition?"

Chloe, who wore her bobcat T-shirt beneath a perfectly tailored taupe blazer (#dressforsuccess), stirred herself awake, uncrossed her legs, straightened her glasses, and stood. Using *Robert's Rules of Order*, she said, "On behalf of Save the Bobcats, I move to reject the ordinance and offer this petition signed by six thousand residents of Bucks County."

"The chair recognizes . . . what's your name, dear?"

"Um. Chloe," Chloe said. "Chloe Turner."

"The chair recognizes Chloe Turner."

"Mr. Mayor and esteemed members of the council. We at Save the Bobcats believe this ordinance has no positive outcomes for the county."

A heckler in the back row wearing a plaid shirt sneered and sighed and said "Bullshit" beneath his breath.

"Continue, Ms. Turner," said Randy McBride. Mayor McBride was one of those work hard / play hard kinds of white male patriarchs who had the courage to shave his head once he started losing his hair. The shiny crystal ball pate was so Mr. Clean mystical, it made it difficult to know whose side he was on. He seemed to be floating above it all like a genie.

Maya could read his mind, though, and knew that he was only ever on one side. The side of getting reelected. As Chloe rattled off the numbers she'd garnered from the park service that proved that the bobcat recovery was *not* so robust that we needed to start shooting them for sport—and in fact bobcats could still be considered endangered by most calculations—Randy was dreaming up red and blue bar graphs and pie charts in his head and remembering how the previous mayor had partitioned the county into districts that would always play out in the Republicans' favor. #gerrymandering . . .

If he wanted reelection he had to side with the red. *The trick was figuring out how this issue would play with the white women. Dammit. How would the old blue-haired biddies who were tired of their recliner-sitting, beer-swilling Republican boomer husbands come out on this issue? Animals were tricky to play. What was it W. C. Fields said about show business? Never work with children or animals. What we got here is a one-two children-animal punch.*

"Thank you, Ms. Turner." Randy McBride interrupted her

before she was finished, thinking, *Damn. She eighteen?* And then added patronizingly, "You sure seem to have done your homework, dear. Love what they're doing over at that New Town High. Go Bobcats. Do we have a rebuttal?"

Chloe blushed and sat down, feeling for the first time the insidious power of a true dismissal from the grown-up patriarchy. *Greta Thunberg would not sit down. She would finish. I'm weak. I wish I could.* Maya knew she had a whole anecdote prepared about what had happened in Wisconsin. As soon as they lifted the ban on hunting the barely recovered wolf population in Wisconsin, the hunters slaughtered them. In two weeks, they killed a third of the wolf population, sometimes even hanging themselves out of helicopters with machine guns to kill as many wolves as possible in one fell swoop. They had to rescind the ordinance just two weeks after they passed it, so that the wolves wouldn't plummet right back into extinction. *Do we want that to happen to bobcats?* Chloe thought.

She tried to stand back up but something about the way Randy talked to her made her legs physically weak and she plopped back into her chair, defeated. Spencer and Sam patted her shoulders and assured her she'd done great. Bobby gave her an encouraging fist bump. Maya thought about somehow sending Chloe the strength to regroup and stand up again, but she reminded herself she was no longer in the business of saving Bobcats. She had to let this play out on its own, which was a little nerve-wracking, because how it would play out was that Donny Johnstone would stand up. Donny was the heckler wearing the plaid shirt.

"Mr. Mayor, I would like you to consider Exhibit A," he said, walking around the town hall passing out a packet of eight-and-a-half by eleven printer paper filled with photographs. On the front was a picture of a mountain lion in California attacking a backpacker. The next page showed a picture of someone's driveway with garbage strewn about. An obviously photoshopped bobcat stood at an impossible angle in the middle of the garbage. The last photo showed a bunch of hunters in King's Pub toasting together to the day's kill. "What you see here is evidence of my three points. Bobcats are dangerous. Bobcats are a menace. And hunting bobcats will boost the local economy. I rest my case."

Someone in the audience let out a yeehaw, and Spencer stood up and said, "But that's a mountain li . . ."

"Do we have a motion to take it to a vote?" Randy asked.

"Aye," said one of the council members.

"All in favor of passing Ordinance 582a, thereby creating an open hunting season for the *lynx rufus?*"

Three Republican council members raised their hands, of course. And the other three Green Party liberals shook their dowdy, unkempt, undyed, and graying heads. (*The liberals might have more success if they pressed their shirts, got some good haircuts . . . used some product,* Maya thought.) Maya and Lucy had this thought at the exact same time. *You never get a second chance to make a first impression,* Lucy thought. "Clothes make the man," Maya said back.

"All opposed?" the chair asked.

The three liberals raised their unmanicured hands.

All eyes were on Randy McBride. The mayor, still feeling uneasy about it, you could tell, shook his head in apology to the right, as he reluctantly raised his hand in opposition to the ordinance. *Kids and animals,* he thought. *It was a one-two punch.* The gavel came down. And it was law. Ordinance 582a was defeated! Open season on bobcats was canceled.

The human Bobcats rejoiced! Chloe and Sasha jumped up and down, while Sam and Spencer hit each other in an overly aggressive high five. Bobby cried. But this time, they were tears of joy.

The Gen X townspeople seemed unfazed by the victory. They hailed from a whole generation of apathetic Stacy-and-Glens: deer-in-headlights underachievers, whose inertia may have ushered in the end of the world. Maybe that was harsh, Maya thought to herself. Anyway, they didn't celebrate, and Maya watched them curiously as they packed their legal pads into their briefcases, talking among themselves about asparagus being on sale at the Walmart this week.

"Cringe! You did it!" Lucy said, hugging her. "You saved the bobcats!"

"*We* did, right? Look at those T-shirts, Luc. They're dope."

She joined the little huddle of the club she'd created and thanked Sam and Spencer before their moms took them out for ice cream. She hugged Bobby for a long time and could tell that something inside him had shifted for good.

I'm so so so so sorry, he thought, and he let himself cry.

Then as she was just standing there minding her own business and doing her own thing, she felt the invisible pulsating waves of the umami force just emanating right at her.

She turned around and there Tyler stood holding a bunch of gerbera daisies.

Maya physically shook off the umami like a dog shaking off a bath, took a deep breath, and graciously accepted his flowers. "What are you doing here?"

"You said we could still be friends. What is friendship for if not to celebrate each other's success?"

Maya leaned into the umami and whispered in his ear, "You really think we can just be friends?"

"I mean. Yeah, there's like a ton of sexual tension, but we can just ride it out, engaging in cute innocuous banter like we're on a sitcom, teasing it out seemingly endlessly until the show jumps the shark and the producers need us to finally come together to save the ratings."

"Like Pam and Jim?"

"Exactly like Pam and Jim."

"I like it," Maya said. "Except maybe not in Scranton."

Album Therapy

A week later, Lucy was "popping up" in Stacy's record store.

With Terry the librarian's help and the funds from the poker game, Lucy was able to rebrand. Her Etsy store went from Gilding the Monster to Monster Paint to just Paint. Terry's market research indicated that she should punch things up brand-wise and delete as many syllables as possible, so, Paint. It embodied Lucy's process but also evoked the idea of color and everything that represents: Art, Inclusivity, Sustainability, Hope. What's more hopeful than a fresh coat of paint?

Terry purchased office cubicle walls from a PR company that was, a little late to the party, transitioning to the dreaded open office workplace, where all the workers would now have to sit together at a long table and get nothing done, because how could you possibly focus? (Maya would definitely be a failure to launch if it meant having to work like that. What's wrong with righteous walls? Introverts unite!)

Anyway, Lucy covered her cubicle walls from the bottom up with a soothing off-white faux fur to distinguish herself as a slightly more feminine brand of street. A softer landing. The walls were trimmed with gold edges. Inside her walls, she strategically placed ottoman poufs that she painted herself with either graffiti or new vavnik faces: Greta, Malala, X González. Casey and Sydney the mannequins stood at attention in the back corner, wearing some fake band name concert T-shirts she and Maya had collaborated on. Sneakers, about a hundred of them, hung over the space in a constellation of soles, each tied to the store ceiling with different lengths of invisible fishing line.

The design that Terry had submitted to a bunch of retail organizations had secured her an entire pop-up tour. After Stacy's store, Paint was popping up at the Brooklyn Flea, Extra Butter, and Flight Club. An unprecedented pop-up coup, because, like everything else, the world of sneaker/street was still mostly run by men, and they were looking for a new voice.

"Look at the new display," Stacy said as Maya walked into the store in wonderment and disbelief. "I'm growing up."

Maya shifted her awe from the thing that was Paint to the opposite end of the store, where Stacy had set up a display case called Album Therapy. The idea was that Stacy would feature a new album every month with photos, news, memorabilia, and merch surrounding the history of the album, and then if you scanned a QR code with your phone, you could listen to Stacy explain the intricacies of how this album and its lyrics worked as a whole to heal your soul. This on its own was so heartwarming to Maya. The fact that her mom was curating and celebrating her expertise. It would probably lead to a book someday or a podcast or at least a TED Talk. It had to. That was heartwarming enough. But the pièce de résistance was seeing the first album Stacy had decided to highlight: *Jagged Little Pill* by Alanis Morissette. It was an undeniable feminist classic.

Stacy saw Maya taking it all in and yelled across the room, "She's still not better than me."

"I know, Mom," Maya said, and she made her way to Lucy's fuzzy cubicle where she found Lucy combing the walls with a giant red comb.

"This shit can get matted, and I need to keep it fresh," she said.

"Makes total sense," Maya said. "It looks so great, Luc."

"Isn't it ironic?" Lucy said with a nod to the Alanis display.

"The display?"

"No, the fact that this is the exact kind of shit that would look great on the Common App," she said, waving her hand around the cubicle. "The thing I created to avoid college is the exact bullshit thing that could get me in."

"Maybe that was in your subconscious this whole time," Maya said, winking.

"Ah jeez, Cringey. Enough with the psychotherapy. Maybe you need to wean off. When you start analyzing your friends it means you've had too much."

"Speaking of that, I need to head out."

"Wellness calls," Lucy said.

As Maya left the store, the familiar sleigh bells slamming against the door as she closed it, she looked to the left to see a line of shoppers queuing up around the block behind some velvet ropes. Jeanne sat on a stool proudly taking tickets. Paint was sick. And dope and fire. Paint was the schizz.

Before therapy, she wanted to talk to Scott, so she took to the woods. Tyler had shown her how to fold little boats out of biodegradable origami paper. She'd write notes to Scott and then send them bouncing down the river, where she knew he'd find them because he'd send her a sign or an answer to her question or some affirmation that she was on the right path life-wise. Once it was a rainbow, which she criticized as being too cliché. "Do better, Scott," she said, so the next time it was a knife wedged into the side of a tree with the freshly carved word "excelsior," ever upward. She'd also found one of his T-shirts from the seventies buried under a bunch of mulch. KEEP ON TRUCKIN', it said, and so she did. What choice did she have.

And she may have been making it up. It may all have been magical thinking, like believing in astrology or wishing on a star, but it didn't matter what was real, as long as she felt a connection. As long as she felt that the web of kindness between us can even bind us to spirits we can't see. There was a wonder in it, or she decided to think there was. It took her a while to remember it because she had been subsequently pumped with drugs, but something had happened to her when she fell from that bridge. She realized that people were good. She realized that "only evil continually" was a story she was telling herself. It wasn't the truth. She'd forgotten her revelation because of all the drugs in the hospital. But the falling, the failing. It gave her some perspective.

In a free fall, there is no time. And there is no sound. And there is no thought. In Maya's soundless, timeless free fall, the universe turned off the volume. It was finally, finally quiet. And what she noticed as she mutely and endlessly drifted toward her probable death was that *goodness* was also great in the earth. Doy! She, of all people, the daughter of an ex–rock star record store owner, should have realized that the universe had a flip side. And the flip side, like the B-side of a 45, was where everything good was happening. "Colour My World" by Chicago was on the B-side. "God Only Knows" by the Beach Boys: B-side. "Strawberry [Fucking] Fields" was hidden on the B-side of "Penny Lane."

Why was the good relegated to the B-side of the universe? Why was it so much harder to sense? Not because it wasn't a powerful force; it's just that the evil was always louder. Like the A-side of a record, it got more play. It got amplified because it was entertaining. It was something to talk about. It was gossip. An illusion. A distraction. The evil was loud. It was maya.

During her quiet free fall to her probable death, Maya got to see a B-side montage of everything that was good in her life. Random mixed-up memories kaleidoscopically zoomed in and out, like an introduction to a bad seventies sitcom. These were the images that existed in the cracks of her consciousness, stuff that her brain collected but refused to register, because the evil had drowned it out.

Like the time Tori (Lucy's supposed archenemy) was absent from math class, and Lucy drove all the way to her house to make sure she was okay. Like the time Jenna, suffering herself in the hospital, was able to check in on Bobby in art therapy, and had been writing him letters ever since. Like the fact that Aidan and Jacob *hadn't* started that CryBobby account. They got it taken down and they followed up with Bobby, inviting him over to cheer him up, recommitting to their friendship. Like the fact that Sasha from Peach created a heartfelt fangirl stan-fest of a video for Stacy that begged her to Please *Rock On*! Like the time Just Maddie organized a letter drive for Bobby when he was in the hospital and then wrote all the letters herself. Like the time Amy, despite all evidence to the contrary, pleaded with the hospital administration to discharge Maya. She yelled, slamming her hand on the desk, going to bat for Maya as if she were her own daughter. Like the time Mr. Benson quietly donated all his winnings from his sad poker night to Save the Bobcats! Like the times Scott secretly did all Sheila's yard work after Antonio died. Like the time Eddie, wrestling boy with the cauliflower ears, designed a better wheelchair in shop class for his brother with CP. Like the time Stacy signed up to volunteer three times a week. Like the time . . .

It went on infinitely, and then it was white.

Acknowledgments

If, as Scott says, making connections is god, then I have been lucky to meet "god" in the generous spirits of so many humans who contributed to the completion of this book.

I struggled to untangle the swollen knots of my long COVID brain to find this story. Without the supreme patience of Sara Goodman and the team at Wednesday Books, *Mysterious Ways* would never have seen the light. Thank you, Sara Goodman, Vanessa Aguirre, Rivka Holler, Zoe Miller, and Cassie Gutman, for believing in this project.

Thanks to my ride-or-die agent team, Sara Shandler and Joelle Hobeika. You know you are my heart and my other heart.

Thanks to a whole posse of grown-ass boss ladies in the South End who met me for artists' dates, walks, and micro-celebrations of the tiniest bits of progress: Sandra Larson, Polly Becker, Dina Mesbah, Cecilie Everly, "Book" Club, Lisa McTighe, Liza Jones, Meg Macri, Tami Huang, Christina Dominique-Pierre, Paulina Zgorzelska, and Dr. Cher Knight, whose supercool band names notebook she keeps with her students inspired this table of contents. Also to 49 Mine. And Dr. Nicole Fanarjian. (insert heart emoji)

Thanks to my Porter Square Books family. Love you guys. Special heartfelt shoutouts to beta readers Jane Nolan, Robin Sung, and Dina Mardell. Also to my BB&N social media intern, Madeline Song.

I'm grateful for the wise writerly counsel of Laura Zigman and Nicola Yoon. And for cheerleading boosts from Gretchen Schreiber, Jessica Parra, Allegra Goodman, and Iva Marie Palmer. One day we'll meet irl.

Ironically, this book is a testament to how little we truly know. I have the strength to embrace and explore the uncertainties in the universe because of one very certain and steadfast force in my life: my mom. As enigmatic as all mother-daughter relationships can be in this here patriarchy, I never once questioned her love for me, and that has given me everything.

. . . Including the power to become the mother of a courageous Gen Z warrior who partly inspired this book. Cadence, you impress me every minute of every day, and I'm so lucky to be your mother.

Thanks to the Rosenblum-Jackman-Menschel-Stoughtons, and, finally, to Gregg Rosenblum, whose grace, sacrifice, good humor, and big Pisces dreaming makes all of this possible and worthwhile. Love you forever.